Murder Almost

The Maggie Monroe Series: Book Two

Helene Mitchell

Green Sweater Girl
Columbus, Montana

Praise for the *Maggie Monroe* series

"Forty years of working in prison systems left me curious to read Helene Mitchell's *Maggie Monroe* books. I found them to be intriguing and captivating. From the first page I was enthralled with the eccentric, mysterious, and engaging characters. The books kept me guessing on 'who did it' while the small details brought me into the storyline. Highly recommend!"

— **Pam Sonnen**
Idaho Department of Corrections Deputy Director (Retired)
Prison Consultant

"I ordered this book because I love the author's humorous blogs. However, this is a whole different genre. I loved it! Couldn't put it down! I'm anxious for the next book in this series. Order yours today. It will not disappoint!!"

—**Linda**
Amazon Customer

"Thirty years in law enforcement, I have seen all kinds of criminal behavior. Helene Mitchell's *Maggie Monroe* books spin those behaviors into quirky mysteries. Fun reads!"

— **Shaun Gough**
Gooding County Sheriff

"I am halfway through and can't put it down."

—**Gary**
Amazon Customer

"Instantly draws you into the story! Unable to quit reading until you get to the end! Full of surprises and can't wait to read the next book in this series!"

—**Sharon**
Amazon Customer

"I like the characters in the novel and the way the author tied in past events with the current situation. The plot was interesting and held my interest."

—**Patty**
Amazon Customer

"Helene Mitchell brings the 'extra panache' with her *Maggie Monroe* books. She weaves a PERFECT tapestry of unpredictable mystery plots with colorful, imperfect, and unconventional characters. After working four decades in law enforcement, I thought I had seen it all. Then along came Helene Mitchell...you will absolutely love these books!"

— **Mike Moser**
Ada County Sheriff's Office (Retired)

This is a work of fiction. Names, characters, businesses, places, events, locales, and incidents are either the products of the author's imagination or used in a fictitious manner. Any resemblance to actual persons, living or dead, or actual events is purely coincidental.

Copyright © 2024 Green Sweater Girl Publishing, LLC

All rights reserved. No part of this book may be reproduced or used in any manner without written permission of the copyright owner except for the use of quotations in a book review.

Edited by AnnaMarie McHargue and Anita Stephens
Designed by Leslie Hertling and Eric Hendrickson

Library of Congress Control Number: 2024902623

ISBN (paperback): 979-8-9895968-1-2
ISBN (ebook): 979-8-9895968-2-9

www.gailcushman.com

Green Sweater Girl, Columbus, Montana

To Anna and Anita,
my editors, my mentors, my friends,
who continue to be the push-me, pull-me critters.
Thank you.

Time is the coin of your life.
It is the only coin you have, and
Only you can determine how it will be spent.
Be careful lest you let other people
Spend it for you.

–**Carl Sandburg**

Acknowledgements

The Push-Me, Pull-Me People

I love to put words on a page; it gives me such a rush. But dispatching words from my mind to the brains of readers can be a challenge. When I first scribed the words "My name is Charlie Walker," I had no idea where Charlie would end up, or even what he would be like. As words fell on the page and the story began to form, I hoped that readers would find him as interesting as he was in the folds of my brain. But the thing is, I couldn't have done it alone. I had a lot of push-me pull-me critters (with apologies to Dr. Dolittle) urging me on.

I am deeply indebted to the many people who have given time and expertise to bring me this far. Thank you, Tom, my first love, for believing in me. You gave me two kids, four grandkids, and a life filled with adventure. Semper fi, Marine! RIP. And thank you, Robert, AKA my new love, my Cowboy. You see things of beauty that I don't and have opened the world to one of adventure and exploration. You never fail to provide love, confidence, and support. You listen and critique, but never criticize.

Thank you, AnnaMarie McHargue and Anita Stephens, Words With Sisters, for guiding me to publication. You were my main push-me, pull-me critters and I appreciate it. Thank you, Leslie Hertling and Eric Hendrickson for your artistic eye and technological skill that makes my typed pages closely resemble a book and a cover to be proud of.

And finally, and perhaps most importantly, my readers, (neighbors, friends, and some anonymous readers), thank you for reading and critiquing my works. I listened and became a stronger writer because of you. To name a few, but not all...Pat Bennett, Charmaine Cates, Keri Collins, Sandy Manger, Clare Montgomery, Sherry and Denny Neifert, Grace Oldham, Patti O'Dell, Virginia Radcliffe, Trish Trinrud, Joan Wenske, and Pat Werhane

I hope you enjoy my story as much as I enjoyed writing it.

Chapter 1

Charlie
Present Day

My name is Charlie Walker. I am forty-three years old and ready to restart my life. I have a couple things to do first though, and I'm in a hurry to finish them. I have not been home in over twenty-five years because I was in prison in Fenwick paying my debt to society, so they claimed, for a crime I mostly didn't commit. Sure, you might say I participated, but I didn't do it. My best buddy did, but he skipped town. So now I resolve to make the son of a bitch pay.

***

I grew up in Barrier, Nevada, a jerkwater town, although the population loomed larger in those days than today. Barrier grew gold as its main crop with no end in sight, until it ended. The multiple mining corporations stripped the gold clean while I served out my prison sentence, and now with the loss of mining, its population has dwindled. Returning to my hometown, I didn't expect much, maybe a few lowlifes who couldn't or wouldn't leave their roots.

I'm a good-looking guy with black, wavy hair, brown eyes, and bushy eyebrows starting to gray. I'm six feet tall, the same as when I entered prison, but I've beefed up a lot. I have a prison physique and can handle myself in most situations. When I wasn't working in the prison library, I bulked up my body and my self-confidence by pumping iron, and when all of my tattoos are exposed, I am especially imposing. Mostly, though, I keep my tats hidden, with one exception: Patsy, with a heart on my bicep. She had been my high school friend and occasional girlfriend when both of us were horny, but I hadn't seen her in a long time.

Right now, my face is mostly covered by a graying beard, but I might shave it off before it gets too gray, going naked as they say in the big house. You need a beard in prison before they'll respect you. No beard, no respect, and the guards aren't any different than the inmates.

The prison gave me a set of civilian clothes when I left, they called them civvies, but I'm sure people will recognize them as prison clothes. A pair of wranglers, a t-shirt, and a plaid flannel shirt, none of them new, but by wearing them, I suppose I looked like a regular Nevada guy. They gave me a new pair of tennis shoes with laces and a green mesh ball cap that read Sammy's Feed Store.

Fenwick, a high security prison located in the middle of the Nevada desert, had no redeeming features. I passed through the town of Fenwick when they first drove me to prison. It had nothing, and, if even possible, was worse than Barrier. When I first arrived, the guards dumped me in the maximum-security unit in a single cell. I spent a sleepless night listening to other inmates shouting and clanking and farting. The hard bed had a flimsy mattress with no springs, and they gave me one blanket and a pillow with no case. Too many lights flickered outside my cell, further interrupting my attempts to sleep. I had finally fallen asleep when the guard awoke me by clanging his keys on the cell door and shouting, "Wake up, Newbie, time for chow." He said this same thing every single day during my time in the joint. After about a year, he replaced Newbie with Walker and a few years later Walker with Charlie.

Three days after Judge Little banged down his gavel and sentenced me to twenty-five years with no parole, I rode the bus to Fenwick. I considered his sentence a lifetime because it was longer than the eighteen years I had already lived. I was angry. I was a kid, just a kid, and I needed help.

I spent most of the first morning pacing my nine by seven-foot pale green, concrete cell wondering what would happen next, until a guard escorted me to the counseling office where the welcome-to-prison counselor, Ms. Clara Moneyjoy, explained what was what. An old, gray-headed lady with a wrinkled face and leopard hands, Ms. Moneyjoy didn't move too fast because she limped in her clunky black shoes. Even still, I noticed she smelled of old books as she passed me. Her charcoal gray pantsuit was speckled with tea or coffee, and her faded, navy blue blouse looked older than she did. I didn't have anything in common with her, that was for sure, and resented having to see her, but what else did I have to do? I had never spent time with a counselor before and didn't think I would like her, but what she said somehow stuck and has remained with me through all these years.

On our first visit, she removed a nickel from her drawer, carefully set it on its edge, and drew her hand away. "This coin is you, Charlie, on your first full day in prison. You can stand tall, or you can fall flat and, believe me, prisons offer many ways to fall." She flipped the nickel onto its side. "Gangs, disobedience, fighting. But prison also offers positive opportunities. While you are here, you get to choose. Nobody's going to select for you. Counseling, education, learning of all types are all available. The gymnasium is a positive outlet for frustrations that might arise, and a chaplain comes to Fenwick several days a week. I call this nickel The Coin of Your Life, as Carl Sandburg said."

I had never heard of Carl Sandburg and wouldn't understand the depth of her lecture for a year or more, but I did get the you get to choose part, which my stepfather, Eugene, who had been a Marine drill instructor, attempted to hammer into my head from the first time he met me. It hadn't worked.

The other inmates heard I had killed a cop, a rumor I didn't work to clear up. I hadn't killed anyone, but if I laid my story out, I would be targeted as a fraud. Inmates hate police in general and honor those committing crimes against cops, which I knew would be useful to me. Telling guards or inmates the truth would have been bad for business, with me being the business.

Doing time is a drag. Bad food. Bad bed. Good gym. Every day the same. I started my time in Fenwick working toward earning my GED. This was part of the sentence mandate, so I complied and worked as fast as I could to get it done. It wasn't hard. While getting that degree, I filled the endless hours of boredom working in the library where I discovered a few books that looked interesting. Reading became my lifesaver. I read everything, particularly biographies. As Ms. Moneyjoy said, You can stand tall, or you can fall. Characters in some biographies stood tall; others fell. I learned from the books and decided I would work to emulate the standing-tall folks.

I didn't know how easy this would be. Were there any other inmates hoping to turn things around? I wasn't seeing it. Most of the prison inmates looked ready for a fight. I had heard terrible things and didn't want to get beaten up or hurt anybody else, so I behaved myself and didn't cause trouble, and the guards left me alone. One guy, who considered himself tough, attacked me once, but I managed to clean his clock, although honestly, I'm not sure how. For an unknown reason, he held a grudge against me and came after me in the shower during my first week at Fenwick. We were the same size, but the fight ended when I threw a knee into his nuts. He had trouble walking for a long time after. From then on, everybody left me alone because they thought if I had killed a cop and had a long sentence, I must be a bad ass. I didn't even get rotated to other prisons like most inmates did and lived in the same cell at Fenwick for my whole sentence.

The staff allowed me to visit Ms. Moneyjoy as often as I wanted, and I learned from her. A grandmotherly type, she treated me kindly and even made me laugh. Several years later she gave me a metal coin, a challenge coin with Time is the Coin of Life embossed on it. It resembled the red and yellow Marine Corps challenge coin Eugene kept in his pocket. She said it violated prison rules for her to give it to me and made me promise to keep it hidden from the staff. I cherished the coin, my singular real possession for the time

Chapter 2

Charlie
Twenty-Five Years Ago

I had recently turned eighteen and acquired a dangerous combination of stupidity and immaturity. My best buddy, TwoJohnny, and I wanted to go to Las Vegas to gamble. We had brand new IDs, hot off the press, and we both knew how to play craps and convinced ourselves that we were pretty damn good. Problem was, we needed a car to drive to Las Vegas. We didn't have a car, so obviously our only choice was to steal one, which TwoJohnny volunteered to do since he had previously hijacked a few cars. He picked a sleek, beautiful, canary yellow Porsche 911 with under 2,000 miles on the odometer. It sat in the old lady's driveway that night with the keys dangling from the ignition. Why would anybody leave the keys in a brand-spanking new Porsche? She deserved to have it stolen. Maybe she wanted to have it stolen.

The theft itself was a cinch, but just as TwoJohnny was driving out of Barrier by way of Highway 376, he noticed the yellow light announcing he was about out of gas. "It looks like we have about two gallons of gas left. And that's if we're lucky."

"We've gotta go back. Nothing's out here," I told him. "On Highway 376, a person could drive 100 miles and never run into a gas station."

I resided at Fenwick. I later learned she told the correctional officers on my floor what she had done and threatened them if they bothered me about it.

The staff also had me visit a re-entry counselor a few times, but we never discussed release from prison, rather what I did to be sent to prison. I didn't hurt Sarah Hudson and wasn't going to admit I did. So much for innocent until proven guilty. Railroaded. That's what I was.

How I arrived at Fenwick is a compilation of bizarre events and boneheaded mishaps, and I paid mightily with twenty-five long ones. Many people in the big house say they didn't commit their crime, but most of them did. Not me though. I really didn't.

He flipped a U-ie and aimed the car back the direction he had come. He glanced over at me and smirked, "Uh, money? Do you have any extra money? How do we pay for the gas?" He could be so clueless.

I barked back at him, "Where do you think? The old lady who owns this car, Dumbass. She has all that money from her dead husband's insurance policy." Devising the best plan that my eighteen-year-old-brain could come up with, I continued, "We go back and ask her politely to lend us a few dollars. We'll pay her back when we take her car back because we'll win big in Vegas. No doubt about it."

"What if she says no?" TwoJohnny snapped. "She might say no."

I shook my head and retorted, "She won't. She's old and not smart. She left the friggin' keys in the car, didn't she? Plus, I kind of know her. She works as the juvenile probation officer. I had to meet with her when the cops arrested me when I was twelve. I'll wait in the car, and you go ask her. Politely. Her name is Sarah Hudson. Mrs. Hudson. Go ask her. I can't go in because she knows me from that bogus arrest, and last week I helped her move crap out of her laundry room and kitchen into the garage. She paid me twenty bucks, so I can't go in. You'll have to do it."

TwoJohnny pulled the car into the driveway and squeezed out of the Porsche, taking the keys with him. He went around the house to the side door. An unlocked screen door met him, and he vanished into the house. A long minute crept by. Then another. Suddenly he burst out the door and shouted, "Go! Go! Go! Start the car. We've gotta go now."

"You have the keys, Dumbass," I shouted. "You took 'em."

He leapt into the car and fumbled with the keys. Finally, he keyed it up and ripped down the street.

"What happened?" I shouted over the roar of the car. "Did you get the money? How much did she give you?"

Chapter 3

Maggie and Brick
Present Day

A quiet town, home to few thousand residents, Barrier drew more than its share of transients looking for an idyllic small town where they could live out their dreams. Speeding tickets, weed busts, and barking dogs had been the town's only high crimes and misdemeanors when Sheriff Maggie Monroe was first elected to office a few years ago. But that easy spell of crime solving ended quickly when she found herself in the middle of a murder case involving the town's beloved priest. When the case turned even uglier, with pornography and pedophilia at its center, Maggie had been baptized by more than fire; it had been a volcanic eruption, shattering her youthfulness and naivety. The entire town had been spellbound by a charismatic priest, but everything changed after his murder. The publicity and community gossip not only transformed Maggie, but it also changed the town's aura, as the whole of its small population seemed to bubble with a newfound cynicism that hadn't lived there before. One good thing to come of the murder case was a whirlwind romance with former LAPD detective Brick O'Brien. A wedding and twins followed quickly.

Brick had come to Barrier in search of a calmer life. After serving in L.A. as an officer for ten years, the number of near misses started to rattle him, and he decided to move on. He arrived in Barrier to head up the high school's basketball team and to teach a few high school classes, a much safer career choice. All that changed when his soon-to-be boss was murdered in cold blood on the very day Brick arrived. So much for a quiet, safer life.

Brick stood around six-foot-three with black hair and blue eyes. From the moment he arrived in Barrier, he was at Maggie's service. With only one deputy to help her, Cagey Garrison, Brick was deeply involved in a murder before he began to unpack.

Today found Maggie at her desk, rifling through a pile of letters and emails that had accumulated during the past week. Nothing seemed important, and she mindlessly sorted them in two folders, to do and done. It seemed enough.

Deputy Cagey Garrison entered her office and closed the door. He held a sheet of paper in his hand and sat down. A no-nonsense deputy, Maggie knew something was up the minute he closed the door.

Cagey waved a paper around and said, "Do you remember Charlie Walker? He was the one who robbed and hurt a local juvenile probation officer named Sarah Hudson. This happened a quarter of a century ago. Back then, he swore up and down he didn't do it. Neither of us was old enough to remember it, but I have heard people talking about it over the years. Anyway, court documents say he assaulted her with an iron. He knocked her out and left her for dead. Because Mrs. Hudson worked as a law enforcement officer and Walker showed no remorse, the judge sentenced him to twenty-five years fixed, a long sentence for a kid of eighteen, especially since it was his first serious offense. The prosecutor called Walker a real bad ass."

"I vaguely remember him from my days at UNLV. We studied a lot of court cases and Walker's was one of them. What kind of iron was it again? A tire iron?" Maggie asked.

"No, it was a clothes iron, as in pressing clothes, the housework type. Walker swung it by the cord and thwacked her in the head, knocking her out, and giving her a concussion. Her eye and face were burned, but she could see well enough to identify him."

"Which prison did he go to?" Maggie asked.

"Fenwick and the bad news for us is that he got out two days ago," Cagey answered.

Maggie said, "The assault happened around the time my parents moved our family to Barrier, but since I was only five years old, the only memories I have about it were from college. God, I'm over thirty. If he had a twenty-five-year sentence, he must have topped his time. Twenty-five years is a long time."

Cagey summarized the rest of the email, "Well, our problem is that he is out of prison. And, on his way out, he told a guard that he planned to go to Barrier, and he's gonna kill the SOB who cost him twenty-five years of his life."

Chapter 4

Charlie

Twenty-Five Years Ago

I couldn't believe what TwoJohnny told me. He started blubbering with snot running out of his nostrils, "I don't know how much money she gave me, whatever's in here. I grabbed her bag and left. We have whatever she had in the purse, that's all. Here, you count it."

TwoJohnny flung the rather large, well-worn handbag at me. I caught it, looked at him, and growled, "Her purse? You stole her damn purse, Dumbass? Why in the hell did you take her purse? What were you thinking? Did you even mention we would repay her?" I dumped the entire contents on the floor of the car and picked out the cash. I counted it, there were primarily tens and twenties. "It adds up to $582," I told him.

"I asked her exactly like you told me. Real polite. I even said please, but she refused. She had an iron in her hand, Man, and she threw the iron at me. I caught it. Right here. See this massive burn mark on my palm? I tried to dodge it, but I caught the hot part of the iron on my hand. It hurts like hell. I snagged the cord and swung the iron back at her. It hit her in the head, and when she fell, the iron sat on her face for a few seconds. Her eye popped out of its socket and hung on her cheek, so gross. There's blood everywhere, lots and lots of blood. I think I killed her, Man." TwoJohnny turned red in the face then yellow. I thought he was going to throw up. Instead, he spit on his burnt palm again and stared down at it; it looked bad.

"Are you kidding? You killed her? I said to get the money and nothing else. Not kill her," I snapped at him.

"I'm scared, Walker. I'm really, really scared," TwoJohnny whined.

TwoJohnny had never been in any serious trouble with the law, but I had. He wasn't exactly Mr. Clean but had managed to avoid law enforcement. He had smoked a little weed at the abandoned castle and porked girls on Saturday nights. He skipped school and did a little shoplifting but never got caught. The police heard the rumors but had nothing on him.

I, on the other hand, managed to find trouble wherever and whenever opportunity showed itself. The worst thing thus far had been that I stole the key to the gold mining office. I broke the lock on the office door intending to borrow some gold, but the local sheriff relieved me of the key and locked me up for the night. I was twelve, and the cop called my mom to pick me up and take me home. I had to talk with the juvenile probation officer, but she didn't do anything. I wrote a paper on the evils of stealing, and the sheriff ordered me to see her a few times, but my mom called her and talked her out of it because of their friendship. My next worse crime happened the next year. I sprayed skunk scent into the deputy's car because he had been hassling me for no reason at all. Following me and stopping me now and then. I pried the backseat window open and let 'er rip. Beautiful. The stench only lasted a few weeks, but he deserved it. He knew I did it but could never put it all together. Other than that, a couple fights. Weed smoking. Joy riding, all piss-ant stuff, but the sheriff didn't have much to do, so he would run me in.

I tried to think fast but couldn't think clearly and was as scared as a fish that had just bit down on a hook. I had never been involved in something as serious. I told TwoJohnny, "We need gas, so keep driving.

We can stop at Patsy Bard's house and borrow a few gallons of gas at the pump by the barn. We can leave her dad a few dollars to pay for it. Five gallons ought to hold us until we get to a bigger town where we can swap cars. This yellow Porsche will draw too much attention, so we need to dump it and steal another. We'll get one that doesn't stick out. A Honda Civic maybe, a shit car."

TwoJohnny blinked back tears, still doctoring his burned hand that beamed bright red. "Get one with gas, will you?" he whined, "I don't wanna have to stop and fill up again."

Chapter 5

Maggie and Brick
Present Day

Maggie left for the office. "Keep track of the twins. They'll both be hungry and will want to eat. Sean will want the macaroni and cheese, and Jimmy will prefer a PB&J but feed them whatever they want," she called from the door. "If they're hungry after eating lunch, give them a banana or an apple." She disappeared out the door.

Playing Dad was a novelty for Brick. The fraternal twins were toddlers, and he wanted to enjoy them while he could. He had been surprised at how amusing they had become. Being twins, they enjoyed similarities but equally as many differences. And they had very different personalities. Jimmy had taken on the clown role, and Sean had received the chatting gene. Brick considered basketball the most important part of his life but discovered Maggie and the boys shoved it to third place. He played ball in college, coached the Police Athletic League in Los Angeles, and now coached high school boys the game of basketball, as well as the game of life. He served as high school principal and hoped his sons would enjoy basketball as much as he.

Leaving the LAPD had been troublesome for Brick because it had been his source of pleasure for ten years. His life's dream had been to keep kids out of trouble, and he first believed that the way to achieve this dream lay in law enforcement. Giving up on his dream had proven difficult, but he found Barrier offered him another avenue to his quest. Involvement with the school allowed him to pursue his dream in a different way. He worked with kids on the front end of their lives rather than the back end, that is, after they made mistakes, sometimes fatal or at least unfixable. As a coach and teacher and later principal, he demanded his students demonstrate positive values, and he taught them how to set goals. Through his coaching and teaching, he encouraged students to respect themselves and other people. Now working in a school system, he was still chasing his dream.

Brick enjoyed life in Barrier and although small, diminutive by Los Angeles standards, he influenced approximately the same number of kids at the school as he did in the big city, a couple hundred a year with much less likelihood of getting shot. People in both locations carried weapons: In Barrier, they had permits and carried pistols on their hips in open view, but in Los Angeles, criminals hid weapons beneath jackets or hoodies, often accompanied by a switchblade knife, making it difficult to predict when, where, and why they would use them.

The town's population hovered at fewer than 10,000 people with no big-box stores to spend their money in. People debated whether a Walmart might build a store, but no one knew anything official. They joked that if a Walmart came in, Amazon would go out of business because so many Barrier residents shopped online. The stores that had weathered the mines' closures served the townspeople well, and they offered things like charge accounts and free delivery. And the clerks greeted you by name.

Several curiosities made Barrier an interesting village, including a castle with a moat, that had been developed into a bed and breakfast with a medieval theme. The castle had been built in the 20th century as a summer home for a Portuguese gentleman who replicated his Lisbon mansion. He erected the four-story structure and covered it with green and white azulejo ceramic tiles, which he transported from Portugal via train, to face its four exterior walls. Now, after roughly a century, the Nevada sun, wind, and neglect faded and chipped those tiles, but still they offered a European flavor to the structure.

When Brick first arrived in Barrier, the castle had been mostly used by teenagers for beer, boyfriends, and whoopie, nicknamed "BBW" by the sheriff as she attempted to quell or slow their drinking habits. Transients, on their way to nowhere, stopped by for shelter and repose. Occasionally the two groups coincided with trouble erupting. The castle's current owner, Jay Guzman, had transformed it into a weekend destination site for California tourists. As a young boy, he thought the castle was enchanting and set a goal of owning it and living there, but he spent most of his time shepherding the activities at the Chicken Dinner Ranch, where he worked, ate, and slept. Each weekend, out-of-town visitors eagerly visited and participated in the shenanigans and idiosyncrasies that Barrier offered.

Jay also owned the local brothel, the Chicken Dinner Ranch, which had existed and thrived for over a century. Currently, the CDR employed a dozen young women in the world's oldest profession. A constant stream of visitors stopped at the CDR, some out of curiosity and others to partake of its pleasures. A John Wayne cowboy bar and gambling opportunity added to its appeal, creating a profitable business. Jay added a spa and upgraded the size and quantity of the gambling operation to appeal to truckers who traveled through Northern Nevada. The popularity of the brothel brought more cars to Highway 50, which had been nicknamed "The Loneliest Highway" in America many years ago but didn't seem so lonely now. It derived its name from the chicken dinners served daily along with all the trimmings. The aroma lured visitors to have dinner, if nothing else.

Just down the street from the CDR was the Panorama Hotel, which offered a cosmopolitan environment. The hotel had two stories (a true high-rise building for the likes of downtown Barrier) with a bar and exquisite restaurant, but no casino. An international menu changed daily. It might be French or Thai or Italian, but seldom strictly American, and they served an expansive offering of tea, but no coffee. All were served by beautiful young women who immigrated to the U.S. from a variety of countries.

The women made their way to the U.S. through a consortium of Las Vegas and Reno casino head-hunters who identified these international beauties and persuaded them to chase their dreams in America. The women were groomed at the Panorama where they learned or improved their English and became Americanized in manners and dress, all so they could hit the ground running once they were ready to work in the casinos. They also learned the various casino games, so they would be ready to advise their clients to gamble and spend more money. The consortium paid for their trip to the USA, their room and board, and education for a year. In return, the women agreed to work and train for the year with little pay before moving to a larger city and more lucrative positions. Most fulfilled their contracts. Jay Guzman also owned the Panorama and treated these ladies kindly during their introduction to America.

The tiny county did not provide a large sheriff's staff. Maggie had no dispatchers or clerks, with only one full-time deputy, Cagey, and one adjunct deputy, Brick, her husband. Brick had more experience than the sheriff and her deputy combined, but he tried not to interfere. He would offer advice if asked but otherwise didn't insert opinions.

The office itself consisted of a mere seven rooms, including four usually vacant cells. At the height of the gold mining boom, the sheriff's office had been bursting at its seams and needed more office and jail space, but now it had room to spare. Maggie enjoyed her own private office, but Cagey worked in the front area, which tripled as a reception area and waiting room. In addition, it contained a small but functional interview room. Brick, when needed, landed in whatever vacant chair he could find. The four basic cells each contained a bed, toilet, and sink, but one cell now served as a storage area, meaning they had three available cells. In her first term, Maggie relied on Brick's experience and was grateful for his patience as she learned her job. Working together, the duo solved the murder of a beloved priest.

After handling that case, she needed less help, but didn't hesitate to ask for assistance, grateful when proffered.

First entranced by her beauty and green eyes, Brick soon discovered her to be a smart and ambitious law enforcement officer. She stood nearly as tall as he with auburn hair that dangled down her back, usually drawn into a ponytail. Her long limbs and athletic skill allowed her to overtake Brick when they ran together. Their unconventional courtship began the first night they met, the night the priest/principal was killed. They worked together to solve his murder and later discovered a child pornography case. Brick first asked her for a date while crawling through a dark tunnel leading to a brothel, and their first date found them swimming and making love in a natural hot spring. Their first days together included nothing ordinary or normal.

On the night of the priest's murder, Brick inherited Bridget, the slain priest's dog. A piebald mutt with pinkish eyes that carried her importance in her posture, holding her head high and proud. She didn't like anybody and didn't go out of her way for anything. With Brick alone as her master, she stood in first position, but when Maggie and he married, she fell to second fiddle. With the birth of the twins, she plunged to a distant fourth. However, she kept her bloodshot eyes glued on the twins, glaring at anyone who came near them, including their parents. After two years, she had slowly accepted her fourth place position and the twins, but still wasn't happy.

The reappearance of Charles Owen Walker worried Brick. He vaguely remembered discussions of the case during LAPD trainings but not the details. Everything he did recall seemed negative, one disaster after another as Walker showed no remorse over his crimes. One quick Google search filled him in on everything he needed to know. It seems his misdeeds had caught up with him. He had done awful things before he injured Mrs. Hudson, and his callousness at the trial had nailed his fate. One of the Innocence Project teams had reviewed his case but dropped it after a few weeks. Brick didn't know why. Although Walker continued to maintain he had not injured Mrs. Hudson, no other person or solution had come to light.

Brick knew this crime not to be premeditated. If Walker had deliberately planned to kill or injure her, why would he have used an iron? An iron was a weapon of opportunity not a purposeful decision weapon, like *I think I'll murder her with an iron*. Walker's fingerprints had not been found on the iron, and his mother and the victim had been friends. Police pulled fingerprints from the iron, but they had been smudged, and nothing had been in the system. Many unanswered questions arose, such as, had he gone insane and tried to kill her, or had the victim tried to provoke him, and he reacted? Walker had been young, and this was his first serious offense, but he had been given the maximum sentence without parole. What was Judge Little thinking?

After doing some initial research, Brick also questioned the use of the inexperienced public defender. Why had the judge allowed Dortha Ling, a recent law school graduate, all of twenty-four years old and inexperienced, try the case and be the lead, rather solo, counsel. Her boss, Phillip Rose had not been involved in trying the case, and the judge failed to assign a more experienced defense attorney or even at the bare minimum enlist the assistance of an experienced paralegal. Ms. Ling now practiced estate planning in Las Vegas and might be of help in sorting through the questions he had.

Brick knew that Judge Little had died three years ago, thus unavailable to be interviewed regarding his thought process in committing Walker to an extensive prison sentence. He was curious whether Sarah Hudson was still alive and, if she was, did she have any thoughts concerning Walker's sentencing and its completion. She and the judge had married before the end of that first year, which loomed large as another curiosity. She quit her job as juvenile probation officer shortly after the trial, and she and the judge built a home in Forsythe rather than remaining in Barrier. Further research revealed that the loss of her eye earned her a state retirement and enabled her to draw Social Security. Walker had left her for dead, but she made a full recovery. Did she still live in Forsythe, or had she moved somewhere else?

Murder Almost

The loose ends in Walker's case seemed long enough to make a substantive addition to the ball in Minnesota's Twine Ball Museum. Brick's phone chirped, and he checked it for the message. Maggie: "Could you come down here? I'll call my mom to see if she can watch the boys." A few seconds later his phone chirped again. "She'll come by in a few minutes."

Chapter 6

Charlie
Twenty-Five Years Ago

We didn't see anyone at Patsy Bard's home, so we pumped a few gallons of gas and continued to search for a spot to ditch the Porsche and steal another less-conspicuous car. We secured one of Mrs. Hudson's five-dollar bills with a rock on top of the gas pump and turned onto Highway 6, but it had even fewer places to steal a car, so we drove for quite a long way. I worried we would run out of fuel, but finally found a small town with three truck stops lined up, two on one side of the street and one on the other, all open and waiting for our business. All three advertised food, but we didn't need to eat; we needed to steal a car.

"Turn into the second truck stop, that one there," I told TwoJohnny, pointing at an orange, two-story adobe building with large front windows. Bright lights illuminated the gas pumps and parking lot, and a large neon sign reading *Gas Eats Showers* spanned its front. A smaller sign painted on the window read *Joe's Eats*. "Drive around to the back so we can see if there's a place to stash this car and swap it for another one that is less obvious."

TwoJohnny continued to blubber, "Get one full up with gas. I hate stopping for gas with the police on our tail." We hadn't seen any police, but he fretted anyway. Gas was the least of my concerns. I just wanted to find a nondescript ride, something invisible, particularly to the police.

Six vehicles sat behind the building. I pointed again, "Any of those will work. Park behind the mesquite trees so we can hide the Porsche from the view of people driving by." A half dozen mesquite trees sat apart from the building and would easily shield the 911 from view.

The six vehicles parked side-by-side in a row behind the diner undoubtedly belonged to the truck stop staff. Two Fords, blue and black. One white Chevy pickup, a red Toyota station wagon, a beat-up turquoise Firebird, and a baby blue Studebaker with rust spots speckled over the hood and doors. I exited the Porsche and tried the doors of the parked vehicles and found five of the six locked. Miracle of miracles, the keys to the Studebaker lay on the front seat. The owner undoubtedly thought nobody would want to steal a Studebaker anyway. An early 1960's Lark model with a dented left rear fender, it wasn't pretty. The *L* on the rear had been broken off, and it read *ark*.

I went into the café and asked for a cup of ice for TwoJohnny's hand before crawling into the driver's seat and firing it up. The V8 engine responded appropriately to my foot on the pedal. The gas gauge read a full tank of gas, enough to get us into Vegas where we might have to steal another. I hoped the gas gauge worked, but it seemed probable that it wouldn't because of its age. I looked at my watch and calculated we would have enough time to drive to Vegas before the owner noticed it missing, assuming the worker's shift ended before midnight.

I grabbed a towel from the backseat of the Studebaker and started wiping off any fingerprints we might have left on the Porsche. TwoJohnny jumped out of the car, patting her on the hood. "Goodbye, old girl. You've been a first-rate ride, and we'll be back for you." I had to rub off those prints, too. Dumbass.

I drove the next stretch faster than TwoJohnny had driven the first leg. I think he worried he would get a ticket or arrested. The ancient Studebaker purred like a kitten, and we arrived in two hours flat. We didn't see much traffic until we arrived at the outskirts of Vegas where we picked up the rush-hour type traffic, even though it was after ten p.m. We passed through town to arrive on the south side of Vegas with fewer hotels and casinos. Neon lights invited passersby to join in the fun as we passed several casinos. We chose the Big V Hotel and Casino because it sat off the highway with a parking lot in the back, out of view to passersby. It had a lot of trucks parked outside, so we figured it would be cheap.

We parked next to an eighteen-wheeler filled with new Buicks. TwoJohnny made an inane comment suggesting we steal one of those. He continued to amaze me with what a dumbass he was.

I registered us at the front desk using our new fake IDs with the names Tony Dow and Jerry Mathers, who had starred in the *Leave It to Beaver* series. I hoped the young female desk clerk wouldn't recall them, and she didn't. Easy peasy. The girl said $14.95, plus a $3.00 tax, meaning we had $500 left. I paid in cash and gave her a dollar tip. So far, so good.

The aging elevator crawled to our sixth-floor room, jerking and creaking along the way. We had no suitcases, nothing except the old lady's purse hidden under my shirt. TwoJohnny grabbed the ice bucket and filled it to cool his burned hand. He had stopped crying, but his face had turned red and blotchy.

"Let's go eat," he suggested, blubbering and whimpering like a hurt puppy. "I'm hungry, and I saw a café downstairs. Or better yet, I'll get burgers and bring them back here. We can eat in the room, and I can soak my hand. What do you want? We passed a burger joint down the road. Burgers, shakes, and fries sound okay? While I'm out, I'll grab some beer and maybe later we can try our luck at the casino. At some point, we'll figure out what we're gonna do about the old lady."

I pulled a small plastic bag out of the ice bucket, and I walked down the stairs to the fifth floor where the ice machine was. As soon as I got back, TwoJohnny stuck his burned hand in the ice, grabbed a handful of the cash from the old lady's purse with his other hand and left. I watched him and the Lark spin out of the parking lot to get our food. I turned on the TV, which flickered and sputtered as it warmed up. It showed a Gomer Pyle rerun I hadn't seen before or at least didn't remember. Another old sit-com came on. Then another. Where the hell had TwoJohnny gone? Had he been involved in an accident? Or did the police recognize the car? What was taking so long? Maybe he forgot the hotel's name, such a dumbass. Three hours passed, and my stomach started to growl. I didn't consider that he had left for parts unknown. My mistake.

I looked in the handbag, which still contained a few dollars. TwoJohnny had grabbed more than he needed, but he left plenty for me. I carried a credit card that I had borrowed a few weeks earlier from my mom but didn't want to use, because she probably hadn't figured out I had it. At least she never said anything. I didn't know for sure if you could trace credit cards or not, but I hesitated to use it as she might kill me. I had enough trouble and still, no TwoJohnny.

I knew TwoJohnny before he was TwoJohnny. He had been plain old Johnny when we met back in first grade in Barrier Elementary. Three Johnnys showed up in the first grade, and the teacher labeled them OneJohnny, TwoJohnny, and ThreeJohnny. I don't know what happened to the other two Johnnys, but everyone called him TwoJohnny after that, except me, because I called him Dos, like Spanish for two.

We had been friends for a long time, and it didn't occur to me he would leave me cold, but it looked like he had.

I drank a few beers at the casino while keeping a sharp eye on the doors, watching for Dos or the police or any other person who might cause me trouble. If he had stranded me, I might kill him. I had a little cash, whatever he left in the purse, but no car and no plan. So, basically, I was in shit city.

Chapter 7

Maggie and Brick
Present Day

Brick strode into the sheriff's office wondering what the emergency was. Maggie seldom asked for help, but the sense of urgency in her text was obvious. With a single deputy, her office could get busy in a hurry. Maggie deputized Brick when he first arrived in Barrier, and even though he seldom used them, he kept the ID and badge just in case. A volunteer deputy with no pay and limited authority, she reminded him from time to time that she, not he, had been elected sheriff.

Cagey Garrison served as Maggie's lone full-time deputy. He had worked for the previous sheriff and continued his employment after the county had elected her to the position of sheriff. Being a big, burly guy, he looked scarier than he was. His muscled and tatted arms and neck made him look formidable. Sometimes he had a beard, other times not. Currently, he had two-day's growth. He could be sullen and moody and didn't talk much, but he knew his job, and she could rely on him to do what she asked. In addition, he had a strong moral compass and superb instincts. He had survived hard times as a teenager and suffered with the issues that emerged as a result. A few had been resolved, others not. The deep-seeded ones never would be.

"Thanks for coming down, Brick," Maggie said. "We hope you can get us on the right track. We received an email, and the Fenwick prison warden also called and said they released Walker a few days ago. He indicated his destination as Barrier. At least that's what Walker told one of the guards before he left. He's threatening to kill somebody named Dos in Barrier. We don't know if Dos is a last or first name, and the warden wasn't sure either. He said Dos, nothing else, so it could be a name or nickname or even three initials, D.O.S. Cagey and I can't think of anyone with that name or with those initials, and Walker doesn't have any family here. His mom left after the mines closed."

Cagey interrupted, "Walker informed the guard he planned to kill the person who cost him all the time in the joint. He could have arrived by now depending on his transportation. He left Fenwick alone on foot, but he used to steal cars and might have found a vehicle to steal."

Brick retorted, "Did you check reports on stolen vehicles yet? If he stole a decent car, the owner would report it. An older car, maybe or maybe not because the owner might opt for an insurance payment. Electronics like door openers, keys, and windows did not exist when he went to prison, and the new technology in vehicles makes them more difficult to steal. Not to mention how car alarms have made it problematic for car thieves to thrive in their chosen occupation."

Maggie replied, "We haven't checked yet, but it's on our immediate to-do list. We were wondering if you could see if there were any kids named or nicknamed Dos enrolled in school when Walker lived here."

"Sure, I'll check," Brick answered while wondering if any rules existed concerning the identification of kids who had attended school a quarter of a century prior. Yet, if it would save a life, he would help. He held the authority as high school principal, but changing laws carried additional restrictions and nuances. "I'll be back in a little while. Doc might be another source. Or Harry Bird. Harry and Doc will know the nickname if that's what it is. I'll check with them, too."

Doc, a retired Latin and Greek teacher, had landed in Barrier forty years earlier. The Vietnam draft had been on everyone's radar, determined by birth dates and General Hershey, who oversaw it, had selected Doc's birth, among others, for the next group to join the Army. Doc had finished graduate school and was ready to go to boot camp when someone miraculously canceled his calling. He fortunately missed his thirteen-month visit to Vietnam. When he and his wife, Janey, had taken a honeymoon trip across America, they happened upon Barrier, which they fell in love with. Running short on money, he called his parents in Connecticut for a resupply, and his mother opened a letter from the draft board. He feared his report-by date had been moved up, but his draft had been canceled. He obtained a teaching position, and Janey offered piano and art lessons.

They didn't match the town in any way. With a doctorate in Greek and Roman art, he seemed a fish-out-of-water. Rural Nevada was a hunting, hiking, and fishing mecca, and Doc was a classical art and history whiz. No similarity existed in any way. Janey also had a music and art background and played several musical instruments. Doc taught Greek, Latin, and humanities for many years, and the principal also assigned him to coach football, because in this small school, every faculty member participated in athletics by coaching a team.

When he retired, Doc began a new career as a chanticleer, a storyteller. Janey enjoyed playing medieval music. They billed themselves as the McCrone Crooners and performed at the local medieval-inspired bed and breakfast.

Harry Bird, the school custodian, waged an ongoing war against dirt. He had been hired to be the custodian on the day he graduated from high school and seldom missed work during the thirty-five years of his employment. Dirt and grime could not defend against his relentless search for cleanliness. People joked the century-old structure stood fast and strong because Harry's cleaning products glued it together. The school might have been ancient, but Harry kept it immaculate. Doc held a Ph.D., but he bragged that Harry held a P.C.D. Pristine, Clean, and Dust Free.

Combined, Harry and Doc's longevity totaled over seventy years. They knew everyone, and everyone knew them. If anyone knew who Dos was, it would be Harry or Doc.

Chapter 8

Walker
Twenty-Five Years Ago

"What's worse than pissed?" I thought. What a piece of trash Dos was. I guzzled a couple more Coors and smashed the cans in my hand. Two turned into six, and before I knew it, my pissed mood switched to mega-pissed. I didn't trust the elevator, so I staggered up the stairs to my sixth-floor room. TwoJohnny had double-crossed me. I waited for two more days and passed the time playing video poker, drinking beer, and cussing Dos out in my head.

When I walked into my room, I saw the message light flashing on the phone. It surprised me that he remembered the names we used when we registered at the front desk, but the dumbass left me a message. It said, "Sorry, Walker. I had to leave. I'm headed to Mexico, but I'm not sure where. I'll see you in a few years. I feel horrible that I killed Mrs. Hudson, but don't tell the police that I did it or where I went." He didn't leave a phone number or address.

I couldn't believe it. He stole my money and went to Mexico, leaving me behind. He killed Mrs. Hudson, and I didn't know where to go and had no car to get there anyway. I counted the cash in the purse, $105 and some change. I had already spent $35 for two nights in a crappy room of this third-rate casino, plus food and drink. I didn't relish the thought of playing craps without TwoJohnny, and I had wasted a few hours at the quarter machines playing video poker but came up dry. At that rate, I'd be out of money in another day. This was getting serious.

I drank too much but couldn't sleep. I knew I needed a plan but couldn't think of anything. I thought and thought, but my brain wasn't working. I didn't think the beer had affected me, but my mind seemed scrambled and probably, in hindsight, the beer didn't help. I knew I needed to do something, but I could think of nothing to do except call somebody. But who?

I obviously couldn't call Dos, because I didn't know where the bastard had gone, and he couldn't be trusted anyway. I could call my other friend Mikey, but he and I had a falling out a few weeks ago, and I doubted he would help me. Then it came to me: My mom would never refuse me. She always knew what to do. My dad had deserted her after I was born, but she survived okay. She'd be furious that TwoJohnny killed her friend and I borrowed her credit card, but she'd help me. Technically, I hadn't been an adult for long, and she wouldn't ignore her parental responsibilities. She worked as a bartender in Barrier but should be home by now. She'd know what to do.

I dialed Mom but didn't call her collect, although I thought about it. Her name was Dolores, and her current husband, number five, was Eugene, but I called him New Gene because husband number three had also been Eugene. New Gene answered and said she hadn't come home yet because she stopped at the hospital to visit a friend, but he would tell her to call me. I recited the phone number but didn't offer any other information.

I didn't want to miss Mom's call, so I called room service for a Coors, which cost another $2.00 plus a tip. I counted $72 left; things added up fast.

I waited a long time, but she finally called. She asked the usual questions like where I had gone and who I was with. I told her Vegas and she shrieked, asking more questions. I told her the truth, that I was alone. I didn't want to mention TwoJohnny as she would go off on me again. She started telling me about her visit to the hospital, which wasn't an actual hospital, more of an urgent care facility dealing with cuts and bruises, but they had a couple beds for short-term visits. Barrier didn't have a real hospital.

She told me her friend Sarah had been assaulted and had a concussion, and her eye was damaged, in fact she had completely lost her sight. Great news! Not the parts about the eye being damaged and the concussion, but she wasn't dead, meaning TwoJohnny hadn't killed her after all. Thank heavens, but I didn't say anything to Mom. She droned on a while longer about Mrs. Hudson, saying she been flown to Reno for two nights to see an ophthalmologist, but he said he couldn't repair it and sent her back to Barrier.

She continued her story of the assailant throwing a hot iron at her and included details, but I didn't listen to most of it. I was happy that TwoJohnny hadn't killed her; he could have ended up in jail for years. The doctor diagnosed a concussion saying she also had a migraine, which was not responding to medicine. The son of a bitch assailant stole her purse and her brand-new yellow Porsche. Sarah would remain in the urgent care until the blood and pus quit oozing from her eye wound and the headache lessened. The doctor predicted her facial burns would cause permanent scarring.

Mom paused in her soliloquy of her friend and asked, "What's so urgent, Charlie? What do you need? I'm calling long distance, and it'll cost me a fortune."

Right at that moment, I found myself stymied. What should I tell her, the truth or should I just make something up? Both had consequences, so I decided to mix it up and tell a little of both.

"It's this way, Mom. I need a ride back home from Vegas. I came with a guy I know, but he dumped me. We came to gamble and win a fortune, but on the spur of the moment, he decided to go to Mexico and left me here. I don't have enough money to rent a car or take a bus, and I need to get back to Barrier because I sort of have a job interview." This was a lie, which she didn't need to know. "Could you or New Gene come to pick me up?"

"What guy?" Mom asked. "Who'd you go to Vegas with? Did you go with TwoJohnny? I warned you that he'd get you in trouble."

I knew my story put me on thin ice, so I decided to reveal as little as I could, "Yeah, Two Johnny, but he's not as bad as you think." I really don't know why I was defending him after what he did to me.

Mom's frustration came in loud and clear over the phone line. "I figured, and now you want me to drive all the way to Vegas to pick you up? I can't drop everything and come to get you. He's a no-good bum. You need to get better friends."

"I know, Mom. I will. I promise. He left with no explanation. He went to get food and didn't come back. He called me from the Mexican border and said he was leaving, but he didn't say where."

"That's sounds like TwoJohnny. Where did he get a car? Does he even have any money? He won't get far without money."

"I think he saved up money from his job at the grocery store, maybe a couple hundred dollars, and he borrowed a green Ford pickup from his uncle." I was lying my eyebrows off, but it should keep me out of trouble. My mom didn't need to know everything.

"I don't have time to talk any longer, and I already told you this is a long-distance phone call," she repeated. "I'll talk with Eugene, and maybe we can work it out. I'll call you later. Wait by the phone because I'm not happy, and I don't want to have to keep phoning and getting a damn answering machine."

I felt relief that she was coming to get me, but I dreaded the ride home.

Chapter 9

Maggie and Brick
Present Day

Brick stopped to get Bridget, who leapt into his month-old Jeep. He had owned a Wrangler when he first arrived in Barrier, but a wife, twins, and all their paraphernalia supported his desire to purchase a new vehicle. He bought another Jeep, a Cherokee this time, with all the bells and whistles. Bridget often sat between the twins where she could eye both, but today, she rode shotgun. With the windows open, her nose twitched in the breeze, and her ears flapped over her eyes, but she didn't seem to notice.

Brick drove into the empty school parking lot. With school out for summer vacation, he didn't expect any teachers to be there. No kids and no teachers. The custodian, Harry Bird (who also served as chief of security, concierge, and whatever else bounded his way), would be working. Brick's assistant, Thumper, who hopped in and out of the school, would come to the school if he needed her. Her school chums shortened her maiden name, Thelma Ampere, to Thumper, and it stuck. She lived up to her nickname with a bounce in her step, moving rapidly from place to place.

Brick knew he would most likely learn what he needed to know from Harry, a real-life data base for all things Barrier since the start of time. He would know Dos and the history of Dos's family, including names, dates, ages, and birthmarks. The population of Barrier reminded me of the old spiritual song *Dem Bones*, "The foot bone's connected to the leg bone," and traveled all the way up the torso, ending with the "neck bone is connected to the head bone." Everybody in Barrier connected to everyone else, and Harry recalled them all.

Sure enough, Harry was at the school. His short stature and bowed legs didn't slow him down. He reminded Brick of the cartoon character Roadrunner while being pursued by Wylie Coyote. He darted from task to task never wasting a motion. His keen eyes zeroed in on any dirt or smudge brave enough to appear when he was on alert, and he was always on alert. Brick and Bridget wound their way through the entire school and into the gymnasium before locating him in the girls' shower area, scrubbing the shower stalls with disinfectant reeking of chlorine.

"Don't get sick on the chlorine, Harry," Brick warned. "Perhaps you should wear a mask or spread out the cleaning days, so you don't inhale too much of it. The stalls look great by the way."

"I heard rumors that one of the girls had an unhealthy toenail infection, so I thought I should scrub the showers to get rid of any germs. I don't think she caught the infection from our showers, but I would be upset if her folks blamed the school. I had extra time and thought it seemed like a chlorine day," Harry explained smiling.

"I appreciate your hard work and know the parents will, too. Nevertheless, I don't want you getting sick from the chlorine fumes. Be careful, Harry. If you get sick, who will do all that you do?" Brick reminded him.

"You sound like the wife. That's what Jean says, too," Harry answered. "I've been doing this for thirty-five years and have taken few days off work because of sickness. I don't count the days off for the time when I broke my arm falling off the ladder while I painted the ceiling in the gymnasium. It wasn't my fault the ladder slipped, and anyway, I could have worked those days, but the superintendent refused. He insisted I hire another guy to paint the ceilings after I fell." Harry shook his head showing his disapproval.

"The superintendent was right. Some tasks should be left to others, not you. Anyway, I have a question for you," Brick began. "Did we ever have a student called Dos? It could be first or last name or part of a name or maybe even a nickname. It could be the initials D.O.S. and called Dos?"

"Hmm," Harry answered. "Dos? No, I don't think so. It might have been a nickname the kids used on each other, but I don't remember it."

Brick said, "Maggie doesn't know for sure. It would have been twenty-five years ago, I think. Do you remember Charlie Walker? Dos might have been Walker's friend or somehow related to the Walker case."

Harry continued, "Of course, I remember Charlie Walker. He tried to kill Sarah Hudson, who's my mom's cousin. She lost the sight in her left eye, but he didn't get the old girl. She was fifty-ish when she lost her eye, and she's over seventy-five now and doing fine, wears a patch over it. He stole her car, but the police caught him, and he ended up in Fenwick for a long time. I don't know whatever happened to him after that. He might be He's probably dead by now. I know he went to prison but haven't heard anything in years. Sarah worked as the juvenile probation officer for the county, and the judge gave Walker a long sentence. Judge Little showed Charlie no mercy because Sarah worked in law enforcement and, although no one knew it during the trial, the judge had a thing for her. They married shortly after Walker went to prison. People talked but no one ever confronted him, including Charlie's attorney. That attorney melted into the woodwork, and we never saw her again. Judge Little died three years ago, but she still lives in Forsythe.

"At just eighteen years old, Walker had already been in more than his fair share of trouble, mostly little stuff which wouldn't amount to much one at a time, but the constant activities and his meanness, made him despicable. He skipped school and did some joy riding. He stole lots of things, including his mother's car one time. I thought she might kill him. He stole her cat and turned it loose in the desert. It came home three or four weeks later, starving and mangy. I saw the cat when it came home, and its paws had sores all over, and it was badly sunburned. I had never seen a sunburned cat. I don't know why he left the cat in the desert. His mischief bordered on meanness. He didn't seem to care if he hurt people, maybe not physically, but in how he treated them."

Brick replied, "Did he have girlfriends?"

"He had one that I know of. He and this girl Patsy had a thing. I figured she would get pregnant, but without telling anyone, her parents transferred her from Barrier High School to a private school in Salt Lake to straighten her out. I wondered if she had gotten pregnant, but nobody ever said anything. Last I heard, she married a guy from Barrier, Gabe Cochran, but I think she divorced him. Patsy Bard, I don't remember her well, but I think she had a couple of older brothers."

Brick pressed further, "What about friends? Did Walker have any friends? Do you remember who his friends were?"

Harry coughed a couple times and stood up. "Let's go outside. This chlorine is getting to me, now that you mention it."

Brick and Harry stepped outside into the cool fresh air where Bridget waited. She scowled when she saw Harry, who eyed her with equal disdain. "I don't know why you keep that dog. She is the grouchiest mutt I've ever seen. Does she also scowl at the twins?"

Brick reached down and patted her on the head. "She frowns most of the time, but she's turned into a guard dog for the twins, although she wasn't pleased when we first brought them home. She got used to being number one before Maggie and I married, but now she's plummeted to number four in the O'Brien hierarchy, making her crankier than ever."

Harry laughed, then said, "About Charlie, he had a couple wayward friends, but they seemed to get in less trouble. They skirted the rules and the law, made the usual mischief, but usually avoided getting caught. His main two friends were Johnny something and Mikey Edenfield. Mikey broke away from him and ended up going to college and eventually became a lawyer. He lives in Florida and has a successful law practice, as far as I know. Johnny…Johnny…Grayson. That's what his last name was. The kids called him TwoJohnny, but I don't know why. Charlie Walker's mom married several times, but I don't know her name now. Johnny ran away from home the same time that Charlie tried to kill Sarah. Johnny's mom had already moved away. I have no idea where she ended up."

Brick nodded saying, "That's not much information, but way more than I had twenty minutes ago. Do you think Doc would remember him?"

Harry answered without hesitation. "I'd sure ask him. I remember a lot of Barrier's history, that's for damn sure, but Doc writes it down. He keeps a written record of everything that has happened in Barrier since he's been here. Notebooks and notebooks. I would definitely ask him."

Chapter 10

Charlie

Twenty-Five Years Ago

Both Mom and New Gene arrived in Las Vegas to drive me back to Barrier. I was right. It was a long trip home. We ate lunch at the $1.99 lunch bar on the way out of town, and I had ham and eggs. Although they'd been married for a short while, New Gene had been more of a dad to me than the rest of her husbands, but he didn't give me an inch. He had been a Marine Corps drill instructor at Parris Island before he met her, and he looked the part. He resembled an English bulldog with wide jaws and protruding jowls that flapped when he talked. His leathered and furrowed brow suggested he worried all the time. When he disapproved of something, a vein in the center of his forehead pulsed purple. He seldom smiled but nodded his head when he approved. He stood at least six feet tall with layered muscles bulging beneath his form fitting t-shirt. No fat at all. He wore a butch haircut, high and tight, and he wanted me to do the same. My mom wouldn't have it, so my bushy hair always shagged a little, but New Gene never said anything.

It started to rain the moment we climbed into the car. The dark sky flashed yellow and white with lightning over the Grand Canyon. I felt sure it predicted what my life would be like when we arrived home. We drove north from Vegas in a downpour and nobody said anything, and I felt glad. The black and gray sky inspired silence. I stared out the window at the blooming sagebrush and watched for coyotes and jack rabbits, hoping the silence would continue.

Halfway to Barrier, the sun emerged from behind the rain clouds and began warming the desert. Slight heat waves quivered over the Earth, and my mom turned on the air conditioner. It had heated up outside, and the inside of the car began to heat up, too, as the quiet ended and everybody yelled and cried and swore, sometimes all at once. My mom cried and threatened to kick me out. New Gene swore and threatened to get me enlisted in the Marines. I yelled and threatened to quit school and leave home.

By the time we arrived home, everybody had run out of threats. I didn't mention TwoJohnny, but they did, and they dwelled on him. They thought he was a bad influence on me, and I didn't disagree because it meant fewer accusations toward me, which was a good thing. I considered sneaking out to the castle to have some beers with my friends but decided they would go ballistic so instead turned on my Walkman and listened to Madonna.

The next morning life at our house had mellowed. New Gene went to work, and Mom and I hung out at home. New Gene worked for the city as the public works guy, plowing roads and filling potholes. He also dug graves with a backhoe when residents of the town died. It paid well, and he liked it, but he worked a lot.

I had considered my situation and decided to tell my mom some version of the truth. I didn't tell her the entire truth, but I spilled out as much as she needed to know. I told her we stole a car, not Mrs. Hudson's, but the Studebaker. She ranted and threatened me again, cussing TwoJohnny. I told her he had stolen a purse with a few hundred dollars in it, but I didn't admit it belonged to Mrs. Hudson. She didn't need to know everything. She went off on TwoJohnny again.

She needed to go to work, so I didn't mention anything else. I would have a few hours of peace and quiet to figure out how much more to tell her, but she spoiled my idea of serenity by telling me to go check on Mrs. Hudson at the urgent care. Uh, oh.

I couldn't tell her no. I didn't think Mrs. Hudson had seen me with TwoJohnny, at least I hoped not. She knew me because she and my mom had been friends, but TwoJohnny had been the guy. He'd hit her with the iron, stolen her new car, and swiped her purse. I hadn't done anything.

When I walked into the urgent care center, Mrs. Hudson sat propped up in her bed with an ice bag resting on top of her head. She had an exceptionally large bandage over her left eye surrounded by black skin, the blackest I had ever seen. The skin was shriveled up like an old tomato, and she had a red mark that loosely resembled the shape of an iron on her cheek and forehead. Her face blotched with red, yellow, and black, and she wasn't smiling. She looked terrible.

"Hi, Mrs. Hudson, it's me, Charlie Walker," I said politely as I inched closer, so she could see me with her good eye. "How are you feeling? I'm so sorry about your injuries. Mom asked me…"

She began to shriek, "Charlie, did you come back to murder me? Don't kill me, Charlie! Why did you try to murder me?" She let out a scream, loud and long.

"No, Mrs. Hudson, you have it wrong. I don't want to kill you. I'd never hurt you," I said while moving toward her to calm her. She had known me for a long time, and I thought I could get her to chill out.

She continued shrieking louder than before, "You liar. You tried to kill me and left me for dead." The nursing staff rushed in and shoved me away. She pointed at me and called me a thief and a gangster and a murderer. The nursing staff tried to soothe her, but she would have none of it. One nurse left to get something, perhaps a sedative, perhaps another nurse.

The head nurse, a sizeable woman, cornered me between the door and the wall, and somebody else phoned the sheriff. A bunch of deputies arrived and snapped the cuffs on me while Mrs. Hudson continued her screeching. One deputy talked to her, and while she signed some paperwork, they escorted me out to their car and drove me right to the sheriff's office.

TwoJohnny and I did not look alike, but in her dazed state, she must have thought it was me. We both stood six feet tall, skinny, tanned, and had dark brown hair worn in a mullet. That day, I wore blue jeans, a white t-shirt with *Tigers* stenciled across the front, and an orange and black school baseball cap, like the one Dos had been wearing five days before.

Chapter 11

Maggie and Brick
Present Day

Bridget trotted beside Brick as they re-entered the school. The parking lot stood empty, except for Harry's pickup with a broken windshield from his hitting a deer a week before. In truth, the deer hit him, instead of the other way around. A fawn leapt toward the car and spread eagled the windshield, shattering the glass. He hadn't repaired it yet.

Brick's assistant, Thumper, had come and gone again leaving him a few notes from parents who had called to complain about their child's grades or next year's class schedule. He sighed. Their urgency didn't dictate Brick's urgency, but he called the parents back. The parents liked Brick and seldom became angry with him; they either wanted to vent a complaint or verify a rumor.

Brick's years on the police force benefited him in dealing with parents of school children because it was the same as dealing with victims of crimes or families involved in criminal situations. Both knew they couldn't change the system or outcome, but desired to gain information concerning how, why, and when he made decisions.

Brick entered the records vault, which bulged with paper files of students and staff dating back over a century. The records had been organized by year of graduation or potential graduation, if the student had not completed school. Starting in the late 1990s, the records had been electronically recorded creating easier and more accurate access. Thumper had been slowly converting the files to electronic records, but she was pre-World War II. Walker's class in the mid-1990s had been recorded by paper and pen. Charles Owen Walker had not graduated from Barrier High School, but there his records sat.

During the four years when Walker had been enrolled in BHS, mining had been at its peak. Student enrollment at that time fluctuated with the transient mining population. Brick was surprised to see how many students started school, left a few weeks later, returned, and repeated the cycle. It must have been difficult for the teachers who dealt with the constantly changing class makeup and size, as well as the uprooted students.

When gold had been discovered beneath the town of Barrier, the mining corporations purchased every house in town and razed them. The assessors and assayers estimated three million ounces with a value of $300 an ounce. The mineralogists had discovered microscopic, trace elements of gold, not gold veins or lumps of gold, but they estimated the value bordering a billion dollars. The companies paid top dollar for houses and land, often more than their market value, and the townspeople willingly sold. With their homes being sold, the residents had to find other living arrangements, but given the profit they made on the sale of their homes and the more plentiful and higher paying jobs, they didn't complain. Where the populace would live had emerged as the unsolvable puzzle. With all the houses belonging to the mining companies, the residents improvised by bringing in temporary housing units, such as campers, metal shipping containers, and tents that could serve as homes. The cheap metal shipping containers hauled easily but were uninhabitable as purchased. Desperate to solve the housing issue, innovative people cut doors and windows in them and added minimal electricity and plumbing. The units had one large room curtained off to separate the spaces for privacy or convenience. Add a flowerpot, TV, and lamps, and the makeshift house felt like a home. The community erected outhouses and common shower houses for small groups of the community. With these basic needs met, the residents could exist for the foreseeable future. The cheap solutions addressed their problems, and they came out ahead financially since the mining companies had paid premium prices for their previous not-so-elegant houses.

Brick found Walker's school record and scanned through it, checking for disciplinary entries that might reveal an association with Dos. He didn't see anything and checked the three years preceding and following Walker's graduating class, searching for anyone with the initials D.O.S. or a name starting or ending with Dos. Nothing appeared. His next stop would be to see Doc.

Chapter 12

Charlie
Twenty-Five Years Ago

When the cops led me into the sheriff's office, all hell broke loose. A dozen deputies crammed themselves into the small interview room that had only one door and no windows. A few sat in chairs, but most stood leaning against the wall. I couldn't have exited the room without stumbling over four or five deputies, all bigger and tougher than I was. They had handcuffed me to a pipe centered on the table. I had reached adulthood and finished growing taller, but I was still scrawny. I don't know why they left the cuffs on me.

A couple of them called me a cop killer. I wanted to remind them that she was neither dead nor a cop, but I would have been in more trouble. I told them the truth: I didn't hurt Mrs. Hudson, but they didn't believe me, and I felt that they didn't want to believe me. I asked for a lawyer, and they agreed to find one, but nobody left to get one, and they continued to ask me questions. I didn't know any lawyers but asked them if I could call my mom or New Gene, but they said no.

All the deputies asked me questions simultaneously. I didn't know who to answer or not answer. My eyes started itching, and I feared I would cry, which would be embarrassing. Finally, a deputy with three stripes on his sleeve entered the room and banged the door behind him; he seemed to take control. He told a couple people to leave so the room felt bigger. His name tag said Daniels, and he didn't fool around. He said, "Mrs. Hudson positively identified you. If you didn't attack her, who did?"

My thoughts jumped and jumbled in my brain. Should I tell them Dos did it? He had proved to be a scumbag, and I didn't owe him anything. He stranded me and left the country, and he deserved whatever I dished out to him, but I didn't want to be charged with car theft either, because that would sure as shit land me in jail.

I blurted out, "I don't know for sure. It might have been Dos. It wasn't me."

Daniels eyed me suspiciously, "Dos? Who the hell is Dos?"

I didn't pause and said, "You know. TwoJohnny."

Daniels shook his head. "Johnny Grayson? You run with him? Where is he? Is he still in town?"

I lowered my head trying to find a line to walk on without ending up in jail. I mumbled, "I dunno. I think he went to Mexico. He was talking about it last week."

"Does TwoJohnny have a car? He'd need a car to get to Mexico," Daniels pressed.

"Maybe. I don't know. Maybe he stole one. He wanted to steal the yellow Porsche on Third Street. He had the hots for it." I hoped I could divert their attention to the stolen car and the possibility of Dos as the culprit. Better him than me.

The cops didn't know TwoJohnny, but they knew the name because it popped up regularly. He didn't have a record because they never caught him for anything. He was slippery as goose poop.

"The yellow Porsche? What do you know about the yellow Porsche?" Daniels asked.

"I don't know nothin'," I lied. "It belongs to my mom's friend, Sarah. She bought it after her husband died last winter. I guess she received insurance money. I don't know anything else."

The cops continued questioning me, but no lawyer appeared. My watch read a few minutes before noon, and I was hungry, so I asked for a hamburger. They brought me one along with fries and a coke. It tasted good. They uncuffed my right hand so I could eat and drink, and they let me eat my burger in peace without more questions being thrown at me. Daniels left but another cop named Reynolds stayed in the room. I panicked because I had sprayed the skunk scent in his car, and I thought he knew. He didn't say anything though, so maybe he didn't realize I had done it.

After lunch, they let me use the john, but they had a guy watch me, which was embarrassing. When I came back, a young woman sat at the table, and she said she was my lawyer. Christ, she looked my age or maybe even younger. She was small, less than five feet, and looked scared like she was the one in jail. She wore a long black ponytail with her bangs cut short, high above her eyebrows. Her voice sounded a little whiny, and she kept scratching her neck as if she had an itch. She wore jeans and a red t-shirt with *Rebels* stenciled on the front and carried a backpack that must have weighed more than she did. Her cowboy boots clacked when she walked. She avoided looking at me, but when she did, she smiled. She introduced herself as Ms. Ling. Dortha Ling. She said she had graduated from law school that spring. Oh, great.

Ms. Ling told Reynolds to leave, and we talked for a while. I told her parts of my story. I told her how TwoJohnny had burnt his hand on the iron and what a dumbass he was. She opened her backpack and drew out a yellow pad, pen, and law book. She wrote my name and today's date on the top line and then wrote a few words down. She kept looking down and wringing her hands with long gaps of silence in our conversation. I liked her okay but wasn't positive about her being a real lawyer. I thought she might have been a plant by the sheriff to weasel a confession out of me. I answered her questions but didn't volunteer anything additional. Maybe later.

Daniels came back in and said, "We called your mom, and she'll come by in a while. She works until four o'clock."

Oh, crap, I thought. *She knows I was in Vegas with Dos.*

Chapter 13

Maggie and Brick
Present Day

Brick and Bridget drove to Doc and Janey McCrone's home, which backed up to Toiyabe National Forest. They migrated to Barrier from New England and had lived in Barrier for forty years. In this rural community, they built their dream home to fit both of their eccentric personalities. Doc's unconventional personality and Janey's creative mind did not match the rough and tumble aura of a mining town; however, the community accepted and honored them for the positive influence they brought to Barrier and the high school.

Doc opened the door with a big smile. "Ah, Rockford, my friend, we are indeed honored to welcome you into our residence. Come in, come in. You, too, Bridget." Bridget followed Doc into the kitchen and made herself at home.

"Hi, Doc, long time, no see," Brick responded, holding out his hand to Doc. "It's great to see you."

Doc called to Janey, "Luvvy, come see who has entered our abode. Rockford has arrived."

"No one calls me Rockford except you, Doc," Brick commented as he grinned widely. His parents named him Rockford after the James Garner character, but his brothers had begun calling him Brick because of his basketball skill deficiency as a youth. When he shot baskets, they teased, his shots fell like bricks. His skills improved through practice, but the name stuck.

"Your use of my real name is copasetic, and it cracks me up," Brick said with a twinkle in his eye. The word *copasetic* wasn't in his high school principal vocabulary, but he had been saving it for Doc. At times, Doc used words requiring a dictionary.

"*Copasetic.* Great word! It's a treat to hear uncommon language. I must say, you made my day. It makes me feel like I'm back at the university," Doc responded with a chuckle asking, "What brings you to our humble cottage?" Their log cabin house was anything but humble. Janey had decorated it to exhibit a unique cultural diversity. Each room expressed a different ethnicity, including Asian, English, Scandinavian, French, and Italian, but with an upscale American kitchen. Six rooms, six cultures. With the furniture and authentic décor, Doc quipped that he could travel the world within his own home.

Janey walked in and bussed Brick on the cheek and cooed, "Wonderful to see you, Honey. We've missed you. How is your enchanting wife?"

"Thank you for asking. Maggie is fine but a busy lady as she juggles her sheriffing duties and twin babies. The babies have grown fast, and they move constantly, running all over the place. We never experienced one child at a time, but we are certain one would be far easier than two. It means double everything and even when we are both at home, it's hard to keep track of everything.

Maggie's sheriffing work remains constant, but she doesn't have anyone except Cagey and me, and I'm not available when school's in session." They sat down in the kitchen while Brick rolled out his question. "This actually brings me to the reason for my visit. Doc, do you recall a student named Charles Walker, who left school twenty-five years ago, more or less? I don't think he was a successful student and perhaps he dropped out or flunked out."

"Oh, my, yes," Doc answered. "I recollect him. He never evolved into a stellar scholar and employed a corrupt set of values. He was one of those academics I longed to forget. He attempted to kill Mrs. Hudson, and she lost her sight in one eye. I knew her because she worked as the juvenile probation officer and came around the school now and then. After her injury, she couldn't work anymore. Walker is incarcerated, as he should be. Why do you reference him?"

Brick responded, "Walker finished his prison sentence a week or so ago. Judge Little stipulated no parole, and he sat out his entire sentence. Before departing the prison, he bragged to the correctional officers that he would go to Barrier to kill a person called Dos, but Maggie doesn't know who it is."

Doc looked puzzled. "Dos? I don't remember anybody named Dos. Are the letters the initials of his first, middle, and last names, as in D.O.S., or his whole name?"

"We aren't sure. All Maggie knows is that Dos might be a person here in Barrier," Brick told him.

"Did you question Harry? He has a great memory bank of Barrier. He might be able to help," Janey offered.

"Yes, I asked him first, but he didn't remember anybody named Dos either. He suggested you might remember him. He thought you might have recorded Walker's trial information that would point Maggie in the right direction."

"I do have a massive amount of information on Walker's trial. I contemplated penning a manuscript about him, but I found myself occupied with other matters. Janey demands far too much." He reached over and placed her hand into his and smiled. "It will take me a while, but I am sure I can locate my Walker chronicle identifying and listing his horrendous acts. If you visit again tomorrow, I will have the notes for you, and I might even be able to convince Janey to fix us cock-a-two tails. Bring your gorgeous bride to join us, won't you? How does five o'clock sound?"

Chapter 14

Dortha Ling
Thirty Years Ago

Alone and afraid, she arrived on the sands of America after a long and treacherous sea journey. The Vietnamese boat people fought over inches and food and cots, too little, too small, and too short. One of the thousands of Vietnamese refugees who arrived in America in the late 1970s, Dortha Ling escaped the treachery of the Viet Cong trying to maintain its own civility and autonomy. At fifteen years old, she spoke little English and knew nothing of America other than what her family told her about *the promised land*. Her youthful appearance and frail frame displayed timidity, yet her determination propelled her to excel in whatever came her way.

She started the journey in a tiny, leaky fishing boat built for forty people, but over sixty-five crammed into it. Traveling from Hue to Malaysia, they exchanged the poorly patched fishing boat for a larger, sturdier one to cross the Pacific to San Francisco. The second boat's capacity listed 140 persons, but its captain allowed twenty more (he reasoned he could fit more refugees into the boat as the Vietnamese people had tiny bodies), which also necessitated tight rationing of food and drinking water, less than a quart a day per person. After three days at sea, a band of Thai pirates attacked the ship, raping several women, murdering at least one man, and throwing seven

Murder Almost

overboard, never to be seen again. Dortha hid in a half-empty barrel of rice (sharing the barrel with two rats) to avoid the pirates, who damaged one of the engines and shot additional holes in the boat. Several ships passed by them until eventually a merchant vessel towed them the last 100 miles.

In September of 1979, she finally set her feet on dry land: America. After the horror of the days at sea, Dortha Ling had given up hope of arriving alive (or dead), but, in the end, she had survived the pirates, the lack of food and water, abuse, and rats, and committed herself to survival.

Dortha Ling was alone in the world; her parents having been killed in the war when she was ten. As an only child she had been farmed out to a widowed aunt who assumed the responsibility of caring for eighteen other orphaned children, her cousins, because their parents had also been killed. They managed to survive the poor living conditions and unavailability of food and potable water. She did what she needed to do to eat and help feed her younger cousins while searching for a benefactor to help her travel to America.

She did not want to be one of the 65,000 Vietnamese slaughtered by the North Vietnamese government after the war, and she sought to escape with two of her male cousins. The chaos of finding and boarding a fishing boat in the dark separated the three and Dortha ended up alone for the dangerous trip; the other two, who had boarded different boats, drowned, which she did not learn until years later. Dortha donned a life vest and stepped into the boat in silence. At her young age, she had seen enough injustices, cruelty, war, and poverty to last a lifetime. On her trip across the Pacific, she promised herself that if she arrived alive, she would seek equity for people on the wrong side of justice. She decided to go to school, learn English, and become a lawyer.

She struggled with college and law school but finished within the usual time frame and accepted her first job with a small public defender law firm based in Reno, seeking to diversify its staff. She spoke

Vietnamese, English, and Tagalog fluently and could get by in French. They hired her immediately. She had barely become used to her new surroundings when her boss sent her to Forsythe to fill in for a manager who had fallen ill. The Forsythe office carried few cases, and her Reno supervisor thought he could place her in Forsythe without difficulty.

Chapter 15

Charlie

Twenty-Five Years Ago

I dreaded her coming, but Mom showed up right on time. She had tried her best, but she had this streak of infernal honesty that popped up without warning. It didn't exist when she dealt with her own problems, but when she dealt with me, she could construct the damnedest barricades to my having fun. She bent her self-proclaimed rules for her own well-being, but from me, she demanded the straight and narrow. With Eugene the Marine in the picture, it would be worse. Count on it.

Daniels escorted Mom into the room. She wore her work uniform with her name on the pocket. Remnants of spilled beer and wine drips stained the front. No other deputies accompanied them, and I wondered where they had gone. My mousey lawyer also came in and sat down beside me. She smelled like perfume.

I asked Daniels, "Can I talk to my mom alone? I mean without you or my attorney? I want to explain to her why I'm here." In truth, I wanted to warn her against saying that I had been with Dos. Ms. Ling didn't say anything.

Daniels responded, "No, not today, another day perhaps, but not today. You can update your mom on what you did and why you did it while your lawyer and I listen."

Mom reached across the table and clasped my hand, but I yanked back as much as the cuffs would allow because I didn't want to hold her hand. I could tell her anger bubbled and boiled, but she controlled her temper by lowering her voice, "What did you do, Charlie? Who is this woman?"

"Aw, Mom, the cops think I hurt your friend Sarah, but I didn't. I didn't do anything. You asked me to go check on her and I did, but she started screaming when she saw me. She thought I hurt her. I promise I didn't. I wasn't anywhere nearby. I swear." I used the word *nearby* rather loosely since I had been in the car parked in the driveway. I added, "This is my lawyer, Dortha Ling. She graduated from law school a few days ago."

Mom looked at my attorney, "I'm pleased to meet you, Ms. Ling." She turned back to me and asked, "Charlie, do you know who hurt Sarah? The doctors told her she's going to lose her left eye because it's badly damaged and can't be saved. She even was taken to a specialist in Reno on Tuesday. Who hurt her, Charlie? Do you know?"

I looked at Daniels before glancing back at my lawyer and shifted them back to Daniels. I drawled my answer out slowly, so Daniels would understand, "No, I don't know. I have no idea, but I am sorry she lost her eye."

Daniels spoke, "You mentioned earlier that maybe TwoJohnny hurt her. Do you know if he went to her house?"

Uh oh. I knew this would happen. I tried to send mental messages to my mom by staring and blinking at her. She saw the signals and said, "What's wrong with your eyes, Charlie? Do you have something in them?"

I didn't say anything for a few seconds, silently cussing her out. But then, I began to stammer, "I told you. He went to Mexico. I don't know anything else."

Daniels picked up the conversation, "He went to Mexico? Did you see him before he left?"

Murder Almost

I knitted my brows and paused for a minute, thinking hard and trying to recall, "No, I haven't seen him in weeks." Would Mom support me or leave me high and dry?

High and dry it turned out. No surprise. She didn't understand my eye signals and said, "What you do you mean? You and TwoJohnny went to Vegas to gamble this week. TwoJohnny dumped you off at a Las Vegas casino and left you stranded. You asked Eugene and me to pick you up because you said TwoJohnny called you from the border, and he wasn't coming back to pick you up. This is serious, Charlie, tell the truth for once in your life."

Dammit, I thought. The one time I needed her to support me, she didn't.

Daniels turned and looked at me, scowling with what I perceived as hate. He pursed his mouth and replied, "Let's start again, Charlie. When did you go to Vegas with TwoJohnny?"

Mom responded to Daniels. Damn her. "He went to Las Vegas on Monday or Tuesday. Today's Friday, and we picked him up yesterday. Sarah was injured on Sunday, but I know Charlie didn't do it. I'm not sure when he left because Gene and I had gone camping until Tuesday. Charlie would never hurt anybody, would you, Sweetie?"

My lawyer interrupted in her squeaky voice, "Charlie, don't say another word. Don't answer any more questions from the sergeant or from your mom. Sergeant Daniels, I don't want Charlie to answer any more questions. I want to talk to Charlie alone."

Maybe Ms. Ling would be useful after all.

Chapter 16

Dortha Ling
Twenty-Five Years Ago

Dortha arrived in the law office of Rose & Reubens in mid-June. The Reno-headquartered public defender firm had a solid reputation among judges, an okay reputation among defense attorneys and defendants, and an excellent reputation among prosecuting attorneys. Scattered throughout northern Nevada, they hired a total of twenty-five staff, including fifteen attorneys. Paralegals and clerical staff filled in the other ten.

Dortha Ling's graduation from law school had been anticlimactic with no family to help celebrate her accomplishment, and she went to work the following day. Summer had arrived, and most of her friends either traveled to Cancun to party or stayed local to study for the bar, but she went to work. She had to face the bar exam, but her immediate supervisor encouraged her to gain actual experience before taking the bar, making the bar exam easier. Understanding the importance of passing the bar, Dortha listened to her supervisor. She liked the idea, and it seemed a good idea to delay the exam.

"Dortha, I'm glad you joined us," the lead lawyer, Phillip Rose, said. "I hear you will take the bar exam in the fall, which is an excellent idea. You can gain practical experience at the same time as taking additional time to study. Coincidently, the office manager in Forsythe is taking a hiatus, and I

Murder Almost

need you to fill in for her. I would like you to go to Forsythe and manage that office for a few weeks or so. Just manage it, don't take any cases. Josh Gaines is an experienced paralegal in that office. Listen and learn and call if you need help. You can live in the apartment in the back of the office. It's small, but it'll be okay for a while, and it's better than a dorm room. It's furnished, and I'll give you an advance on your salary to tide you over for groceries. Better yet, go to David's Foods where we have a charge account and charge your groceries to us. We'll pay for your food while you're there. You'll likely be in Forsythe for a month or two. Josh does all the legal work, so you'll be answering the phone and that kind of thing. Use your down time to study for the bar so you can pass it on the first attempt."

Dortha grew excited at the thought, "Thank you, Sir. It sounds like a great opportunity. I have been worried that I wouldn't have time to study for the bar exam while working in the office. This will be real-life experience before I become an actual lawyer. I truly love this idea. Thank you."

The Forsythe office consisted of two people, an office manager and a paralegal. The office manager/administrative assistant had taken a combination of vacation and medical leave to relieve her stress. The paralegal, Joshua Gaines, age thirty-four, had been a paralegal for several years and enjoyed his job, but he also enjoyed activities that took him outdoors, including hiking, rock climbing, and desert biking. An exercise aficionado, he hit the gym before work and again as soon as the five o'clock whistle blew. As much as he enjoyed recreation, he seemed accident prone, and this year alone he had already dislocated his shoulder and broken his foot and used an abundance of sick days to recover. Phillip Rose had become irritated at all the time Josh had taken off from work.

On her third day in Forsythe, the phone rang and Dortha answered, "Forsythe office of Rose and Reubens."

A deep, but floundering voice said, "Dortha, it's Josh. Hey, I won't be at the office today. I had a little accident, and I'm home now, but it's not good. I broke my left femur last night, and I'm a wreck. I went rock climbing, and one of the knots slipped. I slid at least sixty or seventy yards down Horseman's Bluff, you know, out by the hot springs. My right ankle had not completely healed from the sprain two weeks ago, and I twisted it, too. The urgent care doc said I should not walk on it for at least a month, maybe two. The leg's in a cast, hip to ankle, so, basically, I am a mess right now. I'm renting a wheelchair because I can't use the crutches because of my dislocated shoulder. It's a total bummer. Can you cover for me?"

"Sure, I mean, of course. Are you okay? Do you need help? I could come by after work and bring you some food."

"No, I don't need anything. I can have groceries delivered. All you need to do is watch the office and call me if you have any questions. I'll be home because, obviously, I can't go anywhere. Can you do me a favor, though? Between my broken bones and painful shoulder, I've already used a whole shitpot of sick days, and Mr. Rose might be mad. If he calls, could you tell him that I'm busy or out of the office and will call him back. Call me, and I'll call him from home."

"Sure, I can do that. Just get better. I don't know if I can handle the office for a month, let alone two. I'm not a lawyer, you know."

"You'll be fine, so don't worry, Dortha, and thanks for covering for me. I owe you big time."

Chapter 17

Maggie and Brick
Present Day

Brick and Maggie arrived right on time to enjoy Doc and Janey's cock-a-two-tails, which meant she made doubles. Janey would enthusiastically make two drinks at once, but if she had to deprive herself of whatever conversation evolved, she would be far less eager.

On the coffee table, Doc had placed a stack of journals that were all dated in the eighties and nineties. "Here they are," he said. "My handwritten notes recorded Mr. Walker's various school activities or lack thereof. I followed his arrest and trial closely because I really thought it might be the basis for an intriguing novel. I even retained these newspaper articles that chronicle the story of the automobile theft and maiming of Sarah Hudson.

"The prosecution accused Walker of stealing her canary yellow 911 and her purse containing over $500. Walker told the police that he had been at home when TwoJohnny stole the car and money, but TwoJohnny picked him up at his house afterwards. He said TwoJohnny told him Mrs. Hudson had loaned him the car. The two boys drove to Vegas and abandoned the Porsche along the way before stealing a blue Studebaker Lark to finish the drive to Vegas. Law enforcement never recovered the Studebaker. The sheriff reasoned that Walker dumped the Lark at an auto salvage yard located near the hotel. The auto salvage company had no record, which is not unusual since it likely had negligible value. Another possibility though was that they had dumped it with the keys in it, or it might have already been a stolen vehicle when they happened upon it. TwoJohnny never returned to Barrier, as far as I know, so nobody knew his version of the story."

Maggie sipped her Chardonnay and mused aloud, "I was a little girl at the time and don't really remember anything regarding his arrest or trial. We briefly reviewed his case in one of my college classes, but that was years ago. I know that Walker has denied it all these years, but what do you think really happened, Doc? Do you think he hurt Mrs. Hudson and stole her car and money?"

Doc paused and didn't answer straightaway, but Janey filled the silence, "I would describe Charlie as a mean and wretched person who is capable of anything. He started quite a few fights and bullied his way through school. One of his escapades that happened when he was fourteen or fifteen shows how mean he was. One boy, Freddie something, used a wheelchair most days. He was a young boy of twelve, had been treated for bone cancer in his hips, and couldn't walk more than a few steps without the chair. One day Charlie followed him into the school lavatory and stole his wheelchair when Freddie had entered the stall. Charlie sneaked the chair out of school and put it in his car. The next day he sold it for $20.00. Can you think of anything worse?"

Maggie drew back and wrinkled her brow as she had not heard this story before. "He stole a kid's wheelchair and sold it? That's horrible."

Janey continued, "Yes, he did. To make matters worse, Freddie was his cousin. It's been a long time, but I've never forgotten that incident. Freddie lives here and uses a wheelchair full time. He testified at the trial while Charlie glared at him. I don't think Walker ever understood how meanspirited this theft was."

Doc added, "That's Charlie Walker, a miscreant with no real values and no moral compass. He could be mean or hurtful to anyone. I think his mother tried to keep him straight, but she couldn't control him, and he always found trouble. I can't imagine prison has changed him."

"Was he punished for stealing the chair?" Brick wanted to know.

Doc continued, "No, nothing ever happened. Everybody knew he did it, but his mom came to the rescue. The chair had disappeared, but nobody believed Freddie's story regarding who did it, because Freddie also had a reputation for lying. Charlie's mother alibied him, saying he had already left school to drive her to work, and somebody else stole it. The school had no record of his departure that day, but his mother's statement was enough to get him off the hook."

"I had heard he had a mean streak, but I hadn't heard this story before. The prison system has indicated he is coming this way, and I can't wait to meet him," Maggie uttered sarcastically. "I suppose there's the chance he changed while in prison."

Brick looked at her sideways and rolled his eyes. "Prison doesn't change people for the better; it changes them for the worse."

Chapter 18

Dortha Ling
Twenty-Five Years Ago

Dortha manned the Forsythe office, and for the first two days nothing interrupted her, no walk-ins, no phone calls, and she set herself to work studying for the bar exam. She had taken a bar exam prep course during her last semester of law school but was determined to pass the difficult exam on the first go-around, so she spent her time reviewing all her notes and rereading the textbooks. She enjoyed the sections on taxes and estate planning and thought she would like to go that direction. The criminal law sections, not so much.

Late on the fifth day of her near-dutyless job, the phone rang, and she answered. "Forsythe office of Rose and Reubens."

The voice on the other end of the phone said, "I am Sergeant Daniels with the Barrier Sheriff's Office, and we have arrested a young man who requires the services of a public defender. Do you have anyone available who can help him?"

Dortha paused, not knowing what to say. "Yes, Rose and Reubens has the public defender contract, but the paralegal had an accident, and isn't in the office right now. I can ask him to call you."

"Sure, that would be fine. Could he come to Barrier to see this inmate today?" Sergeant Daniels asked.

"Of course, I'll give him the message." She wrote down the pertinent information and called Josh.

"Josh, a sergeant from the Barrier Sheriff's Office called, and one of their inmates needs a public defender. Can you call him back? They want to see a P.D. as soon as possible."

"No can do, Dortha. I rented a wheelchair to use, but I'm in such bad shape that even that isn't helping. Use of my shoulder is limited, and it is difficult to roll from one place to another. I can't walk because of my broken leg and sprained foot, and I am unable to drive because of, well, everything. I'm thinking that I'm going to be out for at least two months, maybe longer. You'll have to take over the office and cover this case."

"Two months? Are you kidding? How will you keep this a secret from Mr. Rose for two months? I can't do it. I'm not a paralegal or a lawyer. I haven't even taken the bar exam," Dortha answered. "We should call Mr. Rose."

Josh snapped back without hesitation, "No! You can't do that, Dortha. I might lose my job, and besides, the law license is merely a piece of paper. I've seen people much less capable than you in court. You know everything you need to know, you even graduated with honors. Go to Barrier and talk to the inmate. Get the lowdown on his arrest, bring back all of the info, and I'll walk you through the process. What's he charged with?"

"I don't know, the officer didn't say, and I didn't think to ask. I've never done this before, Josh." Dortha protested. "You are a paralegal. You should talk to the inmate, and you should definitely call Mr. Rose."

"No, no, no. It'll be a piece of cake, but don't tell Mr. Rose. He would kick my ass, and I'll lose my job. Drive to Barrier, introduce yourself as a representative from the office of Rose and Reubens. You don't have to tell them your qualifications as a lawyer, and no one will ask to see your bar card. Wear lawyer clothes, act like a lawyer, and talk to the inmate. You'll be fine. Take a briefcase, a yellow pad, and a law book, it doesn't matter which one. Any law book will be fine, just so it's thick. The inmate probably did something simple like a DUI or a bar fight. It's Barrier, and nothing ever happens in Barrier. Phone me when you get back. Easy stuff, Dortha."

"Josh, he can't fire you because you broke your leg, it's against the law, and I don't have lawyer clothes. I have jeans and t-shirts but nothing appropriate to see clients in. Forsythe has no decent clothing stores, and I didn't buy any because I thought I would be in Reno. This is crazy."

"It makes no difference, it's Barrier. They don't expect much."

He hung up, and Dortha stared ahead wondering what she was getting herself into.

Chapter 19

Walker
Twenty-Five Years Ago

Mom and Sergeant Daniels exited the room, leaving Attorney Ling and me alone. I still didn't think she was an attorney and reasoned she might be a spy for the sheriff's office. But to her credit she had plucked me out of the sheriff's questioning so maybe she was legit. I'd take a chance.

Ms. Ling withdrew a yellow pad, pen, and thick book from her backpack. With copies of the arrest documentation in hand, she said, "Tell me what you know relating to TwoJohnny. Don't leave anything out, and don't lie. Start from the beginning." She sounded bolder than she had when Sergeant Daniels had been present. Even bossy.

I told her about TwoJohnny, some of which was the truth. "TwoJohnny told me that Mrs. Hudson loaned him the Porsche and a little money so we could go to Vegas to gamble. We ran out of gas on the drive and had to ditch the car in another town. I don't remember the town's name, but the truck stop had a restaurant called Joe's Diner. We hid the car in a safe place and planned to pick it up when we went back home with our winnings, so TwoJohnny pocketed the keys. We would leave the Lark at the café and drive the Porsche back to Barrier later in the week. A simple plan, but solid. We would have enough money for gas to drive it back to Mrs. Hudson's house.

We borrowed the Lark because we needed transportation, and the owner left the keys on the seat. It had a full tank of gas and ran fine for an old car."

Ms. Ling looked blankly at me before she squeaked out another question, "And Mrs. Hudson? How did she get hurt?"

I needed to shift the blame to Dos, and I had an idea. "I dunno. I can tell you what TwoJohnny said. He told me he went to her house to thank her for the use of the car. When he arrived, she was lying on the floor, bleeding with her eyeball popped out of its socket, and he became scared. When Dos got to my house to pick me up for our trip, he acted kinda funny. He didn't mention her eye until we had driven part-way to Vegas. When he told me she had been injured, I pleaded with him to return to Barrier and see if she was okay, but he didn't listen. We both had seen trouble with the cops before, and I didn't want this blamed on us. We hid the Porsche behind a grove of mesquite trees so it would be safe. When we arrived in Las Vegas, TwoJohnny dumped me at a hotel and said he would go pick up some burgers. He didn't come back and called me the next day from the border. At least that's what he told me. I didn't talk to him, but he left a message."

"Why do you think Mrs. Hudson started screaming when she saw you at the hospital?" Ms. Ling asked. "She assured the sheriff that she recognized you, and it was you who had injured her and stolen her money. Maybe her car, too, she wasn't sure."

I had anticipated this question and knew what to say, "TwoJohnny and I don't look alike but our long, skinny frames are similar to each other, so I guess she might have mistaken me for him. We both have dark hair cut in mullets and wear green Barrier High School baseball caps. I helped her with chores the day before, and she might have had me on her mind. She must have thought TwoJohnny was me when he went to thank her for the use of the car. With her eye damaged and in her dazed state, she likely couldn't see well. She might have been delusional and switched around her times and people. My mom and she have been friends for a long time, and I would never hurt her."

Attorney Ling probed again, "And TwoJohnny? Would he hurt her? Did his mom know her, too?"

I answered, "TwoJohnny's mother abandoned him earlier last spring, and I don't know if they knew each other. I don't think he would intentionally hurt anybody, but he sometimes doesn't make the best choices and can be a dumbass. He said she had already collapsed to the floor, but maybe he lied. He lies all the time, so maybe he lied about going to Mexico, too." I thought I might be on the right track with the liar comments, at least I hoped so. I continued, "You can ask the school, they'll confirm that he was a compulsive liar." I fell quiet before asking, "Do you want to know anything else? I didn't hurt Mrs. Hudson. I would never hurt her. Can I go home now?"

Ms. Ling warned, "Charlie, I hope you told me the truth. Without TwoJohnny as a witness or available to be interviewed, it will be difficult to shift the blame to him. Mrs. Hudson will make an effective witness. She has worked as the juvenile probation officer for a long time, has helped many kids, and is respected in this community. Despite losing the sight in her left eye, she claims that she saw you, not TwoJohnny, come to her house and injure her. She is positive you hurt her, and I doubt the prosecutor will change her mind. She will swear under oath, and the police will charge you with harming her. The police spoke with Mrs. Hudson during lunch, and she says she doesn't know who TwoJohnny is. She's never met him."

"Are you serious?" I roared. "This is bullcrap. I didn't do anything. What's the punishment for hurting someone?"

Ms. Ling answered, "I believe they will charge you with several offenses: attempted murder, mayhem, and car theft, and I doubt they will let you out on bail."

"Murder? That's bullcrap. I didn't try to murder her, and I didn't steal the Porsche. TwoJohnny did. I don't know what mayhem is, but I didn't do that either."

"Did TwoJohnny steal the Porsche, or did Mrs. Hudson lend it to him?" Ms. Ling pressed.

I bowed my head and revised my comments, "He might have stolen it. He told me she lent it to him, but he's such a liar. Maybe he stole it."

Dortha liked Charlie and felt oddly drawn to him, but sensed lies, "If you don't want to go to prison, Charlie, you must tell me the entire truth. To answer your question, mayhem means permanently injuring someone, in this case, the loss of her eye. The penalty for attempted murder is two to twenty years, but they can tack on an additional ten years for the eye. With her being in law enforcement, the judge could opt for the longer time. And for stealing the Porsche 911, you could be sentenced to another five years. However, for your first offense, the judge might be lenient and give you a combined sentence of ten years, but I don't know for sure. I do know I have my work cut out for me. You have tumbled headfirst into a pile of deep shit, my friend."

Chapter 20

Maggie and Brick
Present Day

Brick and Maggie arrived home to enjoy a leisurely dinner with the twins. Bridget had been on guard duty eyeing Maggie's mother suspiciously with intermittent growls that expressed her distrust. Although she still wasn't accepting of the twins, ironically, she had become their protector. She yapped at Brick and Maggie, who wondered if she reprimanded them for leaving her behind or if they had been transferred to her suspicious-people list.

"Cagey has been trying to get ahold of you, Maggie," her mother offered. "He didn't say why though, but he wants you to call him."

"Maybe Walker showed up," Maggie guessed. She dialed the office number, and Cagey answered. "What's going on? Is Walker in Barrier?" she asked.

"Not Walker, but we have another issue," Cagey responded. "Could you come down here? A guy from Los Angeles insists on seeing the person in charge, which is obviously you."

"Who is it?" Maggie asked. "I just got home. Can it wait?"

"No, I don't think so," Cagey answered. "He's been in our office for what feels like a very long hour and is still hot. You might want to bring Brick with you."

"I'll be there in a few minutes," Maggie sighed and disconnected the call. "Mom, can you watch the twins for a while longer? Something is going on, and Cagey thinks both of us need to go to the sheriff's office. We'll take Bridget, so you don't have to deal with her."

"That dog hates me," Maggie's mother complained glaring back at the dog. "I don't think she trusts me."

A forest green VW van with California license plates sat in front of the sheriff's office when they arrived. Maggie and Brick entered the office and greeted Cagey and the visitor.

The visitor growled, "I'm Vincent Ivan Pierson, but most people call me Viper. I'm from Los Angeles and want to file a criminal complaint against one of your residents here in Barrier."

Maggie looked at Cagey before responding. She wondered why he couldn't take care of this complaint himself and why he felt it necessary for Brick to join them. Her manners proved stronger than her frustration as she extended an invitation to the visitor. "Let's go into my office, Mr. Pierson, and you can tell me what's on your mind." Brick remained in the outer office also wondering why his presence was requested.

Viper was a small man with massive black hair twisted into seven dreadlocks cascading to his waist. The braids intertwined a variety of gray and green ribbons reminding Brick of snakes. Maybe that was the viper part. He wore multiple silver earrings, which lay on one side of his head making him appear a bit lopsided. He wore black jeans with three zippers on the front of each leg that served no purpose. A black long-sleeved turtleneck, black cowboy boots, and a black, leather, flat-brimmed Stetson hat completed the image. The Stetson currently rested on Cagey's desk.

Brick asked Cagey, "What's he want? Why am I here?"

Cagey, who had never been keen on Brick, answered slowly. "His strange accusation involves my brother, Jay. I thought you might be able to help explain why he alleges Jay did something wrong. It makes no sense to me, and I'm certain it's a false accusation. At least Jay's never said anything in all the time he's owned the Chicken Dinner Ranch."

Brick asked, "What's his accusation? Did someone hurt him?"

"No. He says he's been robbed, not here, but in L.A.," Cagey revealed.

"L.A.? Why is he making the complaint here and not in L.A.?" Brick queried.

"Do you remember those paintings that hang in the upstairs hall of the CDR? He claims he painted them. He says he's a graffiti artist in L.A., and somebody stole his works from the streets. They now hang in the CDR outside the girls' rooms. He says he painted those seven, plus at least three others that aren't upstairs."

"Some of the graffiti in L.A. is amazing, but I'm not sure how you steal graffiti," Brick answered. "The artists use buildings, doors, and walls as their canvasses. Most people look at the graffiti as vandalism, but others view it as a source of art or even beauty. Business owners try to keep ahead of the artists but aren't successful most of the time. Besides demolishing parts of buildings, I don't see how graffiti can be stolen."

Cagey clarified, "I asked him the same question. He says thieves steal parts of structures. They cut apart a wall or a door and sell it online. He alleges that Jay stole his walls."

Chapter 21

Charlie
Twenty-Five Years Ago

After my so-called lawyer left, Daniels escorted me to a cell and read me my rights. Up to that point, I didn't believe they were serious about arresting me. I thought they would harass me like they had done before and send me home. Ms. Ling didn't help much either. I wanted to go home, but it looked like Daniels would keep me in a cell for the night. Things had gotten worse, not better. Damn, this was getting serious.

I ate a mac and cheese dinner, but ignored the green beans served with it. The dinner wasn't tasty nor tasteless, but I ate it and didn't complain. Adding hot sauce would have improved it immensely. After dinner, Mom showed up with New Gene, and Daniels said I could talk to them alone. They re-handcuffed me and moved me to the same room where I had been before, but this time, I noticed a huge mirror on the wall. I didn't know if it had been there earlier, and I wondered if it was a two-way window like they have on TV cop shows. I didn't know for sure but thought I should watch what I said in case the cops planned to listen.

New Gene wanted to kill me, and Mom wasn't far behind. "What did you do, Charlie?" New Gene roared. The bulging vein in his forehead pulsated hard and reminded me of flashing purple neon light. I fixated on the vein for a minute before New Gene brought me out of it.

"God dammit, Charlie, what is going on with you? You're going to end up in prison. I don't believe your innocence for one second, and anything you do with TwoJohnny can only mean trouble. Didn't you and TwoJohnny think any of this through? How could you harm that sweet woman? Do you have any idea what she will have to go through? Oh, yeah, you didn't think, as usual. Did you forget that she was a law enforcement officer? Killing or harming a law enforcement officer is a felony and can have the death penalty. I realize you didn't think or consider what she would go through, but now she has no left eye, permanent injury. Losing an eye is a big deal and will change her life forever. She may not be able to work or drive a car anymore. Dammit to hell. At age eighteen damn years you became an adult. You know better and need to man up to whatever you and TwoJohnny did."

He ranted for a while longer with his vein pulsating the whole time, but I didn't say anything. When he paused, Mom started in. "Eugene's right. We want to believe your story, but we just don't. You and TwoJohnny have found yourselves in jams since first grade, but this takes the cake. Sarah has never done anything harmful to you; she's always been kind to you. She insists you did this and, frankly, I believe her. Why would she lie? They're going to send you to prison, Charlie. Start telling the truth."

I opened my mouth to talk, but they both interrupted me with more angry reprimands. They weren't going to listen to anything I had to say, so I clammed up and said nothing. My eyes swelled up, and I felt tears close to the surface.

Mom and New Gene did not believe me. The sheriff's office called me a liar and wanted to throw the book at me. TwoJohnny had disappeared. Mrs. Hudson blamed me, and everything had crashed down on me. I had mostly told the truth but didn't see any way out of the muck. I had not hurt Mrs. Hudson and had not stolen her car or money. To make matters worse, Dortha Ling was a fucking incompetent lawyer.

Chapter 22

Maggie and Brick
Present Day

It wasn't long before Maggie and Viper exited her office, but he didn't look any happier than he had when he entered. Maggie introduced Brick as a reserve deputy. For professional purposes, she used her maiden name, Monroe, so Viper might not have noticed their marital connection.

Viper and Brick shook hands, and Maggie relayed a shortened version of the story Viper told her. Viper looked back and forth among the three of them, nodding and saying "That's right" a few times.

Viper asked, "How long do you think it will be before you give me back my stolen art? They've been gone a few years, but they're mine, and I want them now. The manager of the whorehouse must have stolen them. There were ten paintings total, but only seven are hanging on the walls, so he must have three more stashed elsewhere. Does he own another whorehouse?"

Maggie answered, "No, he has one brothel, but he has other businesses. We'll investigate and call you as we progress, or you can call next week if you haven't heard from us." She handed him a card listing her name and phone number. "We'll be in touch, Mr. Vincent. One other thing: Do you have insurance and an appraisal of their value? Without a dollar value, it will be difficult to verify their worth. Can you give us an idea?"

Viper thought for a minute and eyed first Maggie, then Brick, followed by Cagey, and lastly Bridget. He cocked his head and said, "My art is unique, but people don't recognize why. I encrypt two pictures into one painting with one obvious image, but the other is subliminal. Many people never see the veiled images, but those who do, realize their uniqueness and value. The covert images may be as small as a honeybee hidden in the design of a costume, but other images depict more elaborate imagery, such as something painted by a Renaissance artist. For example, I once concealed the likeness of Mona Lisa's eyes in a peacock's tail. That work remains in L.A. Since I usually paint on buildings at night, I paint rapidly, which is part of my joy and intrigue. When I finish a painting by dawn, I hide to enjoy the looks on the building owners' faces when they see the paintings for the first time. It makes me laugh.

"As for insurance, Sheriff, I paint street art on public buildings, so they have no insurance. They've never been appraised, but I can tell you what they have sold for in the past."

Maggie had no idea of the value but would have guessed a couple hundred dollars. Maybe. It was street art, after all.

Viper smiled at Maggie and repositioned his Stetson on this head, "My most recent painting, offered through an online auction, sold for $700,000."

Chapter 23

Charlie
Twenty-Five Years Ago

The prosecution promoted holding my trial without delay, and it occurred within a few weeks of my first visit to the jail. It lasted only two days. The whole town attended, and everybody I knew testified against me. The mid-summer heat poured into the courtroom, which had overhead fans but limited air conditioning. The bailiff opened the windows and occasionally a cool breeze stirred the air, but overall, it was a stifling forty-eight hours.

My attorney brought me different clothes, including a suit, shirt, and tie. I didn't own a suit, so I'm guessing she bought it at the rummage store. It fit okay and didn't stink, but the too-tight shirt had a spot on it, and the tie didn't match either the suit or the shirt. I wore my prison-issued sneakers because that's all I had.

The main witness, Mrs. Hudson, testified first. She sat in a wheelchair near the front of the courtroom, and when the bailiff called her name, she gave out an oral sigh that resembled a small shriek. Her daughter wheeled her to the front of the courtroom, and she appeared incredibly frail. Her hair had grayed since I had seen her, and she hunkered down in the chair with her hands clasped on her lap, her head tilted to one side. I didn't think she needed a wheelchair and considered it a part of an act. She wore a damn black pirate patch over her eye that emphasized her injury. I didn't know if the patch was real or a prop, but later a doctor testified that her eyeball had burned so, of course, she would never regain her sight. Judge Little looked up from his notes, stared down at me, and frowned. I felt sorry for her, but I hadn't done it. Ms. Ling asked how she knew that I had injured her. She explained I moved stuff for her the day before, and she had known me for a long time, adding that I had done a lousy job, was useless, and she didn't know why I tried to kill her. The prosecutor showed her the clothes I had been wearing when I went to visit her at the urgent care facility. She said they looked the same as when I struck and burned her with an iron and when I had visited her a few days later. It was total bullshit. I sank lower into my chair.

My attorney asked Mrs. Hudson if she knew TwoJohnny, and she said that she didn't. Ms. Ling told the judge she had no more questions and sat down. The prosecutor smiled.

Sergeant Daniels testified next and reported they found my fingerprints in Mrs. Hudson's house. Of course, they had; I helped her move stuff to her garage the day before she was hurt. The prosecutor inquired of my character, and Daniels mentioned that he had been to the house a few times when my mom and I had disagreements, and things grew out of control, but nothing ever came of it. He rattled off a bunch of things I had done as a young teen, like when I tried to steal gold from the mining office when I was twelve years old. I thought the court sealed minors' records, but the judge made an exception, and my attorney didn't object to that either. I thought he would mention the skunk smell I sprayed in Reynolds' cop car, but he didn't. Of that I was glad.

The prosecutor next called Mrs. Hudson's boss, Jim Rutherford, the head of juvenile probation, who testified as to Mrs. Hudson's character and described how many kids she had worked with and turned around. He stressed that she had a wonderful reputation, loved kids, and had been quite successful as a juvenile probation officer. He gave several examples of her successes, but I wasn't listed. He said I had skipped out on the probation requirement at twelve years old, even though Mrs. Hudson's office was in a different town, and I didn't drive. In truth, she and my mom had been long-time friends, and my mom arranged to have me excused after the initial visit. Mr. Rutherford proceeded to inform the jury I held a grudge against her because of my previous probation situation, which wasn't true either. But that might change.

My cousin, Freddie, wheeled himself up to the witness stand and glared at me as he went by. Dressed in a suit and tie, he resembled a Mormon missionary, not the weasel he was. He had never grown tall, and he looked small, fragile, and rather spooky. His eyes bulged, and he had no eyebrows. I had a hard time looking at his polka-dotted pimply face. His testimony damaged my case, as he swore that I stole his wheelchair, making the jury gasp. Their eyes almost bored a hole straight through me. I didn't think it was a big deal at the time, but in hindsight I guess it was. I should try to repay him the twenty bucks sometime. Ms. Ling asked him how he knew I had stolen the wheelchair, and he paused and said, "He bragged to the kids at school." I don't think I did brag, but most of the kids knew.

The prosecution called one of my teachers, Mrs. O'Dell, to the stand, and this confused me, as she had been one of my few quality teachers. I wondered what negative remarks she could make. I liked her, did the assignments in her class, and she never gave me a poor grade. The prosecutor asked her to define my character, and she didn't answer at first. He probed a bit more, and she admitted she had doubts of my honesty. It seems she had missed a few dollars from her purse, and another student suggested I stole it. Of course, I hadn't taken it, but her story created doubt in the minds of the jury. Ms. Ling didn't ask her any questions either.

Finally, my attorney laid out her case. She looked like a legitimate attorney that day, with a black suit and fancy shoes, an improvement over the jeans, t-shirt, and boots she wore when we met. She actually looked hot, and I found myself wishing we had met under different circumstances. She had told me that she would rely on character witnesses. My mom took the stand as her first character witness, and she didn't wait for any questions, blurting out that I lied all the time. She then recited the story of her stupid cat getting lost in the desert. She rattled on, telling of the time I borrowed her car. She acted like she owned a Corvette, but it had been a piece-of-trash diesel Chevette, and I hadn't wrecked it, so I don't know why she continued to be so angry. Ms. Ling said my mom would be a character witness, but her testimony didn't help me at all. She said I often skipped school, but that wasn't true because I had skipped school just three times during the school year. Three times wasn't often.

Ms. Ling called New Gene to the stand, and I figured my life had turned to burned toast. As it turned out, he gave the most honest testimony of any witness, saying that I had the potential to be a wholesome kid, but I needed more discipline. He suggested to the judge I join the Marines to straighten out because they didn't call it *Uncle Sam's Misguided Children* for nothing. He and the jury laughed aloud. He said, if the judge would allow it, I could enlist, and in four years, I would be a changed person, upstanding and honest, plus I would learn a trade. He looked at me and nodded, meaning he was pleased, and his forehead vein had quieted down. The Marine Corps would change me; you could be sure of it. I had never liked anyone as much as I liked him at that moment. I could have kissed him.

Ms. Ling asked every witness a few questions, but every time she was even close to reaching her goal, she failed to drive the point home. In the end, I didn't think she made any progress with my not-guilty plea with either the judge or the jury.

I wanted to testify on my own behalf, but Ms. Ling thought it would damage my case because I didn't have an alibi, and no one would believe me. She thought the story of TwoJohnny and me going to Vegas would be viewed as bogus, trying to cover my ass. TwoJohnny couldn't be found, and she didn't think that blaming an absent person who had never been in trouble would help me out.

Judge Little closed his eyes through much of the trial, making me wonder if he had fallen asleep. Every now and then, he fluttered his eyes and cast a sideways glance at Mrs. Hudson, smiling and adjusting his tie each time. His bald head with a gray fringe crowned him like a half-halo, and as he watched Mrs. Hudson, he licked his fingers and slicked down wayward hairs. Then he would look at me, and his eyes seemed to pierce straight through me, and I would duck down in my chair. He had a pen and pad on his desk, and he tapped the pen on the pad but never wrote anything down. After the testimony had finished, he sent the jury out without making any comments except what evidence they could use to decide. In no time at all, they came back and announced that I was guilty of everything. I couldn't believe it.

Ms. Ling, my attorney, stood up and sniveled, "We want to file for a mistrial," and sat back down. It was the first smart thing she had said all day.

The judge asked why she thought a mistrial would be in order, and she stood up again but didn't say anything. He answered no and proclaimed he would sentence me that day. He started to lecture me and emphasized Mrs. Hudson's position as a well-loved and capable law enforcement officer several times. He sounded like he considered her to be the best law enforcement officer in the country and announced that I would never change because I was without a doubt the worst person in Barrier. He praised Mrs. Hudson and addressed how she had been irreparably damaged. Ms. Ling sat in her chair looking flustered as the judge ranted for half an hour. Without notice, he slammed the gavel down and announced twenty-five years with no parole. My mom shrieked, and I threw up.

Chapter 24

Maggie and Brick
Present Day

"We work in the wrong business," Maggie stated after she watched Viper exit her office and enter his van. "People pay $700,000 for street art? You must be kidding. I mean it's interesting, but still, it's street art."

Brick commented, "In Los Angeles, the graffiti artists have become a cult. I dealt with a significant number of graffiti artists during my time on the police force there. Depending on how you view graffiti, the artists either vandalize or embellish all kinds of buildings. Sometimes their work is even political, taking sides on issues or political parties or events and often focuses on societal injustices like poverty and racism. Other times, it can be used as sales promotions, advertising products or services. I once saw several pigs painted on the side of a meat processing company. A graffiti artist tagged the building by painting it in the middle of the night, but the owner liked the concept so much that he began using a similar picture to advertise his business. While many people consider graffiti vandalism and a destruction of property, there are quite a few people who consider some graffiti as plain old-fashioned fun, like cartoon characters or movie icons. Donald Duck and Marilyn Monroe were the most popular when I was in L.A. The artwork in the CDR falls into that category, caricatures of the movie stars of the 1950s and 1960s including, Marilyn Monroe, Jane Russell, Elizabeth Taylor. All women, no men. Most graffiti artists remain anonymous, not wanting to be arrested for or involved with vandalism, so I find it odd that Viper came forward. Did he visit the Chicken Dinner Ranch and see them, or did he learn about them elsewhere?"

Maggie answered, "He said a friend told him of the paintings hanging at the CDR after they recognized his work. He traveled to Barrier this week to see for himself, and when he saw them, he became irate. Luckily, he didn't try to take them off the wall or personally accuse Jay of theft but came here instead. If he had threatened Jay, he might have had a fight on his hands. Jay's a lot bigger than he is and would have cleaned his clock. I warned Viper against returning to the CDR and hope he takes my caution seriously, but I don't know if he will or not. He seemed iffy on his answers to my questions regarding his going back to L.A. Cagey, why don't you keep an eye on him until he leaves Barrier?"

"On it, Boss," Cagey answered as he grabbed his hat and keys and went out the door.

"Thanks, Cagey. Brick and I will head over to the CDR to speak with Jay. Why don't you stop by, too?" Maggie invited. "Shall we take Bridget or leave her to guard the office?"

"She can guard for a while. She's had her dander up all day, and this will give her reason to adjust her attitude. The first time we walked through the CDR, I noticed the paintings on the second-floor walls. The Marilyn and the others don't fit the rest of the brothel's western décor, but I honestly paid little attention to them. I guess I should have been more observant," Brick lamented as they walked to her vehicle.

"Yes, I noticed them, too," Maggie replied. "The full-sized, floor-to-ceiling caricatures are vivid and intense. I never thought about it, but they definitely don't seem to fit with the Ranch. Did you notice if they had autographs?"

"No, I didn't look, to be truthful. We were in the middle of figuring out the pornography case. I remember I was wearing running shorts and banged up my knees in the tunnel," he answered. "The idea of asking you for a date had taken priority over scrutinizing the paintings. Hard to believe, I know," He grinned at her recalling their hike through the tunnel.

They arrived at the Chicken Dinner Ranch, and this time they entered through the front door instead of the secret tunnel they entered through the last time. The bar was in full swing, but the noise faded as customers became aware of them. Heads turned, and the crowd seemed restless. Maggie wore her uniform with her various police paraphernalia hanging from her belt. Brick had on his signature blue jeans and t-shirt. They both stood tall, and when standing together, they became an imposing and handsome couple. Maggie asked to see Jay, and the hostess beckoned him on the phone. They sat down to wait, and the din rose again.

"How the hell have you been?" Jay roared as he burst in the room. He towered over them with his bigger-than-life personality, "You haven't visited for a coon's age. Glad to see you!" he continued, while eagerly grasping their hands with hearty handshakes. He scanned the people in the bar and called to them, "Don't mind these two; they're friendly." He laughed aloud and gestured for Brick and Maggie to follow him to his office that was located behind the large ranch-style kitchen. The alluring aroma of fried chicken and fresh-baked bread filled their nostrils, reminding them they hadn't eaten.

"What can I do for you?" Jay bellowed. "Want a cup of coffee?" Before Brick could answer, Jay called, "Nat, we need coffee now. Three cups."

"Yes, please," Brick answered. "Your cook makes amazing coffee."

The coffee arrived, and Jay introduced Nat. "Nat, I want you to meet these folks. Sheriff Maggie and Deputy Brick, who doubles as the high school principal. Ain't that a kick? Nat is my new bouncer. He arrived in Barrier a few days ago and so far, he's been able to handle the job, and I'm hoping we can keep him."

Nat was a tall, burly man of about forty-five with a belly that protruded over his belt. Sleeve tats covered his arms, gold jewelry dangled from his neck and left ear, and several fingers held gold rings. He had shaved close and wore a gray CDR uniform with black and red patches sewn on both arms. His name was embroidered on his front pocket.

Brick and Maggie both rose to take the coffee. Brick said, "I'm Brick O'Brien. My pleasure." Brick's eyes locked in on his tats and said, "Have we met before? You look familiar."

Nat shrugged, "I doubt it since I've never been in Barrier before this week. I spend most of my time in Vegas."

Maggie shook Nat's hand, and as she looked him over, the nape of her neck tingled. She glanced over at Brick before tendering the first question to Jay. "Could we see the murals in the upstairs hall again? Someone had some questions and came to see us about them, and I'd like to see them again. I haven't been upstairs since our initial visit, more than two years ago."

"The murals? You mean Marilyn Monroe and Jane Russell?" Jay knitted his eyes in puzzlement. "Sure. Why not? What's the question, and who posed it?"

"The question comes from an artist who claims he painted them. He says they were stolen from some L.A. buildings a few years ago and somehow landed here. The artist's name is Vincent Ivan Pierson, but he calls himself Viper. Have you heard of him?" Maggie asked.

Nat's head jerked upward at the mention of Viper's name, but he recovered and pursed his lips together. He shifted his eyes to each of the other three, but no one seemed to notice his sudden twitch, or at least no one said anything.

"Viper? I don't think so. I could check the records to see if he slithered in though," Jay answered with a loud chuckle. "I don't recall any of my employees or guests reporting such a critter."

Maggie smiled at his pun, asking, "How did you obtain the murals? Did you buy them, or did someone give them to you? Do you know their origin?"

"I did not steal them, if that's what you're asking. I bought them from a Beverly Hills art dealer a few years ago. I went on a graffiti art tour, one of those funky things you can find in California. I liked the works and thought they might brighten up the upstairs hall and asked to buy them. A few days later an art dealer called me and offered them to me. I bought them. I hadn't owned the Ranch long but had made a ton of money. They cost a couple thousand each, but I bought them. I think I purchased ten of them, so $20,000 for the lot. I repeat, I did not steal them."

The four of them climbed the wide staircase to the second floor and began to review the murals. Maggie photographed each of them. Brick searched for signatures on the paintings, photographing them as he found them. Jay and Nat stood by, neither of them saying anything. The veiled signatures were difficult to see, but they were there. Viper had scripted his name into each.

Chapter 25

Dortha Ling
Twenty-Five Years Ago

The Charlie Walker trial did not strike the radar of the central office of Rose and Reubens because during his two-month respite, Josh checked into the Reno office every day by phone and indicated that nothing was happening, never spilling the beans as to Dortha's role in the Walker trial. He and Dortha collaborated, but Josh never comprehended the dynamics of the small-town case, and his advice to her proved to be sketchy at best and sometimes flat out wrong. When the trial ended and she had lost Charlie's case, she had become frustrated and disillusioned with the law and her naïve trust in Josh who had lied throughout the entire process.

She had lost her first big case, and with the bar exam looming over her head, she called Mr. Rose and resigned her position as a public defender, claiming she needed time to study for the bar exam, which she passed with flying colors.

Fearing her credentials, or lack thereof, could be investigated and she would go jail, she left Barrier for Las Vegas and accepted a position with a personal finance law firm that dealt in writing wills, explaining taxing options, and building capital estates for clients. The agency hired her, and she gained the reputation of being the *go-to* attorney for corporate executives seeking advice on expanding their estates.

Chapter 26

Charlie
Present Day

That's how I arrived in prison and spent a quarter of a century behind bars waiting for the truth to come out, but it never did. I plotted for the entire quarter of a century on how to find that son of a bitch TwoJohnny and hurt him. I didn't know where he had gone but would start in Barrier.

When they released me from prison, the correctional officers (they didn't like to be called guards, even though that's what they were) warned me to stay out of trouble. I plan to do exactly that after I locate Dos and pay him back for what he did to me. I want to kill him, there was no question about that, but I don't want to get tossed back in prison. But if I beat him up, I'd only be sentenced to jail for a short time, a piece of cake after what I finished a few days ago.

When I walked through the gates of the prison, I felt a rush of something, not sure what, but I knew I felt free, really free, for the first time after what seemed like a lifetime. I poked around my pocket for the coin Ms. Moneyjoy had given me during my first few months of incarceration. It looked different than it had the day she gave it to me. Originally, the embossed words *Time is the Coin of Life* lay on one side of the coin with *From, Ms. M* on the other side, but as I rubbed it every day, the words eroded to T C L with barely perceivable scratches between the words. The words had disappeared, but its influence remained.

I wanted desperately to buy beer and pizza, not the flat-tasting frozen shit that they serve in prison, but a real honest-to-goodness pepperoni pizza that oozed and bubbled and burned your tongue, along with an ice cold Coors. I walked to the town of Fenwick but didn't see a restaurant or bar, so I gave up on the food and drink. A couple cars buzzed past me, but the sign on the highway that read *Don't pick up hitchhikers in this area.* deterred them from opening their hearts and car doors, and I realized I would have to get a ride some other way.

I walked south on U.S. 93 for a few miles before spying an old GMC pickup at a ranch outside Fenwick with nobody in it. As luck would have it, the keys dangled from the ignition, so I borrowed it. I felt impenetrable with the windows down and the radio blasting away. At long last, out of prison, I enjoyed every minute of the drive and my new-found freedom. Highway 50 lay down the road and the gas gauge in the pickup said half full, enough to get me to Barrier.

At the turnoff onto Highway 50, an easy ride to Barrier, I abandoned the pickup at a nearby rest stop. I decided to spend the night there and walk into Barrier in the sunlight the next morning. I stuck a dollar in the user fee box, so I wouldn't get a ticket. I slept soundly but woke up aching from my cramped position on the front seat of the pickup. The owner of the pickup had left a half-dozen tiny candy bars, most likely Halloween leftovers, a sleeve of Girl Scout Do-si-dos, and a jug of water on the floor. I scarfed them down when I woke up. I tossed the wrappers in the garbage bin and wiped the pickup down so the sheriff wouldn't find any fingerprints. I left a thank you note to be polite, but I didn't sign it. The prison had given me $100 when I left, and I had saved a similar amount from my job at the prison library. I would use part of it to rent a room for the next night.

Barrier looked different than it had when I left a quarter of a century before: It had shrunk and looked older. I knew the gold mines had dried up but hadn't considered that the businesses they supported had vanished with them. The old Woolworth's Five and Dime had disappeared, replaced by a pet shop and an ice cream parlor. The Thom McAn shoe store, Blockbuster Video, and the Sears catalog store had boarded up their windows and appeared ragged and lonely. That whole section of the town seemed like a ghost town.

Wallace Johnstone's General Store seemed to be open for business and thriving. Back in the day, they had sold everything from clothing and medical supplies to guns and groceries. I still wore my prison-issued sneakers and was ready to swap them out. Fenwick had issued me one set of clothes, those I wore, so I would need to buy new duds as well.

The Panorama Hotel also had survived, and I thought that maybe I could rent a room in the hotel for the night. The lone grocery store seemed to be the Safeway store. I wondered what had happened to David's Foods, which had been a large grocery chain when I left. It, too, had boarded windows.

The castle stood tall with its ceramic tiles, but many had faded and cracked and appeared weary. The fence had disappeared, and the moat had been cleaned up and cemented with water flowing through it. The owners had paved the dirt parking lot and installed outdoor lighting. There were quite a few cars that sat in the lot. A sign hanging above its arched entrance read *Barrier B&B,* which baffled me. Another brothel?

I continued walking because I wanted to see our old house. I knew Mom had moved from Barrier, and I didn't know where she was. She wrote me irregularly, and one year she said that she had split with New Gene. He might live here, although he'd be pretty old by now if he was still alive.

I hustled past the sheriff's office averting my eyes to the other side of the street. I didn't want to see the sheriff, although the one decent correctional officer who worked at Fenwick recommended that I check in with him. I hoped the sheriff wasn't Daniels, although I thought he likely would also be dead. Whoever had been elected was probably a prick because most sheriffs were. Just ask anybody in prison.

Murder Almost

I passed Mrs. Hudson's house, which brought back a flood of horrible memories. I wondered where she was. I knew somebody lived in her house because a car sat in the driveway, and three or four kids played in the yard, but the mailbox didn't have a name.

I easily found my mom's house. The mailbox had a Marine Corps sticker attached to it, and the faded, washed-out letters spelled Gene Jacobs. New Gene. He might still live here, but I had no way of knowing since I had not heard from him the whole time I had been locked up. Although I never had a dad, he had filled that role, but I had never told him. The tan adobe house looked fatigued and needed a coat of paint. The shake roof looked like it wouldn't stand many more windstorms, but its whiskey-bottle walls still twinkled in the sunlight, even though they were coated with dust. The yard needed mowing, and my mom's favorite flower beds sat empty. I walked to the back of the house to see what else remained.

Without warning, an old man holding a shotgun flung himself out of the rear door and pointed it straight at me. Damn. I wasn't doing anything except standing in the yard, but my hands flew above my head, and I dropped to my knees as I had been taught in prison. New Gene. He looked fit, but his grizzly white beard aged him. His face carried wrinkles and blotches and his arms were dotted with dark spots, age spots, I guessed. He wore a red plaid flannel shirt, blue jeans, cowboy boots, and a blue baseball cap with City of Barrier stenciled on it.

"Who are you, and what do you want?" he shouted.

"New Gene," I called. "It's me. Charlie. Charlie Walker. Don't you recognize me? They released me from Fenwick yesterday, and I came home. I didn't know you still lived here."

New Gene slowly lowered the shotgun. "Damn, Boy, I almost shot you. I didn't know you had gotten out. Your mom doesn't live in Barrier anymore. She lives in Carson City now. We divorced, and she moved, and I haven't seen her in a long time."

I dropped my hands and stood up. I didn't feel welcome, but I wanted to talk to him. He was the first person I came in contact with who knew me before I went to prison. "New Gene, you look great. Do you still work for the city?"

Gene said, "Hell, no. I'm retired from the city and the Corps, but I still do a few odd jobs for folks who need help. You want a beer?"

I smiled and said, "It's morning, but yes, I'd like a beer. I haven't had one since I left Barrier, but I've been wanting a cold one for twenty-five years."

I started to follow him into the house, but he turned and peered at me saying, "You wait here, Charlie. I'll get the beers and bring them outside. We can have a talk. I'd like to hear about your plans."

Chapter 27

Maggie and Brick
Present Day

Jay leaned toward the paintings and squinted to scrutinize the signatures. "I never noticed the artist's signatures before. They're obscure and blend into the artwork, but perhaps I didn't examine them closely. I'm not an art connoisseur, I just know when I like a painting. Or don't. Clients seem to enjoy these as we get lots of compliments, but nobody's ever indicated that they recognized them from L.A."

Nat remained silent in the background while the others examined the paintings, but didn't hesitate to voice his concerns as soon as he had the chance, "How can you be sure this Viper guy didn't autograph them today while in the CDR. Do you really believe him? He sounds like a crackpot to me. I mean, who names himself Viper?"

Maggie shifted her head to look at him, "That's a possibility, Mr...um... what's your last name again? I'll need it for my report."

"Griss. I'm Nathan Griss with two s's. But call me Nat."

"Thank you, Mr. Griss," Maggie answered formally. Something in his manners bothered her, but she didn't know what it was. "It's a helpful observation, and we will investigate that possibility. Viper's anger seemed out of control when I met with him, and I did not consider that he might have signed them when he came in. Jay, you said you purchased ten paintings, what did you do with the other three?"

Jay explained, "I stored the others. I purchased them from the Beverly Hills dealer, as I said, but I left the selection up to him. These seven paintings worked fine for the upstairs hallway, but two of the others weighed too much to be hung, and one painting, done in pastel colors, looked out of place with the rest. I planned to sell the other three but never managed to find time. Hanging them in the B&B was another option, but they didn't fit into the medieval décor."

"No, they definitely don't. We need to see them though, so where did you store them?" Maggie asked.

Jay said, "I own a warehouse here in town and a couple other storage units, one in Reno and the other in L.A. I don't recall where I stored the other three paintings, but if you give me time to check, I'm happy to locate them. I might need to borrow Cagey, if I may."

Nat interrupted, "It's quiet downstairs, and it would be my pleasure to search for them, Jay. I'll check the Barrier warehouse first, followed by Reno. If they aren't in either of those, I'll make a trip to L.A. If you'll give me the key and address of the warehouse, I'll get it done in no time."

"That sounds like a plan," Jay responded. "I'm swamped today, and it would be difficult for me to leave, so I appreciate the offer. Hopefully, I stored them here."

Maggie scrutinized Nathan and responded, "Thanks, Nathan, but I'd like to accompany you to dispel any accusations of improper police work. Checking the local warehouse and going to Reno would be simple but traveling to L.A. would take a little more planning." She thought of the twins and glanced at Brick. She hadn't left them for longer than a day, and a trip to L.A. would take two days for sure, maybe three.

Jay gave Nat and Maggie the warehouse address and the key to the padlock. Maggie offered him a ride, but he preferred taking his own vehicle, a sleek, black Jaguar convertible. The Jag and the usual Barrier vehicles, SUVs and pickups, were incongruous, and Maggie understood why he preferred the Jaguar over her cruiser.

Brick asked Maggie as they exited the brothel, "Do you want me to go with you? He's a big guy and kinda squirrelly. I don't trust him, regardless of what Jay said."

"No, I'm fine. I'll keep in close contact." She drove Brick home before stopping by her office to verify Viper had left town. She had a bad feeling about Nat, but her radar focused on Viper, preferring that he go back to L.A. rather than remain in Barrier. Cagey assured her he had left town, and everything had quieted down.

When she arrived at the warehouse, she parked next to the Jaguar near the front door, but Nat did not appear to be in the area. The door to the warehouse sat ajar, and she figured he had already entered. *I wish he had waited for me,* she thought to herself, *although I didn't tell him not to go inside.* The gray wooden warehouse, located apart from the center of town, looked bigger and taller than she thought it would be. Its two stories dwarfed her car, and it had elevated garage doors with one passageway for people and no windows. The inside remained black even with the open door, and since she didn't know where the light switch was, she went to her cruiser for a flashlight.

Maggie passed through the door to the dark warehouse and called out "Nat, where did you go?" She flashed the light in front of her, first over the wall, looking for a light switch but didn't see one. She noted stalls and crates, along with a few ATVs and trailers but didn't see Nat. A wooden staircase sat to the left.

Nat didn't answer, and she hesitantly walked a few more paces and flashed her light up the staircase to the upper story and called out again, louder this time. "Nat answer me. It's Sheriff Monroe." She heard steps and a rustle behind her. She started to turn, but everything went black, blacker than the windowless building. She fell to the ground with a thud.

Nat used her flashlight to light the way, dragging the sheriff to the far corner of the warehouse and binding her wrists with duct tape. A few drops of blood had trickled across her forehead, but it had clotted quickly so he didn't think it would cause a major problem. He wanted her out of the way, but not dead. He checked her pulse to confirm that she was still alive. She didn't move, but had regular, though shallow, breaths. He smiled at his relief. He picked up her flashlight and stripped her of her pistol, her phone, and the other accessories that hung from her belt. He exited the building, padlocking the door behind him. Her keys remained in the cruiser's ignition, so he grabbed them and locked it, as well.

Nat hadn't planned to leave Barrier in a hurry, but he didn't want to go to jail either. He had avoided jail all these years and didn't intend to get caught now. He hadn't expected Viper to show up in Barrier, but he had shown his face today staking claim to several graffiti paintings Viper had created. They had spent time together in Mexico and had done a couple heists but had avoided the law and had agreed that it was best to part company. Had Viper reneged on their agreement and followed him to Barrier, or had his appearance been happenstance? Whichever, he didn't intend to hang around to find out.

Nat texted Cagey using the sheriff's cell phone, "Nothing here. Going to Reno with Nat in his Jag. Never ridden in one. Back later. Might go to L.A. Call Brick."

Nat spun out of the parking area and wound his way to the highway leading to Las Vegas.

Chapter 28

Charlie
Present Day

I had no plans except to settle the score with the bastard TwoJohnny. Dos, the lying rat. Maybe New Gene could tell me where to find him, but I'd take my time and ease into that line of questioning.

"Thanks for the beer, Gene, it tastes better than I imagined it would after all this time. I'm not familiar with this kind of brew. NB beer? Do you know who makes it? Back in the day, I used to drink Coors all the time because the smooth taste and aroma made it one of my favorites. This beer has a strong bite, but I'm not complaining since I haven't had a beer in a quarter of a century, and I truly will welcome anything," I said, although I had zero urge to talk about beer companies.

"The beer market has changed. Coors and Bud ruled the Nevada beer world for a long time, but local companies entered the marketplace. Now local companies brew and sell their own beers. They call them designer beers, micros, or craft beers. A small company in Reno named Nevada Brews created this beer, and they don't sell anywhere except in northern Nevada. I like it, but you're right, Coors remains number one," Gene said holding his bottle up as if toasting the Coors brewery.

"Barrier has changed quite a bit. It shrank. What happened?" I asked. I hadn't talked to anybody regarding Barrier since I went to prison, except one correctional officer who had attended school here several years after I went to prison. He had told me the mines had shriveled, and the companies relocated to other sites.

Gene explained, "The closure of the mines mainly caused the town to shrink. But each mining company has a skeleton crew that continues to search for gold and maintain the claim to their property, in case they find another vein or strike. They take samples from the ground and test them to try and find trace elements of gold and other minerals. These extractions pay for the crews that remain, but most of the workers left for greener, or should I say *golder* pastures, changing Barrier into more of a community than a town. It has a small city government staff and, of course, the school, although that has also shrunk. Not many stores have stayed in business because people shop online and have their stuff delivered."

I had never used a computer because prisoners did not have access to computers, but I anticipated finding a whole new world. I had heard of online shopping but didn't realize how much people used it and had never seen anyone order anything.

"Shop online? Can anybody shop online?" I asked, wondering what else had changed.

"Shopping online became popular a dozen years ago. People use their computers and the internet to order what they want from Amazon or any other online store, and it is delivered within a few days or maybe even the next day. They've added satellite delivery centers and have great customer service. It's easier and less expensive than driving to Reno or Vegas to shop, and you don't have to deal with the traffic or go to one of the big boxes," Gene answered.

I stared at him with disbelief. "What happened to catalogs? Mom ordered my school clothes from Sears and Roebuck or Montgomery Wards."

"You've heard of Amazon.com, right? You can get anything and everything from Amazon.com. It's like a catalog on steroids. You can order groceries, books, clothes, anything you want. This week I ordered a filter for my refrigerator, and it arrived the next day, cheaper and quicker than driving to Reno and locating an appliance store. The big boxes try to copy Amazon with quick delivery. You probably haven't been to a big box, so we'll go to Reno or Vegas sometime to check them out. Best Buy. Home Depot. Lowes. Walmart. And plenty of others." Gene answered laughing, "But with Amazon, you can get what you want at a fair price, and it will arrive on your doorstep the next day. I've read they plan to use drones to deliver, but I haven't seen that yet."

"I read about drones, they're like a combination of electronic kites and remote operated toy planes from what I understand. It's a whole new world from the one I knew, isn't it, New Gene? Everything has changed," I lamented.

"Yup, a whole new world. Things have changed a lot," Gene said. "How did you get along in prison? The community was shocked at Judge Little's extreme sentencing and didn't understand his thinking. After he married Sarah Hudson, people gossiped, but nothing ever came of it. By that time, your mom and I had split, and she probably didn't know how to file an appeal. The Hudson incident was your first real adult run-in with the law, and your attorney seemed far too inexperienced to handle your case. I thought you received a raw deal, but the fact of that matter is that you shouldn't have hurt Sarah."

"Mrs. Hudson married Judge Little? I didn't know that. I noticed him flirting with her on the bench, although I couldn't complain to anyone. And now, after all this time, the thing that shocks me the most is that you still don't believe me. I am telling the truth when I say that I didn't hurt Sarah. Dos did. It is so frustrating that no one believes me, and I'm even more livid that I lost so many years of my life for something I didn't do. As far as my time in prison went, I quickly learned to manage myself, although I had huge challenges. The key to survival is keeping out of trouble and making sure the guards keep you safe. When other people dictate what you do, you'll be in trouble. Most inmates think the guards are the enemy, and gangs hold the key to keeping you safe, but that's not true, quite the opposite actually.

"I didn't do much except read, and I read almost every book in the library, even the almanacs. The tiny library, maybe 2,000 books, served as my safe haven, and I was grateful when people donated new books. While in high school, I didn't like to read, but in the joint, I found they helped me pass the time, and I learned about myself and life in general. I became interested in other people's lives and read every biography I could. Lots of famous people had difficult situations at the start of their lives, like I did, but they figured out how to get themselves out of it, and I figured I could, too. The staff assigned me to work in the library, and I was able to save a little money. I earned a high wage, for prison, that is, $1.00 an hour. I didn't have any way to spend it, so I saved it. The prison gave me $100 when I left, and with my savings from my library job, I should be okay for a while, but I want to get a job," I said. As I said it, I wondered how much the prices of things had changed since I left.

We chatted most of the day and drank a few more beers. I talked about my time in prison while New Gene listened. Finally, he asked, "What plans have you made? Did you learn a trade while in prison? What kind of work can you do?"

"They don't teach you anything useful in Fenwick. I earned my GED, and they made me go to their useless counseling sessions. There was only one counselor who really helped me, Ms. Moneyjoy. Even though she was old, she really got me thinking about things. She presented me with this challenge coin shortly after I arrived. It's like the Marine Corps coin you carry." I handed my coin to Gene.

Gene rolled it over in his hand and said, "T C L? What's that mean?"

"The letters wore down from my constant rubbing through the years. It used to say, *Time is the Coin of Life*, but the lowercase letters disappeared. Ms. Moneyjoy explained that time was like money, and I could spend it wisely or foolishly, but I had only one chance to use it. After I spent it, it was gone. She explained it in a way that made sense to me, and that's when I decided to make the most of the time I had in prison. She reminded me of you and your lectures while I was in high school. I should have listened to you, but obviously I didn't, and I blew it. I'm sorry, New Gene."

"Will you do me a damn favor, Charlie, and stop calling me New Gene. You're an adult now, and the other Gene is dead, so enough of the New Gene. I'm just Gene."

I mock saluted and said, "You've got it, Sarge. Fenwick didn't offer a lot of classes, but Ms. Moneyjoy suggested that I self-educate by reading and learning. I enrolled in vocational classes but liked reading better because most of the other guys in the classes just screwed around. I enjoyed a course in first aid and later started the advanced course which could lead to EMT certification, but I didn't finish it. I should have, but I didn't like dealing with blood. I haven't made any plans, but I thought I might look up my old friends. You know, Mikey and TwoJohnny. Maybe they can help me find a job." I looked at Gene and wondered if he could see through that lie. He just looked at me and nodded.

Gene handed me back the coin and said, "Ms. Moneyjoy sounds like a smart counselor, and I'm glad you listened to her."

"Yes, she helped me a lot, but she died in my tenth year of doing time. I was meeting with her one day and left the room to go to the bathroom. When I got back, she had died, right there at her desk. Heart attack, they said. She was eighty-two. She taught me so much, and I have really missed her."

"That's hard, but it sounds like she helped you turn yourself around. As for your old friends, Mikey Edenfield ended up in Florida. He's a lawyer. I'm not sure where, maybe Tampa. He comes back every two or three years to hunt or fish. You should have run with him rather than TwoJohnny. TwoJohnny came back from Mexico a year after you went to prison, but he disappeared again. He came to visit for a couple weeks, but I didn't see him. I know the sheriff talked with him, but nothing ever came of it. He visited your mom but never mentioned Sarah. No one expected anything since you had already been convicted and sent to prison. Over and done," Gene explained.

"Gene, I didn't hurt Sarah. TwoJohnny did. I'm going to find the son of a bitch. He owes me. He owes me twenty-five years."

Chapter 29

Nat and Viper
Twenty Years Ago

Nat first met Viper in Tijuana twenty years back. He'd passed into Mexico on a lark to enjoy beers and entertainment at one of the clubs catering to American servicemen from the Navy base in San Diego and the Marine base at Camp Pendleton. The beers were cold, and the women seemed hot, so he'd stayed engaged with the depravity longer than he planned. He'd been fascinated by a bar that billed a *dog-and-pony show*, where young Mexican girls and boys did illicit acts with dogs and ponies. Although licentious, it also intrigued him, and its bawdiness drew him back many times.

Vincent Ivan Pierson worked in law enforcement as a lawyer and judge from Utah and was married with four kids. While attending a judicial conference in San Diego, he slipped away and trekked across the border for a little R & R from his strait-laced life as a Mormon judge and happened upon a club with a dog-and-pony show. He found himself fascinated by the coarseness and realized he enjoyed it and so returned several times during his two-week conference. Coincidently, his wife flew from Brigham City to San Diego with plans to surprise him with a romantic interlude when she discovered his absence. Other judges told her he had gone to The Zoo in Tijuana, but she found that odd because San Diego had a fantastic zoo.

Nevertheless, she trailed him across the border where she learned of his fetish for these illegal shows. She divorced him within the month. The divorce scandal ruined Judge Pierson's reputation in the community and judicial circles. He lost his judgeship and was forced to find a new career. The scandal also had ruined his legal standing with his clientele, and he foolishly let his law license lapse while he looked for other employment opportunities.

Vincent's older sisters tagged him "Viper" as a child to torment him, but he had rid himself of the label while at BYU preferring his given name. By chance, he met an up-and-coming heavy weight boxer searching for an agent. With his legal training, he convinced the boxer that he would be an excellent promotor and fell into a new career as boxing agent and fight promoter. He gained two more clients and reclaimed his old moniker Viper, as his new career called for a robust name to depict strength and passion.

It was then that he began his career in graffiti. He had loved drawing and painting but had never done any serious artwork. He began sketching caricatures of his fighters and posted copies around town to promote them and their bouts. Meanwhile, Hollywood had been releasing more action-packed films, so on a whim, he sketched a few posters for the local theaters, and it soon became his passion. The entertainment industry sought after him for legitimate artwork, but he preferred living on the edge and began his nightly routine of painting on public buildings. Law enforcement called it graffiti, but he called it art. It was his way of getting back at the society that had destroyed his career.

Chapter 30

Charlie
Present Day

Barrier's weather remained pleasant into late June when it heated up during the day, before dropping to cool, even cold, nights. June's long days meant early morning sunrises, but the heat could be relentless until after sunset.

I hadn't slept since my release from prison, and after several beers, my eyes drooped. I hoped to make progress on my quest to find and punish TwoJohnny, but Gene insisted he no longer lived here. I wasn't so sure. Maybe Gene was lying, or maybe he was senile. Just because Gene said it, didn't make it so.

After drinking my fourth beer, I excused myself and headed to the Panorama. I had to pee, but Gene didn't offer his bathroom. I had been anticipating a pepperoni and onion pizza before hitting the rack. The Panorama still stood as the lone hotel in town, as far as I knew, and the pizza shop lay directly across the street. I figured I could get a room for the night for under $20. The last room I had rented, the one in Las Vegas, had been $14.95, so even with inflation, it shouldn't be much more.

"That'll be $40, Hon," the desk clerk said, "or two nights for $75, if you want to prepay for both nights."

Unbelievable. "Forty dollars? The room costs $40? Don't you have anything for less? I'll be close to flat broke if I spend that much money," I said.

"No, Hon, $40. You can pay with credit cards if you like. I'm not allowed to negotiate. Do you want the room or not?" the clerk snapped at me.

"I don't use credit cards," I told her, not wanting to say why I didn't have a credit card. "Does Barrier have other hotels?"

"No, the Panorama is your only choice, unless you want to sleep at the Barrier B&B, but I think it costs more. I've never stayed at the B&B myself, so I am not sure of their rates."

"I'll pass for the time being, but I might be back," I answered as I walked out the door, thinking, *Damn, what will I do now?* Had the castle been converted to a brothel? Did B&B mean brothel and bordello?

I retraced my steps to my old house, wondering if Gene would help me. He hadn't let me enter the house for the beers though, so I wasn't sure if he would put the welcome mat out, but maybe he would let me sleep in the garage.

Gene answered on the first knock saying, "Now what do you want, Charlie? I thought you went to the hotel."

"I planned to, but the rooms cost $40 a night, twice as much as I thought they would be. It will take nearly all my money to sleep there for two nights. I don't know what to do. Do you have any ideas?" Gene had been kind to me but seemed hesitant to assist me now.

"Forty dollars? The Panorama cost that for one night? I had no idea. I figured it would be $20 or $25, but I guess I'm out of touch with the hotel market. What are you thinking?" Gene asked.

Ms. Moneyjoy's politeness training kicked in, "I am wondering, Sir, could I stay here for tonight? I could sleep in the garage or in a sleeping bag if you have one. It's warm tonight so sleeping outside won't hurt me. I don't want to be any trouble, but I am exhausted, and I need sleep before I start my job hunt and try to find Dos. I haven't slept since I left Fenwick. I thank you for the beers, but they wore me out."

Gene looked me up and down and didn't say anything at first, "I'll tell you what, Charlie, if you give up the search for TwoJohnny, you can sleep in your old bedroom, and you'd have a bathroom and everything, and I'll even feed you breakfast in the morning. If you can find a job and get yourself back on your feet, I'll help you out, help you adjust to life outside prison. I'm sure your mom would like to see you. Finding TwoJohnny isn't going to get you anywhere except into more trouble. But you must promise because I'm not helping a murderer, and I'll hold you to it. What do you say, Charlie?"

Chapter 31

Maggie and Brick
Present Day

The warehouse had no light and was pitch black when Maggie came to, so she couldn't get her bearings. Her head throbbed, and she ached all over. She had lost track of time, and her brain didn't want to be bothered. She tried to look around but saw nothing but black and couldn't locate her flashlight or phone because her bound hands and feet didn't allow her to do anything other than roll around on the gritty concrete. She couldn't stand and tried to yell for help, but only weak, garbled words came out of her mouth. She struggled against her binds before lapsing into another deep sleep.

Brick waited at home for her call, but it never came. Maggie always kept in contact, at least every hour or two, making him wonder if she trusted him with the boys. He was new to the parenting gig, but so was she. Maggie's mother served as the main source of the what-to-do's, and she enjoyed the opportunity to be with the twins. The boys had fallen asleep, so Brick phoned his mother-in-law to see if she could babysit the boys again. He didn't want to alarm her, so he fibbed, telling her that Harry needed his help. Maggie always made it a point to stay in touch with Cagey and her family. Her lack of contact worried Brick.

Murder Almost

Brick and Bridget drove to the sheriff's office but found it closed. With one deputy, the office shut its door on occasion, available by telephone only. Cagey and Maggie shared and alternated on-call duty responsibilities, and Brick filled in when he could. Today Maggie had accompanied Nat, so Cagey owned the office responsibilities.

"Hi, Cagey, it's Brick. Have you heard from Maggie since the first text? It's not like her not to call," Brick said into his phone.

Cagey answered, "No, I haven't heard anything since her text saying she was going to Reno with Nat, and I'm starting to worry. I tried her cell phone, but no one answered, and it went to voicemail. If they went to Reno, they should have arrived by now, and she should have checked in. Our office policy is to check in at least once an hour when we are investigating."

"It's been six hours," Brick reminded him. "Where's her rig?"

"I'm not sure," Cagey said. "Her text said she went with Nat, so she must have left it in town."

"Let's see if we can locate her. I'll check to see if she left it at the warehouse while you circle through town to see if it's somewhere else. Stay in contact."

The two lit out to find her. Cagey drove through the streets looking for her rig, but before he had gone far, Brick called. "Her cruiser is parked at the warehouse, both are locked. Do you have an extra set of keys to open the cruiser? I'll see if I can get into the warehouse."

Bridget hopped out of the Jeep and scampered over to Maggie's cruiser. She circled the vehicle, sniffing the tires and doors as she went. She ran back to Brick, circled him, and nosed him as if to say to hurry up. She scrambled to the warehouse door and began dancing and scratching at the dirt. The dancing was following by whining, followed by yapping, followed by barking. Bridget headbutted the door a few times expecting it to open, but it didn't. Brick tried to kick it open, but it didn't budge. Bridget wasn't an athlete, but she began to run back and forth between Brick and the warehouse whining and yapping.

Cagey answered, "I'll stop to get the keys to the cruiser and be right there. I'll stop at the CDR to get another key to the warehouse if he has one. If he doesn't, we'll use a crowbar. Do you see any sign of her at the warehouse?"

Brick answered, "No, but Bridget has started going crazy. I've never seen her act so squirrelly. Call Jay and tell him we need a key now. I tried to kick in the door, but it didn't budge. Ask Jay if he's heard from Nat and get his cell number. Hurry, Cagey. There's a chance that Maggie is in the warehouse, and she could be hurt."

Chapter 32

Charlie
Present Day

I fell into a quandary. In one instant, I had vaulted from being a teenager running with TwoJohnny to being an adult, or what sometimes felt like being an old man. In fact, I had changed the moment the judge slammed the gavel on his desk and sentenced me: "Twenty-five years, no parole." Thwack! With those words, in those seconds, my life changed. From that moment on, I became a convict, not a teenager or a son or any of the other titles I had previously owned. It reminded me of the stories of Marines I had heard from Gene when the young Marines first arrived at Parris Island and stood on the footprints that were painted on the pavement. Every Marine said they became different men the instant they stood on those footprints, even before the drill sergeant barked orders. I became a different man in the courtroom that day when the judge had announced my fate. Yes, I had changed, but I my anger at TwoJohnny still haunted me.

My first days in prison had been difficult. The system, whether guard or schedule, dictated every minute of every day without exception, and I didn't like it. The food tasted starchy and flat, and there was no coffee or orange juice. The kitchen served water, occasionally with ice, but more often without, and tasteless Tang-like substances. I discovered hot sauce improved the food, and I put it on everything when it was available. I heard and heeded warnings regarding nutra-loaves served to non-cooperating inmates. They consisted of the daily menu pureed in a blender and baked and served like a loaf of bread, sans butter, peanut butter, jelly, or hot sauce. The thought of it turned my stomach.

The other inmates thought I had killed a cop, which gave me status, and I didn't tell them any different. I started to use the gym every day, and within a few months, I had bulked up and my beard had grown out. Luckily it came in fast and heavy, so I didn't look like an eighteen-year-old, which also gave me status. The other inmates left me alone. I began reading more and earned a position at the library where they paid me a few dollars every month. I figured out that silence was golden and listened more than I talked because I didn't want them to know I wasn't a cop killer.

Perhaps I had grown up, become a man. With the help of Ms. Moneyjoy, I had managed to avoid trouble during my incarceration, a 180-degree turnaround from my days as a teenager. She had inspired me, and I appreciated her time and wisdom. Without her talks, I would have been like any other convict, angry and seeking revenge. I had been in and out of trouble as a kid, and it made me cringe to think of all the arrests I had narrowly escaped. I had loved my mom, who tried to keep me out of trouble, but she didn't have the discipline in her own life to guide me down the right path. My teachers and school staff also tried to guide me, but I didn't listen. Gene alone had provided me with the structure I needed, but it was too little, too late.

Gene knew what he was talking about. If I found TwoJohnny and took out my revenge, which he deserved, I would be headed back to prison, no doubt about it. Yet, I had understandably carried anger toward him for a long time and casting my resentment off would be difficult. When something bad happens, it lasts for a lifetime. But the thought of becoming an inmate again sickened me as I considered Gene's offer.

My mind was racing as I made my vow: "Okay, I'll try, I mean I evaded trouble for the whole damn sentence, and I definitely don't want to go back to prison. I'll never forget what TwoJohnny did to me, and I doubt I can ever forgive him, but I promise not to go after that weasel. I don't want him costing me more years of my life. Ms. Moneyjoy had another favorite subject. She said two kinds of people lived in the world: those headed somewhere and those headed nowhere. I plan on going somewhere, even though I haven't figured out where yet. But you have my word: When I finally cross paths with TwoJohnny, and I am certain that I will, I promise that I'll leave him alone."

Chapter 33

Maggie and Brick
Present Day

Lights and siren blaring, Cagey screeched into the parking lot of the ancient warehouse. He jumped out of his rig in a flash with the key to the padlock in hand. He panted with anticipation. "Jay had to search for the key. He's not sure, but he thinks this is it. I also have a crowbar if this doesn't work. Do you think she's in there?"

Brick answered, "I think so; at least Bridget does. She's been racing around like crazy and keeps pawing at the door and whining. She's never done that before."

"Maybe the mutt's useful after all," Cagey said. The key opened the padlock, and he yanked it from the hasp. "Damn, it's dark in here. I'd better get the flashlight, or we'll never find the light switch."

Bridget didn't wait for the guiding light from the flashlight and charged through the door before it swung fully open. Brick opened his cell phone's flashlight to follow, but it was a dim lamp, and he couldn't see much. He tried to trail Bridget closely, but the moment she homed in on Maggie's scent, she followed her nose to the far end of the building leaving Brick and Cagey in the dark. Bridget arrived at Maggie's side in seconds, barking and whining and enthusiastically licking Maggie's face. Maggie stirred and moaned before Brick and Cagey could reach her.

"Maggie, are you okay? What happened? Did Nat do this to you?" Brick knelt and moved Bridget away from Maggie's face. He wanted to ask a hundred questions, but those loomed most important.

Cagey extracted his Swiss army knife from its holster and sliced the tape from her hands and feet. Brick lifted her to her feet and braced her to keep her from falling.

She stammered, "The physical pain isn't that bad, but my pride is busted to bits. I'm okay though. I have a killer headache, and I feel like I was hit by a small truck." Looking down at Bridget she continued, "And my face feels slimy. Other than that, I'm good. How long have I been here?" She struggled to talk but pieced together the story of what had happened, as much as she remembered.

"Did you see who hit you?" Brick asked. "Was it Nat?"

"I don't know. It might have been because he had already opened the building when I arrived, and I didn't see him. His Jag was parked outside, and he had unlocked the warehouse door. I remember calling out to him, but that's all I remember. He didn't answer, and I never saw him. Do either of you know where he is?" She rubbed her scalp and found a large bump that hurt when she touched it. "I have a big knot on my head, either from falling or from whatever hit me, and it hurts." She pulled her hand from her head, noting it was sticky with blood.

Brick said, "I'm going to take you to see a doc because you could have a concussion. I'll drive you over to Forsythe. It's only half an hour's drive with lights and sirens, and we'll radio ahead to assure a doctor will be on duty. I'll call your mom and tell her to take the twins to her house for the night or plan to spend the night at our place. She'll worry, but I want to tell her what happened. She'll be okay if I'm with you." Brick barked orders fast and furiously. "Cagey, take pictures of everything here and wipe down the area for fingerprints. See if you can find the overhead lights to the warehouse so you get high-quality pictures. If you can't find the switch, call Jay. Also check to see if we have Nat's prints in the system. He said his last name was Griss, but it's possibly an alias. Take fingerprints from the sheriff's car door and steering wheel to see if this whacko left any prints."

Cagey struggled to straighten his thoughts, perturbed that the sheriff had been injured and that Brick had apparently taken over, but he didn't protest, "I'm on it. Don't worry about a thing; I know what to do. I'll find out if Jay has any information on this dirtbag. I'll get Nat's cell number and see if I can track it. What do you want to do with Bridget? She's risen from a mutt to a champion in my book. We might not have acted so hastily if she hadn't gone crazy."

Chapter 34

Charlie
Present Day

With the noise, all the clanging, and hollering, my sleep while incarcerated became fitful and full of interruptions, and I constantly tossed and turned. Sleeping in my childhood room, I slept longer and harder than I had since I left, and I woke up to the aroma of fresh coffee. Fenwick didn't serve coffee because of the caffeine, so this tasted amazing, even though it was a bargain brand. I'd never had the new flavored coffees, so I didn't know any better. Gene fixed me corned beef hash and fried eggs, and it tasted like manna from heaven.

Gene, both excited and leery at my visit, had reservations regarding my commitment to avoid trouble. He had always liked me, but when the sheriff arrested me, he gave up on me. Maybe he would give me a second chance. I hoped so. Gene had phoned my mom to inform her that I had been released from prison and was now staying with him. She hadn't known I had been released. He also inquired about TwoJohnny. Did she know of his whereabouts, or had she heard from him? She hadn't.

Gene had a list of things he wanted to talk to me about. First and foremost, he wanted to know how I would handle the rest of my life. He had asked the same question, in different ways, two or three times.

Since he'd asked repeatedly, it must have been important to him. "How'd you sleep?" he queried. "Did your bed feel okay?"

"You'd better believe it. The prison calls their beds *bunks,* but that's an exaggeration. My so-called bunk was a wooden box with two drawers below the two-inch thick mattress, better than sleeping on the floor, but not much. I slept over 9,000 nights on that stinkin' bed with the same mattress. It had worn thin by the time I left. My room was nine by seven feet, sixty-three square feet, barely big enough to turn around, with a mostly functional toilet and sink. I had no windows, but every day I could go outside for a little bit, which I enjoyed. The recreational area was as big as half a basketball court with a mostly concrete floor that had weeds poking up through some of the larger cracks. It was fenced on all sides with four walls, a ceiling, and concertina wire was attached both midway and at the top. No way could anybody get out of there, except through the door. The metal door to my cell had a hole for food delivery, which I put my hands through if they wanted to handcuff me," I told him. "They turned the light on in the morning and out at night."

"That would be dreadful on the long haul. Boot Marines don't have it much better, but Basic Training only lasts for a few weeks, not years. When I talked to your mom this morning, she said she's anxious to see you. She's also curious whether you will stay in Barrier or if you will move on to another place. She married again last year and seems to be getting along okay. She lives in Carson City now. You could take the bus, or we could take a road trip if you want. It's a three-hour drive."

"How many husbands has she had? You were number five. Is this one number six or did she have more husbands in between?" I asked. "She didn't write or call much, so I have no idea what is going on with her."

"I don't know. She had at least one after me that I know of, Darryl, but he died, so this one would be seven or so. She likes the idea of getting married, but not doing the work it takes to stay married. Before this morning, we hadn't spoken in quite some time, and I haven't seen her in several years.

Thankfully the old contact info I had for her still worked. Anyway, how about if we take a tour of Barrier this morning? You can see the town, and we can talk about jobs. Since the mines closed, the job market dried up, but I know of a few positions you could apply for, if you decide to live here," Gene offered. He seemed preoccupied with me finding a job.

After we cleaned up from breakfast, we climbed into Gene's banged-up pickup and aimed it toward town. He chattered the whole drive. A Marine's Marine, he didn't put up with much foolishness.

"We'll do a quick tour of the town, and then I'm going to take you to meet Jay Guzman. Barrier residents recognize him as the most influential person in town. He owns three businesses, including the CDR, the Panorama, and the Barrier B&B, as well as serving as the mayor. If anyone can help you, he can," Gene told me.

"The most profitable business in town is sadly the Chicken Dinner Ranch. Do you remember it? It's the brothel just on the outskirts. It employs a dozen people plus the dozen or so ladies who participate in its main business. Jay hires groundskeepers, maintenance guys, kitchen help, a bookkeeper, and several flexible workers who do whatever Jay needs done. Jay's a first-rate guy, fair to his employees, but he has trouble keeping them. Lots of ne'er-do-wells and drifters travel through Barrier searching for ways to achieve their dreams. But they don't want to work at anything for long and soon leave town searching for ways to solve their new problems. What most of these drifters don't understand is that they cause their own problems, and the solutions lie within themselves. Does that make sense to you, Charlie?"

My mind flashed back to my teen years. "Sure, it makes sense. It reminds me of a guy I met in Fenwick with the name of Sam Ready. He is thirty or thirty-one years old now. He received a four-year sentence for drug abuse in Idaho when he was aged twenty and would have been eligible for parole in less than two years. Because of overcrowding, the Idaho prisons transferred him and 199 others to a new prison in Winnemucca, Nevada. They had finished the prison, but they hadn't yet built the fence when the low risk

Idaho prisoners arrived. The prison warden assigned the Idaho prisoners to construct a fence surrounding the new prison. They were, after all, low risk offenders, and the warden thought they could be trusted. They built the fence and secured it. As directed, they positioned the garbage dumpsters outside the fence, so the trucks could access the large trash bins without entering the prison grounds. However, any person taking garbage cans from the prison to the dumpsters needed to pass through the gate. The rule said that correctional officers would accompany the inmates through the gate to the dumpsters.

"The prison assigned Sam to permanent garbage detail because he had been in a few scuffles, and the staff identified him as a troublemaker. At the same time, everybody liked him, and after a time, the correctional officers began to trust him. He was hot to escape and awaited the opportunity. It seldom rained in Nevada but when it did, it poured. A few months into his stint with the Nevada prison system, it rained, coming down in buckets. The correctional officer didn't want to get wet, so he gave Sam the keys and sent him to the dumpsters alone. Since no problem arose the first day, the correctional officer continued sending Sam outside alone every day to complete his work.

"One day, though, the staff shift change came while Sam had gone outside the fence to complete his task. He knew the usual guard had forgotten him, and his replacement didn't realize that he was outside the fence. The town lay a mere mile away, so Sam sneaked into town to look around and noticed a sign on the Western Auto store that said, *Help Wanted Apply Inside* and thought *why not?* He went in and applied for a job before going back to prison. When Sam returned to the store a few days later, he learned he had been hired and would be paid minimum wage to stock shelves and sweep the floors. He accepted the job and became adept on how to use the Western Auto key-making machine to copy keys. He used his new skill to duplicate the keys to the prison. Having a set of prison keys made his life easier, to say the least.

"Sam continued to go to work at the Western Auto Store on his assigned days and returned to the prison after his shift. He did this for several months, and no one grew wiser. It was the best job he ever had, and he became a model employee, even earning a raise. Every payday Sam cashed his check at the store and deposited his cash into his prison commissary account. An observant bookkeeping clerk noticed he had accumulated over $1,000 in the account, while most inmates had no more than $50. She reported the discrepancy to the warden, who investigated. Nevada charged Sam Ready with escape and re-sentenced to five additional years. He managed to turn a four-year sentence with possibility of parole, into nine years with no parole, and they shipped him back to the Idaho maximum-security prison. The correctional officer went to prison in Fenwick for aiding and abetting an escape. Sam said he learned not to save money.

"To finish the story, Sam completed his time in Idaho and was rehired at his old job at the Western Auto store and surreptitiously started making keys for inmates. He felt bad about the guard, who had been incarcerated at Fenwick and tried to slip him a key, but the correctional officers caught him, and now he is back in Fenwick for another five years.

"I will never forget that story. When I met Sam, he was trying to figure out what went wrong with his goals. I didn't want to be like him. Instead I learned patience and spent the coin of life that Ms. Moneyjoy had given me wisely, serving out my sentence and never bucked the system."

Gene said, "That's quite a story, and I'm happy you learned from it. It's hard to believe somebody could do that, I mean, sneak out of the prison to work on the outside. Did you believe him?"

"Yes, I believed him, especially after I had lived at the joint for a few months. Prisoners can do practically anything they want. The honest correctional officers hold limited power over their prisoners, and the dishonest COs may take bribes of either money or sex, but when that happens, the guards hold zero power over the inmates. The inmates act kindlier to those guards, but it's a system of manipulation. I was lucky to have been left alone by the other prisoners and by the guards."

"But now, Charlie, you've finished your prison sentence. You say you've changed and are ready to start your life over? I know what you told me, but are you a man of your word?"

In answer to his question, I pulled out my TCL coin from my pocket and flipped it into the air, "Yes, I am."

Chapter 35

Charlie
Present Day

"I recall what Ms. Moneyjoy taught me," I told Gene. "You need to use time wisely to create a good life. If you don't, you'll be like a caged guinea pig on a treadmill, working hard but going nowhere. Ms. Moneyjoy just said it differently."

"I think that Ms. Moneyjoy was a wise woman," Gene said. "She had a strong influence on you. In life, you never know who you're going to influence and how your words will affect people. Years ago, I met a man who had a tough childhood, didn't speak English, dropped out of school at age fourteen, and went to work hoeing beets. When he was fifteen, he accidentally chopped off his thumb while working. His grandmother tried to help him, but she had twelve other kids in the house and couldn't take on another responsibility. She said to him one day, 'Why don't you go back to school and learn English? You have good brains, and maybe you can make something of yourself.' So, the next day he enrolled in GED classes for no other reason than his grandmother said he had brains. He learned English, earned a GED, and then the GED counselor asked him, 'Why don't you go to college. You can handle it.' So, he enrolled in junior college classes thinking he might want to be a teacher. He graduated and went on to get his teaching credential. Shortly after, he landed a teaching job but quickly recognized that he didn't like teaching school and wasn't good at it. The principal of the school said, 'You could be a lawyer, so why don't you go to law school.' He accepted the advice, went to law school, and graduated in three years. He worked as a lawyer for a few years when a client said, 'I think you have so much more potential; why don't you try to be a judge.' So, he did. He won a judgeship and ruled from the bench for a few years before another judge told him, 'You're a great judge, and I think you should run for the Supreme Court.' And so, he did...and that's where he is today. Sitting on the Nevada Supreme Court all because his grandmother told him he was smart. I think Ms. Moneyjoy did that for you. I like seeing that."

They drove past the ancient cemetery, and Gene gestured toward it. "You could get a job with the city because they're always hiring somebody for something. My old job might be open, but you'd have to dig graves when there's a death. Jay will know the job openings, and you can talk to him. Would digging graves creep you out? I put quite a few people in the ground."

I answered. "Digging graves? Do they dig by hand or with a backhoe? I don't know how to use a backhoe but am quite experienced with a hand shovel. I could dig them by hand, and I don't think it would creep me out, but six feet deep is a big damn hole."

"They dig with a backhoe, and you could learn how to operate one, if that job appeals to you. Running a backhoe only takes hand-eye coordination. Another possibility might be the B&B," Gene continued. "Jay owns it also. He put this nice lady in charge, and it is booming. People come from all over to experience its medieval theme, including real-life jousting and that sort of thing. Like I said, he is always hiring grounds crew, hotel staff, waiters, and who knows what else. Maybe cooks. The grounds crews work full time, but others work part time, as the B&B customers usually rent rooms for a weekend, not an entire week. You should try to be hired for a full-time job, not part time because it will be better for you. Jay also owns the Panorama, where you tried to get a room last night. He doesn't hire anyone in the hotel because he brings in women from other countries, trains them, and helps them to be hired in Vegas. I think he earns a finder's fee because they come and go often, usually within a few months of when they arrive. The ones I've met seem to be pleasant young women, but they leave before you really get to know them."

Chapter 36

Maggie and Brick
Present Day

The doctor confirmed that Maggie did not have a concussion, rather a large lump caused by the thwack on the head with whatever weapon Nat used. She assured Maggie the headache would disappear in a few days and advised her to take a few days to rest. She attributed the small scrapes and abrasions to rolling around on the hard, gritty concrete floor while trying to loosen her duct tape binds. The doctor cleaned and treated the small wounds before sending her back to Barrier.

Cagey returned to the warehouse and finally located the light switch but found nothing. He photographed everything including the Jaguar's tire tracks and lifted fingerprints from Maggie's vehicle and submitted them to Reno for identification. He found another set of keys for her rig and drove it to the sheriff's office lot.

Brick and Maggie arrived home before midnight and found a note telling them the boys would be spending the night with Grandma. The house felt empty, even spooky, without the twins and their gentle breathing.

Maggie and Brick had purchased their house from the school district after the priest/principal had been murdered in the house as he watched Judge Judy. It contained five rooms, two bedrooms, a living room, a bathroom, and a kitchen, meaning no extra bedroom for Grandma or anyone else.

Murder Almost

In the 1800s, wood for construction meant long trips over rough roads and high costs, so builders used alternative ways to construct solid houses. An abundance of empty whiskey bottles inspired people to develop a system of *whiskey walls* in the houses they built. They positioned the bottles on their sides and tamped them with mud creating a strong wall that would sustain the weight of the rest of the building and roof. The intriguing side effects were the shimmers of light creating sparkles on the walls and floor during the day. On clear nights, the moon and stars sprinkled small specks of light creating an ambiance that wooden walls could not possibly have.

Their house, a *murder house*, emitted an aura of evil, but Brick and Maggie painted, installed new flooring, and replaced the kitchen appliances and cabinets to modernize the cottage and make it into a friendlier home. However, it remained old, tired, and out of date and would always carry the character and reputation of a *murder house*. Because the mining companies had razed all the houses back when gold ruled, housing became scarce, and this small cottage had been the solitary house available to buy. Both wanted a larger house, a different house, but they placed the idea on hold for now.

The following morning, Brick and Maggie picked up the boys and Bridget and fed them breakfast. Maggie's mother offered to babysit so Brick and Maggie could go to the office together, but Maggie would have none of it. As soon as her family was settled back at home, she headed into the office and left Brick at home to tend to the kids. She was determined to talk to Cagey and learn what he had discovered with his investigation. Cagey's brother, Jay, the proprietor of the Chicken Dinner Ranch, supplied him with woefully incomplete information. "Sheriff, you shouldn't be here," Cagey warned when she walked in. "Take time for yourself until you feel better."

She snapped, "Stop already! I've heard this recommendation three times this morning; I'm feeling okay, and the doctor said it wasn't serious. If my headache kicks in again, I'll knock off."

Cagey frowned at her response but gave in to her request and started to read off his notes, "Jay copied Nat's driver's license, and his given name is Nathan Griss, which we already knew. The address he gave Jay was bogus, and he doesn't answer his cell phone."

She felt a bit dizzy and sat down in a visitor's chair. "No surprise," she said. "What about references? Did he have any?"

Cagey said, "Yes, he supplied two references, and Jay followed through on them before he hired him. However, when I called the numbers that he provided, both were disconnected. Jay hired him just two weeks ago, so there is definitely something curious going on."

"Things are looking pretty bad," Maggie said. A sharp pain stabbed through her head, and she winced but ignored it and hoped Cagey had not noticed. Her irritation level had risen, not with Cagey but at the lack of information on Nathan Griss.

Cagey leaned back in his chair and shook his head, "And my next bit of information is also bad: Jay recorded the license plate number of the Jaguar, but when I ran it through the state police, the system identified it as stolen out of Vegas. The finger-print check seemed more helpful because it reported he had been involved in robberies in Henderson, Nevada, a few years earlier, and those cases remain open."

Maggie asked, "Did the state police send the case file? What else does it say?"

Cagey looked at his computer and paused while he opened a document. He jumped up with a big grin on his face, "Well, well, well. They just now emailed the case file to us, and holy shit, Sheriff, I think we hit the motherlode."

Chapter 37

Charlie
Present Day

"What do you recommend, Gene? It sounds like this Jay fellow has his fingers in several pies. How well do you know him?" I asked.

Gene answered, "Yes, he is one of those movers and shakers that you hear about. He serves as mayor now, but he previously held a seat on the city council, and that's how I met him. He's an interesting guy and knows everyone. He is a fine businessman, too, even though he runs a brothel. His business is legitimate, but issues can arise, mainly with health and cleanliness, but he stays on top them. The state inspections always come out clean as far as I know. I'll buy you lunch before we go to his office at the CDR."

We ate at the local pizza place, the Eldorado Pizza Shoppe, which served one kind of pizza: pepperoni. Similarly, their only available beverages included Olympia beer and Coca Cola, so Gene and I opted for pepperoni and Coca Cola. The past and present owners said people would eat and drink anything offered, so they limited the available drinks to two long-time favorites: Olympia and Coke.

The Chicken Dinner Ranch had been in business for over 100 years, and part of its charm was its history. It hadn't always been a brothel, rather a variety of businesses. A stage company had transferred it in pieces by horse-drawn wagons from Salt Lake City to Barrier, where it functioned as a stage stop for people traveling through northern Nevada to or from San Francisco and Salt Lake City. Located a few miles from the Pony Express route, a stage depot employee would ride to the designated delivery spot, and the rider would fling a mailbag to whomever waited. The addressees later claimed their mail at the stage stop.

When Union Pacific built its railroad, the Chicken Dinner Ranch (then called the Barrier Stage Stop) served as temporary housing for the construction crew, including the many Chinese who were involved in laying its tracks. It later became a layover for train passengers, and before long, prostitution gained popularity among the predominance of male travelers. As the automobile increased in numbers and popularity, it became more accessible, and for a time, maintained the position of the lone rest stop, complete with a bar and restaurant. Travelers, farmers, ranchers, and later miners kept it going at full strength. After the government constructed the Interstate Highway System and Las Vegas gambling surged, both in the 1950s, its popularity dwindled, but it retained a loyal, thirsty population. Lately, the CDR has attracted truckers, farmers, ranchers, and the curious and business continues to thrive.

The CDR edifice was a two story turquoise, adobe building that had been expanded throughout the years. Downstairs lay an old-fashioned cowboy bar with a carved wood-framed mirror and wooden booths, tables, and chairs imitating those seen in B-rated cowboy movies. The reception area for brothel customers held couches and dimmed lamps with a large eat-in kitchen nestled behind it, serving family-style meals. Within seconds, Jay could access any part of the establishment from his office behind the kitchen. Upstairs lay a dozen rooms for women practicing the world's oldest profession, the same number of bathrooms, and a small but busy spa used by truckers wanting to have massages, baths, haircuts, and beard trims.

The Chicken Dinner Ranch was named after its most famous meal: fried chicken dinners with home-baked bread, green beans, and corn on the cob (in season). Freshly made apple pie and berry cobbler rounded out the offering. They served the same meal daily with a few other options occasionally appearing on the menu. The appealing aroma enticed patrons to eat a meal before departing, and no one left hungry.

Jay had visited Barrier as a child and fell in love with the town, particularly the castle. He earned a basketball scholarship to UNLV but lost it following an automobile accident that damaged his knees. After his college graduation, he revisited Barrier hoping to buy the vacant castle, but it wasn't for sale at the time. The Chicken Dinner Ranch, however, had been for sale, and he bought it on the spot. He didn't know anything about running a brothel, but he decided to put his business degree to work. He had learned enough about business to know honest, fair treatment would help him succeed. He also knew a brothel needed to maintain an ultra-clean environment, and he followed the state laws regarding his new venture. Jay brought a fun atmosphere to his business; the word spread, and his business boomed. He retained the name and the rustic nature of the CDR and operated it for several years before his brother K.G., nicknamed Cagey as a youth, visited Barrier and became the deputy sheriff.

Gene and I parked near the picket fence and entered the CDR. I had never been in a brothel and was curious what it would be like. Gene asked the receptionist for Jay, and in seconds he appeared with his usual boisterous enthusiasm, "I'm glad to see you, Gene! How the hell have you been? It's been a while. How's retirement treating you? We sure do miss you down at city hall. Want some coffee?"

"Sure, thanks, Jay, I'd love coffee. I want you to meet my former stepson. Jay, this is Charlie, my ex-wife's son. I never had a kid myself, but Charlie was the next best thing." Charlie's mind flashed to the day that Gene and his mom met him in the jailhouse when they indicated that he was the next worst thing.

Jay shook Charlie's hand saying, "That's a real compliment coming from Gene. He has high standards, all those years in the Marine Corps, I guess. I am glad to meet you, Charlie."

I responded cautiously, "Yes, Sir, he was kind to me." Aware of bias against ex-cons, I thought before I spoke. "Gene's a special one. My mom divorced him, but I think that was a mistake."

Gene and Jay talked and laughed a little more about the old times at city hall when Gene repaired roads and dug graves, and they reminisced about the situations encountered while the crew worked. Finally, Gene told Jay the purpose of our visit and said, "I brought Charlie to meet you for a reason, Jay. He came back to Barrier after being away for quite some time and is looking for a job. I thought you might be able to help him and get him headed in the right direction."

Jay looked me up and down, pausing to stare at my bulging biceps and asked "What skills do you have, Charlie? Do you have a trade?"

I decided to bite the bullet and be honest with Jay, "I've been in prison and don't have any definable skills, Sir. I completed my GED and a class in first aid and started an EMT class but didn't finish. My best work qualities include following directions and doing what I'm told. I'm a changed person since I first went to prison. I learned to use my time wisely, so I'm willing to learn any job I might be presented with, and I'll work hard. I'll show up every day on time and won't leave until the job is done."

Gene looked at me in amazement and said, "Thanks for being honest about your time in prison, Charlie."

Jay thought of his roster of employees and the difficulty he had with hiring and keeping them. If this were true, anybody who would *be there, be there on time, and do what he or she was told* would be hired in a heartbeat and immediately become his favorite employee. Most of his employees violated one, two, or three of those job requirements regularly. He nodded, "Charlie, it takes a big man to be honest regarding your past. Where did you do your time? Fenwick?"

"Yes, Sir, Fenwick. I finished my sentence this week and am anxious to go to work. I'll do anything you have available."

"What did you do to end up in prison, Charlie?" Jay asked.

Pleading my innocence wouldn't get me anywhere, so I said, "The judge sentenced me for hurting a woman here a long time ago. I could give you the long version, but I'd rather tell you I went to prison at age eighteen and am not the same teenaged kid I was. I gave Gene my word to avoid trouble, and he'll hold me to it." I looked over at Gene as I said this. Gene was apparently astonished at my truthfulness and honesty because he nodded and leaned over and patted me on the back. No vein showed, but he nodded.

Jay had an immediate opening and need for a bouncer because his last bouncer had flown the coop. "Okay, Charlie, I do have one job available at the CDR. You're a pretty big guy and look like you can handle yourself."

"Yes, Sir, I went to the gym every day while in Fenwick. I did a little boxing and can definitely hold my own."

"The job is to work as a bouncer, taking care of people who get out of line in the bar or with the girls. People lose their temper when they get drunk or don't win big at the games, or they might like to rough up the girls, which I won't allow. You might have to get physical, but it's better for everyone if you can talk sense into them. Talking is the best strategy to calm a person down, but if it doesn't work, getting physical does. Do you have a parole officer keeping track of you? I guarantee a parole officer won't be happy if you work in a brothel."

"No, Sir, no PO. I finished my sentence," I replied quickly.

Jay paused before saying, "Good. You're hired but on a probationary status; that is, you will keep the job if all goes well. Can you start tomorrow or better yet, tonight? We get busy at five o'clock so come to work by four. I'll have a uniform ready for you and will show you what to do."

Chapter 38

Maggie and Brick
Present Day

Cagey read Maggie the email message he had received from law enforcement in Reno. "The two guys who were involved in the art store theft were identified through fingerprints. They were none other than Vincent Pierson and Nathan Griss. How about that?"

Maggie sat up straight, "You've got to be kidding. Those two knew each other and robbed somebody? Nat didn't say anything while we talked about Viper, but I felt uncomfortable with him while studying the paintings. You really did find the mother lode. Excellent work, Cagey. It's no wonder Nat volunteered to help Jay find the other three paintings."

Cagey continued reading, "This email describes how they allegedly robbed an art supply store a few years ago. The police never caught them, and the case remains open."

"It's ironic that they stole the art supplies that Viper used to paint his now-stolen art. Are they sure these two did it?" Maggie asked.

Cagey laughed out loud, "Fingerprints don't lie, so they would seem involved. To add to the intrigue, according to this email, the Feds arrested these two when they tried to transport a young Mexican girl to the U.S., and a border patrol agent stopped them. Unfortunately, the system lost the girl, and the feds dropped the charges. She had been working in Tijuana at a bar called The Zoo, a sort of a strip bar that used kids, and Pierson and Griss recruited her to work in a similar role in San Diego County. It is all pretty sick stuff."

Maggie said, "Those charges would be federal." She thought for a minute and continued, "Brick might have heard of them. LAPD has handled quite a few child abduction cases that happened at the Mexican border, so he might know something."

Before she could speed dial Brick, her office phone rang, and she answered, "Sheriff's office. How can I help you? Oh, Mr. Pierson, I mean Viper. I just picked up the phone to call you. We've made progress on your case, and I would like to talk to you in person. Could you possibly come back to Barrier?" She looked at Cagey and winked at him. "Tomorrow morning? That would be perfect. See you then."

Maggie's excitement skyrocketed, "Viper's coming tomorrow morning. I know it's risky asking him to come here, as he could easily abscond, but he is very anxious to get the paintings back, so I have a good feeling that he'll show. We don't know where Nathan Griss went, but I'll bet he does. We'll have to convince him to tell us, but we have a huge bargaining chip because he's gonna want those $700,000 paintings back."

Chapter 39

Charlie
Present Day

I had a job! Although being a bouncer wasn't a job I had ever considered, I could do it. Gene drove me to Johnstone's dry goods where I bought a few new items of clothing. I would wear a uniform at work, but since I had no other change of clothes, I purchased the complete works of socks, underwear, a new shirt, hat, and pants, and I felt I had made headway with getting a new life. I kept the prison shoes. Gene suggested that I trim my beard to appear less grizzly, and we stopped at the barber shop.

"You look civilized," Gene complimented. "I am proud of you for the way you answered Jay's questions. Your honesty about Fenwick must have impressed him because he hired you on the spot, and he takes care who he hires. He didn't even ask you for references."

"You referred me, Gene. And thank you, but I've had a long time to consider how to answer questions that people would ask when I applied for a job. I know ex-cons who fabricate everything. They would lie about the color of their socks, but I'm different from them," I answered. "I am going to make this work, and according to Ms. Moneyjoy, honesty is the path to success."

"Well, it worked for you today, that's for damn sure. If you run into problems, talk to Jay. He's seen it all, so be proactive. He's easy to work with, and he manages the CDR well."

I had no driver's license and no car, so Gene provided me with a lift to my new job. The receptionist escorted me to Jay's office where a uniform was waiting, all clean and pressed. It was gray with several red and gray badges sewn on the sleeves and front pocket. "I have one uniform because the last guy didn't bother to return his. He was nearly your height, and it should fit except for the waist, which might bag as he was chunkier than you are." Jay handed me a belt, "This will help."

I looked at myself in the mirror and noticed my resemblance to one of the correctional officers who also wore gray uniforms with patches sewn on. I laughed out loud at the irony.

Jay said, "This uniform has the former bouncer's name on it, but you'll have new uniforms with personalized nametags soon. I already ordered them, and Amazon.com is speedy. The last guy's name was Nathan, but he went by Nat."

Jay toured the building with me and introduced me to several other employees. He didn't mention my last name or that I had been in prison, which pleased me and gave me newfound confidence. I knew for sure the old timers who lived in Barrier would remember Sarah Hudson and the Charlie Walker trial.

I wandered throughout the brothel, as directed, looking for issues requiring my attention. Two people called me Nathan, but I didn't correct them because I thought it to my advantage if people didn't know my real name. Even though it was common, the name Nathan was familiar to me. I knew someone named Nathan at some point, but couldn't remember if it was someone in school, in prison, or somewhere else. It weighed on my mind.

The new uniforms arrived the next day. They fit well, but Amazon had erred with the nametags, and they read *Nathan* rather than *Charlie*. Jay swore a little, but I had no problem with it, and I assured him it was fine. The less attention drawn to me, the better off I was.

My first bouncer encounter came on my third day when two young women burst into the CDR screaming, "Slavers! Let the prisoners go! Slavers!"

One stood tall with a blonde ponytail, and the other petite with massive black hair pointing in several directions. They both wore heavy make-up with hot pink lipstick and inch-long black eyelashes, which had to be fake. Their language and demeanor defined their anger and indignation about something. They both wore black leggings and oversized pink t-shirts, and they carried themselves with surly confidence. They could have been attractive, but the angry look on their faces made them appear mean and vicious.

"May I help you, Ladies?" the receptionist asked politely.

"Slavers! This place is a slave house. How many girls do you have imprisoned here?" they shouted their accusations.

"No prisoners or slaves work or live here," the receptionist answered calmly. "We are a legitimate, legal business, and employees can come and go as they please, in addition to earning a fair salary. No one is a prisoner or a slave."

"Liar. That's a lie. We want to see the slave quarters. Show us where they live. We want to see where you force them to work," Blondie yelled as she yanked out her phone and began snapping pictures. Pointy Hair turned on her heel and headed for the stairs to the second-floor rooms. The receptionist moved more quickly than she, grabbed her shirt sleeve, and yanked her back.

The din in the bar lessened as the patrons watched the receptionist confront the two women, wondering what the issue was. Someone yelled, "Bouncer!" and I burst into the room and placed my right hand on Pointy Hair's shoulder and yanked her left arm behind her saying, "Come with me, Miss, you should talk to the owner." She kicked me in the shin and tried to knee me in the groin, but I caught her before she could hurt me again. Meanwhile, Blondie jumped on my back as she attempted to dislodge Pointy Hair from my tightening grip. They were strong, but I was stronger, and I flipped Blondie off and placed her face down on the floor while holding Pointy Hair under my arm. They both continued to yell and struggle. Their yowling turned into swearing with more accusations. They seemed to be running their mouths about everything under the sun. Jay heard the commotion and listened for a bit, then called the sheriff's office hoping to find Maggie or Cagey. He wanted to learn what these women's issues were, but it would be better to let them cool their heels in the sheriff's office. No one answered at the city office, and Jay called Brick at home.

"Brick, I'm looking for Maggie or Cagey and can't find them. Do you know where they are? They're not answering their phones."

"No, she called me a while ago saying they had made some headway on the graffiti case, but I don't know where they went," Brick said. "I know they are together, but don't know what they are doing. What do you need?"

"We have a situation, and I need help. Could you break free to help me out with a couple young women who want to close us down?" Jay asked. "They accused us of being slavers and imprisoning women, and they are so riled up that I won't be able to convince them of anything different. They need time to cool off. My bouncer has them restrained and under control, but that does not include their anger. They claim to belong to a group called SWS, Saving Women from Slavery, but I've never heard of them. They also rambled about someone named Viper who suggested they would find thieves, slavers, and liars at the CDR. What are the chances there's more than one Viper?"

Chapter 40

Viper
Present Day

The following morning, Cagey and Maggie came back from having another look at the warehouse when Viper arrived. He was clad in the same black outfit except he had exchanged his black turtleneck for a sleeveless black shirt with AC/DC stenciled on the front. He was waiting outside her office.

"What did you find out?" Viper asked as way of a greeting. "Where's my artwork?"

Maggie replied, "I didn't say we found it. I said we had made progress, but for right now, I am placing you under arrest."

Viper stared at her in disbelief. "For what? Since when is it a crime to try to get your stolen stuff back? This is fucking bullshit."

Maggie read him his Miranda rights and said, "I have a warrant from Henderson, Nevada to arrest you and Nathan Griss for the robbery of an art supply store. Does that sound familiar?"

"No, you have the wrong guy. I didn't rob anybody, and I don't know anyone named Nathan. I have no idea what you are talking about," Viper defended himself. "You have the wrong guy, and you lied about making progress on my stolen paintings."

Cagey handcuffed Viper and escorted him into an interview room. He attached him to the table before sitting down. Cagey didn't say anything, but Viper started swearing and threatening lawsuits against the sheriff's office. He threw out a bunch of legal terms making Cagey wonder if he had knowledge of the law. Cagey sat in silence while Viper continued to rant about his innocence.

After a while, Maggie stepped through the door and said, "Mr. Pierson, I've been on the phone with the Henderson Police Department. They have an interest in talking to you, but they can't retrieve you for a few days. In the meantime, I have a few questions myself, and I'm going to record my questions and your answers and comments.

Maggie: "Mr. Pierson, please state your whole name and address for the record."

Viper: "Vincent Ivan Pierson, Citizen of the World."

Maggie: "Do you know that this conversation is recorded?"

Viper: "Yes."

Maggie: "Can you be a little more definite about where you live?"

Viper: "I live on the planet Earth. That's as definite as I want to get."

Maggie: "Have you ever been to Henderson, Nevada?"

Viper: "Is it a part of the world? If so, I might have been."

Maggie: "Let's try a different question. Why did you contact me last week?"

Viper: "The whorehouse has my paintings. The owner stole them, and you promised to get them for me. You lied to me, and I want it on the record. I repeat: You. Lied. To. Me. You haven't done anything yet. I told you where MY paintings are, but you and your deputy can't get off your lazy asses to get them back."

Maggie: "What is your occupation?"

Viper: "Artist."

Maggie: "Do you earn money for your artwork?"

Viper: (Silence)

Maggie: "What I mean is, do you get paid for your artwork?"

Viper: (Silence)

Maggie: "Where do you draw?"

Viper: "California, generally."

Maggie: "What kinds of pictures do you draw?"

Viper: "This and that, whatever I feel like drawing."

Maggie: "What kind of canvas do you use?"

Viper: "Now that's a fucking stupid question, Sheriff, Ma'am."

Maggie: "If it's such a stupid question, could you please answer it?"

Viper: "No, I'm not going to demean myself by answering your stupid questions. I'm done here."

He started to stand before remembering he was hooked to the table and started swearing and threatening again.

Maggie: "I'm going to turn off the recorder, Mr. Pierson. The deputy will place you in a cell. We'll talk again later. She flipped the recorder's switch to off."

Cagey unhooked him from the table, and Viper leaped up, simultaneously swinging his left arm toward Cagey, catching him unaware. He almost missed Cagey with his left but landed more solidly when he jabbed with his right, striking Cagey's left shoulder. Cagey recovered as Viper repeated his attempts to strike him. Viper danced light on his feet, but taller and stronger Cagey moved quicker. He caught Viper's arm and curled it behind him, twisting him to the floor. On the way down Viper head-butted Cagey's groin and leapt to his feet while Cagey winced and crumpled to the floor. Maggie thrust her knee against Viper from behind and shoved him to the floor, face down. She plunged her knee to his back and held him down, snapping the handcuffs on his wrists. She said, "We're adding assault on a police officer, resisting arrest, and attempting to escape your charges. You might be our guest for a long time, Mr. Pierson."

Chapter 41

Brick and Charlie
Present Day

Brick called his mother-in-law, and thankfully, she had already left for Brick and Maggie's home with homemade dog biscuits for Bridget as a reward for rescuing Maggie. She'd had a change of heart and now viewed Bridget as a hero. She had spent years caring for her Alzheimer's stricken husband and thoroughly enjoyed turning her energies to her *chicos*, as she called the twins, which now included Bridget. She welcomed tending to her young and lively grandchildren who gave her new energy.

I had positioned the two women on the floor, separated by a few feet. They glared at me and looked ready to leap to their feet. I didn't have handcuffs, but I kept a close eye on them and hoped Brick would hurry.

Brick, wearing his deputy badge, reached the Chicken Dinner Ranch pretty quickly. I'd been watching the two protesters while Jay smoothed over the temperament of the bar. I noted the badge and stood more erect not knowing what to expect. Brick introduced himself to me, and I said, "I'm the new bouncer. I've been on the job a few days. It's my pleasure to meet you, Sir."

Brick noted the name badge on Charlie's shirt and said, "I thought the last bouncer's name was Nathan."

"That's correct, Sir, but I'm wearing his old uniform. Jay didn't get any new name badges yet."

When Brick entered the office, the two women started to stir. Pointy Hair rose to her knees while Blondie scrambled up as well, but I wrestled Blondie back to the floor. "No, little lady, you will sit right there." Pointy Hair sat down again.

Brick turned his attention to the two activists, "Tell me your names and what brings you to Barrier, ladies?" He looked more foreboding than I did, and they responded better to him than me.

Pointy Hair snapped at him. "Slavery of women. That's why we came here, while you cops sit by and do nothing. I'm Rhoda Knight and oppose prostitution and slavery of women."

Blondie joined in with, "Liars. All of you lie. No woman in her right mind would be a prostitute, so you must be restraining them unlawfully and then lying about it. You probably have them chained in their rooms or chained to their beds. Viper told us you had slaves, and now that we've met Jay, the guy who's the pimp-bossman, we know Viper's right."

Brick perked up at Viper's name and asked, "Who's Viper? Why did he tell you that?"

"Viper is a famous Los Angeles artist and our friend." They began to chant together, "No more slavery. No more slavery." They repeated the verse, growing louder with each phrase.

Brick gave up on his attempts to quiet the pair, and he tossed me a pair of handcuffs, "Hook 'em up, and let's take them to the sheriff's office. Sheriff Maggie can deal with them." My experience with handcuffs was on the other end: being hooked up, not hooking up.

"I've never put handcuffs on anybody, but there's a first time for everything. Sheriff Maggie? The sheriff's a girl?" I asked. "I've never heard of a female sheriff."

"It's easy, you just snap them on. And, yes, the sheriff is a woman and an excellent, well-trained law enforcement officer. She's out of her office working on a case and will be back in a while. I'll watch these two ladies at the sheriff's office until she or her deputy arrives. By the way, if your name isn't Nathan, what is it?"

Chapter 42

Brick and Charlie
Present Day

"I'm not from around here," I answered, avoiding Brick's question as I thought I might put Brick off. I didn't know if the deputy would know my real name, but I knew the prison had announced my return to Barrier to the sheriff. I made a huge mistake when I told that correctional officer about Dos. Topping my sentence meant I had no parole hanging over me, and I wanted to keep things that way. If law enforcement began to watch me, I might get into more trouble.

Brick looked up from his desk. His experience with people not answering simple questions meant one of two things: wanted by law enforcement or hiding from somebody or something. Brick looked at me and thought the former. "I'm asking again, what is your name? I assume it's not Nathan."

I had rehearsed many possible scenarios of answering questions upon my release from prison, but I hadn't anticipated being caught avoiding a simple question like my name, and it scared the daylights out of me. My mind raced through possibilities that would border on the truth. Charles, Chuck, CW, COW all flashed through my mind, but I said, "Owen. People call me Owen." I hoped Jay didn't call me *Charlie* in front of the deputy, at least until I thought of a better name.

Brick repeated, "Owen. I'm pleased to meet you. I'm Brick O'Brien, one of the sheriff's deputies here. I need your assistance in getting these two ladies to the sheriff's office. I'll wait with these two, but you need to let Jay know that you are coming with me. You can come back to the CDR as soon as we book them into custody. If Cagey or the sheriff isn't at the office, you'll need a ride back."

I said, "Sure, I can help. I'm new so I am not sure how this works. I don't want to get fired during my first week. Let me go talk to Jay, and I'll be right back." And I left.

Owen was my middle name, but I had never been called Owen in my life or even know why I had been given that for a middle name. I had no relatives or ancestors named Owen that I knew of, and I sure as hell didn't know why I had blurted it out.

I passed through the kitchen and went out the backdoor of the CDR without thinking. Part of my brain said to leave the building and start walking to Vegas. Surely, I could hitch a ride, particularly with my uniform on. The other part of my brain pounded with Ms. Moneyjoy's words: Honesty, honesty, be honest. The two parts competed against each other, but when I reached the front of the building, I saw Jay standing in the window of his office watching me, and I realized which part of my brain I needed to use. When I had been honest with Jay about my crime and prison time, he rewarded me with a job, a real job, a good job, my first job ever. Would honesty work again? I hoped so.

I did a U-turn and aimed toward the kitchen to seek out Jay. I hadn't done anything wrong; I feared law enforcement but that wasn't a crime. Jay cocked his head as he watched my quick turnaround. I had no duties requiring me to go outside, and he knew Brick was paying attention to the women. I'm sure he wondered what I was doing.

"Sir, Mr. Jay, I have two questions for you," I stammered as I entered his office.

Jay smiled and said, "Sure, Charlie, and you don't have to call me Sir or Mr. Jay. Jay is fine. What's up?"

I said, "Yes, Sir. First, Deputy Brick asked me to help him take the two women to the sheriff's office, if it is okay with you. I mean I'll be back as soon as I can although I might need a ride back if the sheriff isn't there."

"That's no problem," Jay answered. "We work with the sheriff's office as much as we can. Barrier is a small town, and the sheriff's office doesn't have much manpower. If you need a ride back, call me, and I'll have someone pick you up. My number is on here." He handed him his card that included his cell number. "What's your second question?"

I looked at my toes and murmured, "Well, it's the sheriff's office, Sir. You see, if they know my name, they might get interested and start hassling me. I don't want that; I want to be a regular, anonymous person here. I lied when I told Brick my name. I told him Owen, not Charlie, but now I think I should have told him my real name."

"Damn straight, you should have told him your real name. Lying about your name will make the sheriff suspicious. Let's go figure this out. I'll go with you. Brick's a reasonable person and so is the sheriff."

Chapter 43

Charlie
Present Day

The two women continued to act out when Jay and I entered the brothel office. Brick was threatening to put them in a jail cell where they couldn't hurt themselves or anyone else.

Jay said to me, "We can talk to Brick later but go with him now to put these two women in jail. I don't appreciate all of their accusations."

They positioned the two cuffed women in the back seat of Brick's jeep for the quick ride to the office. Brick tested their handcuffs and seatbelts and noted the child safety locks engaged so they couldn't get out of the car during the five-minute ride. Brick drove while I twisted myself to watch the women.

Maggie and Cagey had their vehicles parked in front of the office when we arrived. Brick and I escorted the two women into the office, and Cagey recorded the incident and put them in separate cells. They fumed and blustered a bit but calmed down when the door to their cells slammed shut.

"Would you like a cup of coffee, Owen, before we take you back to the CDR? You've earned it. Do you take cream and sugar or have it straight up?" Brick asked me. "By the way, you did a great job back there. Is this the first arrest you've ever been involved with?"

"Coffee, black and hot, as long as you are offering. I could use a cup," I answered not knowing how to address Brick's question. It certainly wasn't the first arrest I had been involved with, but it had been the first arrest I had been an external party to. The last time I had been in the Barrier Sheriff's Office, I wore handcuffs with tears gushing down my cheeks like a broken pipe, and it hadn't been pretty. I had tried to put my arrest and prison time behind me, but now it bounced back, big and bold, facing me front and center. "I need to tell you something, Brick. I made a mistake back at the CDR and lied to you about my name. It isn't Owen."

Brick said, "I figured that when you hesitated before answering. Most people answer that question without delay; it rolls off their tongues. What's your name?"

"Charles Walker. My name is Charles Owen Walker."

Brick had been gazing out the window but jerked his head up studying me from top to bottom. "You are Charlie Walker? The warden called the sheriff and said you might come this way. How long have you been in Barrier, Mr. Walker? Is that why you gave me a fake name?"

"Yes," Charlie answered, avoiding Brick's eyes. "Jay knows the truth, and he told me I should be honest with you, so I am. I did my time and don't want to do any more. I'm living with my stepfather, Gene Jacobs, and I want to get a fresh start on life.

"I didn't hurt Mrs. Hudson, but no one believes me. When the prison released me a few days ago, I was hell bent on locating Dos, the guy who did it, but Gene made me swear I wouldn't go after him, so I promised. He introduced me to Jay who hired me on the spot, and Gene allows me to live with him if I don't get into trouble and if I am open and honest in everything I do. I don't want to screw up my chance of success."

Brick said, "You have gotten yourself off to a terrific start, Mr. Walker. We wondered if you'd return to Barrier. I know your mom doesn't live here anymore but didn't realize Gene Jacobs was your stepfather. He's a good guy."

Maggie strode out of her office and said, "I've been on the phone with Jay Guzman. I don't believe I have met you, Mr. Walker."

Chapter 44

Charlie
Present Day

In the small village of Barrier, everybody knew everybody, which I remembered from my past. I didn't know how much the sheriff knew of my case of harming Mrs. Hudson, but I assumed she knew it all, either from rumor or from the former sheriff's files. I looked Maggie directly in the eyes and said, "No Ma'am, Ms. Sheriff, we haven't met, but I'm certain you know who I am. Some of it is true, but some of it isn't. I'm not on parole because I did my time, the whole thing. Mr. Guzman hired me as the bouncer at the Chicken Dinner Ranch, and I intend to work hard and not cause you any trouble. No trouble at all."

Cagey and Brick focused their eyes on me, and in harmony, both raised their eyebrows. My reputation as a youth had been shady at best, and they had no reason to think I had changed. It was well known that people didn't change for the better in prison; rather their criminal ways strengthened and deepened while serving their time.

Maggie said, "I hope that's all true, Charlie, because I don't like trouble either. Barrier is a quiet town, and we'd like to keep it that way. Let's talk again, but right now I need to visit with our guests, give them dinner, and settle them for the night. Brick, could you drive Charlie back to the CDR while Cagey and I spend time with our three guests? Please don't leave town, though, Charlie. We do need to talk."

By the time Brick returned, Maggie and Cagey had checked on the prisoners in their cells. Viper did not know the two young women had been arrested, and the women remained unaware of Viper's presence. Cagey would spend the night in the jail keeping watch.

Maggie declared, "We've never had a full house since I became sheriff. If this keeps up, we'll have to hire another deputy or jailor. Maybe build more cells."

Brick said, "Charlie insists he didn't hurt Mrs. Hudson. He comes across as sincere, but if he's the conman Doc and Harry claim, he's lying to us, as he has done for the past quarter of a century. On the other hand, what if he told the truth, and he didn't hurt her? Could that be true? It's something to consider. We know the Innocence Project reviewed his case, but we don't know how thoroughly. The Project began in the 1990s, and they became overwhelmed with the quantity of cases that inmates, attorneys, and family members asked them to review. Every inmate claims to be innocent, and they had to review and prioritize all of them. The Charlie Walker case might not have risen up to the top of the pile. This is, after all, Nevada."

"We can call the investigators and learn what they discovered and why they stopped investigating," Maggie suggested. "As far as I recall, they never made their findings public. UNLV uses its criminal justice department to investigate the wrongful accusations. We can start there."

"No," Brick cut in with sound advice. "Let's not get ahead of ourselves. The first person we should talk to is Charlie. He's the most important person in this case, and he now has threatened to kill somebody named Dos. We should have pressed Charlie about Dos' last name, but you can talk to him again and try to pluck it out of his craw. Dos didn't attend school or work in Barrier, so we don't know who he is. If we can locate Dos, we'll be better able to learn whether Charlie lied or told the truth."

Maggie nodded, "You're right, Brick, but I want to read the court records before we talk to him. Cagey, could you find the court records containing the Charlie Walker trial? Perhaps after all these years, something will pop out at us. I'll call his public defender, Ms. Dortha Ling. She was inexperienced at the time, but perhaps she'll be willing to talk to us. From what I understand, she practices law in Las Vegas and does estate planning."

"Okay," Brick said. "It sounds like a plan. I'd like to be here when you question Charlie on the death threat against Dos. We don't know if Charlie is dangerous or not. Let's find out who Dos is and what Charlie's intentions are."

Chapter 45

Viper
Present Day

Cagey accompanied Viper into Maggie's office as soon as he had finished his breakfast. The Panorama provided breakfast to the prisoners, today serving Crepes Suzette with fresh mango juice. The hotel served a different cosmopolitan menu each day, always a gastronome's paradise. Crepes Suzette on Tuesday and Wednesday would be another adventure.

"So, Viper," Maggie said, "you answered none of my questions yesterday, so I'll ask you a couple different ones. We want to talk to the other guy, Nathan Griss, who allegedly assisted you in robbing an art store in Henderson. Do you have any thoughts as to where we might locate Mr. Griss?"

"No, I've met Griss, but don't know where he hangs out. He told me that he lived in Vegas, but I didn't believe him because he lies a lot," Viper answered.

"Where did you meet him?" Maggie continued.

"In Mexico. Tijuana." Viper answered. He paused before adding, "We both liked animal shows and hung out at The Zoo. People rave about the San Diego Zoo, but it's nothing compared to The Zoo in Tijuana." He raised his eyebrows and curled his upper lip into a sneer, not realizing Maggie would comprehend his double entendre.

"I can only imagine," Maggie said sarcastically, continuing, "Does Griss have connections in Vegas, like a family, a girlfriend, or a job?"

"I can't tell you. I don't know the answer to that one. I've met him but don't know him well," Viper rebutted.

Maggie continued, "We'll come back to that in a minute. Your name has emerged in another investigation. How do you know Rhoda Knight and Anne Bell?"

"Don't you mean A Bell?" Viper quipped. "Your grammar skills are seriously lacking, Sheriff. You should use 'a' before a word starting with a consonant and 'an' before a word beginning with a vowel. I'm not from the south, and I don't know a belle. And Rhoda Knight? Get real, it sounds like an activity, not a name." He again curled his lip, evolving into a sadistic smile.

Maggie ignored his smart aleck answers asking, "I repeat, Anne Belle and Rhoda Knight, do you know them?"

"No, I don't think so," he lied. "I've never heard of either Ms. Bell or Ms. Knight."

Maggie stood up and grasped his arm, "We're getting nowhere, Vincent, and you can go back to your cell. Enjoy your day."

Chapter 46

Maggie, Brick, and Cagey
Present Day

The sheriff's office had unexpectedly become swamped, and everything was linked to the Chicken Dinner Ranch. Charlie Walker had been released from prison and now worked at the CDR, taking the place of former CDR employee Nathan Griss, who had bopped Maggie on the head. Viper's artwork hung in the upstairs hallway of the CDR, and he claimed it had been stolen by Jay, the CDR owner. Anne Bell and Rhoda Knight had created a ruckus at the CDR and were linked to Viper. Trouble was rare at the brothel, but the last three days had been hectic and bothersome.

Maggie, Brick, and Cagey regrouped to determine how to approach the three prisoners, plus Nathan Griss and Charlie Walker. One by one, they discussed the possibilities.

Maggie led the discussion, "Let's start with Charlie. His case is cold, but we can review it to try to see if it will be productive to conduct a formal inquiry with Innocence Project support. He has completed his sentence, but if he really didn't hurt Mrs. Hudson, the person who did may still live here. I'd feel better if I knew that it had been properly evaluated. It doesn't appear any formal review has ever been completed, and I'd like to clarify who really injured Sarah Hudson, Charlie or an unknown person."

"I agree," Brick answered. "I can take on that project. Do you want to talk to Charlie and tell him our plan or do it without his knowledge?"

"Let's keep him informed because if he trusts us, he will provide us with more information about what happened. If he's telling the truth, additional info may emerge. Your tackling this project is a lovely idea. It can be your summer job. Sans pay, of course," Maggie said winking at him. "Cagey and I will tie up the Nathan-Viper issues. He thwacked me, and Viper is a real puzzle waiting to be solved. So far, he hasn't given us much help, but that could change."

With a twinkle in his eye, Brick repeated, "Sans pay? Of course, I would expect nothing more."

"Of course, because you're still on probation," she joked.

Cagey exclaimed, "I'd like to get cracking on the Nathan issue. If I can find him, I might crack his head like he cracked yours. He's a mean and wicked man. He could have killed you."

"Viper will lead us to him. The two of them have committed more than one crime, and Viper is the key to finding him and solving these cases," Maggie answered. "When we first went to the CDR, Jay praised Nat/Nathan, whatever his name is, noting what a talented employee he had been. When Jay insisted on locating the other paintings, Nat eagerly offered to assist, perhaps too eagerly. Instead of finding the paintings, he thwacked me on the head, tied me up, and disappeared. I wonder if Jay can shed light on Nat and this situation. We should visit Jay again and find out what he knows. I'll do that."

"I'll talk to Jay," Cagey said.

Maggie disagreed, "No, I'll talk to him. You're his brother, and I think it would be better if I dealt with him in this situation. He's never lied to me."

"Okay, you're the boss. What should we do with the two women?" Cagey asked.

Maggie said, "Viper and the women are connected, but Viper's not admitting to knowing them. I want to bring the three of them together and see what happens. Let's handcuff the ladies to the interview table, and you can bring Viper in and see how they respond to each other. It'll be interesting to see what fireworks erupt. Brick, can you bring the girls in? After we situate them, Cagey can add Viper to the mix. It might be a splendid show."

Chapter 47

Rhoda, Anne, and Viper
Present Day

Brick retrieved Rhoda and Anne from their cells. Although handcuffed, they tried their best to be disruptive during the short walk from their cells to the interview room. They tried spitting on him and even attempted to headbutt him, but he foiled their aggression. He affixed both women to the interview table by attaching their hands to the center bar. Maggie watched from the two-way mirror as he secured them before entering and turning on the video recorder.

Maggie started to sit down across from them, but Rhoda spat at her, and the two voiced their chant again, "No more slavery. No more slavery."

Maggie said sharply, "Enough of the spitting already, I will muzzle you, and you won't like it one bit. By the way, you have a visitor, your friend, Mr. Viper."

The aggression turned sharply to submission, and they abruptly ceased talking when the door to the interview room opened, realizing Viper stood in the doorway glaring at them. His hands were handcuffed behind him with Cagey grasping his elbow.

Viper scowled at them, "What are you two doing here? I told you not to leave L.A., you stupid cunts. Do what I tell you, do you understand? And don't say a word about anything to the sheriff or anyone else."

The two girls dropped their eyes, and Anne whispered, "Don't get mad, Viper. We didn't mean any harm. Don't hurt us."

Rhoda hung her head and murmured, barely audibly, "That's right, Viper. We won't say anything; please don't hurt us again."

Viper said, "You'd better not, if you know what's good for you."

Maggie said, "No threats, Viper. Cagey, please take him back to his cell."

Cagey clasped Viper's shoulder and guided him back to his cell. Viper, though small and wiry, twisted and jerked the entire way, trying to release himself from Cagey's strong grip, but Cagey prevailed.

The two women calmed as Viper left, and Brick separated them, accompanying Rhoda to her cell while leaving Anne attached to the table. When Brick came back into the room, he seated himself next to Maggie, and they began asking her questions.

Brick asked, "Anne, can you tell us about Viper's comments? How does Viper hurt you?"

Anne remained silent, head bowed, staring at the table. Her fingers were clasped together so tightly they had whitened, and she acquired a slight tick in her cheek.

Brick continued, "How do you know Viper? Where did you meet him?"

"He's our friend, and we live with him when he's in L.A.," Anne whispered.

Maggie said, "We understand that, Anne, but if he's your friend, why and how does he hurt you?"

"I made it up and didn't mean anything by it," Anne said, "He doesn't actually hurt us. He loves us."

Maggie thought for a moment before saying, "I don't think so. I think he does hurt you. Do you have any bruises or other signs of abuse?"

"He's never hurt me. He wouldn't do that," Anne said on the verge of tears. Her cheek tick amplified, moving up to her eye.

Maggie pressed on, "I see. How often does he require you to have unwanted sex with him?"

Anne jerked her head up with tears starting to stream down her face, "How did you know that? I never told you that. I never told anybody. I mean he never... How did you know?"

Maggie didn't answer but gestured for Cagey to escort Anne to her cell and return with Rhoda.

Learning that rape had been at the core of their issues, Brick and Cagey retreated from the room while Maggie interviewed Rhoda. Maggie repeated the questions she had asked Anne, including the one about rape. Rhoda stammered at first, but after a moment she began to talk, giving details of the last rape that had occurred. She admitted that she had been beaten on occasion and showed Maggie her back with several scars and bruises.

Maggie escorted Rhoda to her cell, and Brick escorted Viper back to the interview room. Brick led off with the questions.

"Viper, my friend," said Brick, "you told us..."

Viper snapped at Brick, "I am not your friend."

Brick continued, "I realize that; it was a figure of speech. If you don't know these two women, why did you threaten them."

Viper didn't say anything.

"You told us you didn't know Anne or Rhoda, but they claim you do. In fact, they claim you live with them and have sex with them on a regular basis. Unwelcomed sex. Is that true?" Brick asked.

"I must have misunderstood your questions at first," Viper said. "If you want good answers, you have to be clearer with your questions."

"Fair enough," Brick said. "Here is a clear question. A yes or no question: Do you know either Rhoda Knight or Anne Bell?"

"I want to call an attorney," Viper said. "A real attorney, not someone from this fucking pissant town. Ask me no fucking questions and guess what: I'll tell you no fucking lies."

Chapter 48

Maggie and Brick
Present Day

Maggie and Brick discussed how to question Charlie during the interview. Speaking with him could prove to be challenging. With no parole attached to Charlie's release from prison, law enforcement retained no control over him and his activities, and although he wanted to prove his innocence, they could not step on his rights. Their interest was simply to discover the identity of Dos and why Charlie wanted to kill him.

Puffy clouds filled the sky and pumped humidity into the desert air. At noon, Brick dispatched himself to the CDR to retrieve Charlie. Jay agreed to let him leave at lunchtime. They could request his cooperation but had doubts of whether they would receive it. While Brick and Maggie viewed this as a routine, post-incarceration visit, they felt confident that Charlie would not see it the same way. It could evolve into a touchy situation, but they merely wanted to identify Dos.

Both law enforcement officers involved themselves with the interview, and Maggie's first question was, "Mr. Walker, we have a few questions, mainly what plans you have made now that you completed your sentence. We know you topped out your sentence, and from the reports at Fenwick, you became a model prisoner. It is to your credit that you obtained a job and acquired a place to live."

"Thank you, Ma'am. I avoided trouble while at Fenwick, and now that I have been hired at the CDR, I hope I can continue the same path. Gene agreed to let me live with him if I have a job and am honest, and that's what I plan on doing. I will pay him room and board money after I get paid."

Maggie pressed on, "We want to know about a person named Dos who lives in or has ties to Barrier. The warden called me the day you left Fenwick and said you made threats toward Dos, in fact, you threatened to kill him. We don't want a murder, and I'm sure you don't want to go back to prison. We don't know who Dos is, and we're requesting that you can assist us."

Charlie repeated the story he had told many times before, "Dos? You want to know about Dos? His name is Jonathan Grayson, a high school friend, but not anymore. He attacked Sarah Hudson and injured her eye, which I told the sheriff when he arrested me, but no one believed me. The sheriff, Mrs. Hudson, and most of the people in Barrier blamed me 100 percent, and the jury convicted me in a quick two-day trial. Even my mom didn't believe me, and I wasn't sure my lawyer believed me. She had graduated from law school a few weeks before she defended me and didn't like or know criminal law. Hell, she wasn't much older than I was, maybe twenty-three or twenty-four years old. She never confronted the other attorney or judge, and her meek and mild ways did not help my case. I didn't blame Ms. Ling though because she did the best she could, but the judge should have replaced her.

"Judge Little didn't believe me either and slammed the gavel down. My trial ended just like that, over and done with. Ms. Ling said he gave me such a long sentence because of Mrs. Hudson's job with law enforcement, but I think he gave me a long sentence because he liked Mrs. Hudson. She was a juvenile probation officer, not a cop, for hell's sake. If I had done this, which I didn't, it would have been my first big offense, and my last, I might add. Before that, I had done kids' stuff, like truancy and smoking a little weed."

Murder Almost

"Jonathan Grayson? Why did you call him Dos?" Brick asked.

"I concocted the name Dos. The teachers at school called him TwoJohnny in first grade because the school assigned three boys named Johnny to the same teacher. She first called him *number two* but then nicknamed him *TwoJohnny*. Everybody else did, too, because it made us laugh and somehow fit him. His mom deserted him while in high school, and he had no support at home. After his mom left, he went to work for Mr. DeClarke at the grocery store. Dos and I hung out together, but I called him Dos after the 'Two' in TwoJohnny, you see. Dos was sneaky and did a lot of mischievous stuff but never got caught for anything, while the police caught me for everything."

Brick and Maggie listened with interest but also with skepticism. While the Charlie Walker case had been reviewed and used in law enforcement circles to demonstrate various issues that had arisen, they had never heard of Jonathan Grayson. Harry had mentioned TwoJohnny but apparently nobody except Charlie knew what the name Dos meant. Brick would have to make another trip to the school to look at records and revisit Doc McCrone and Harry Bird.

Maggie asked, "Do you know what happened to TwoJohnny? Did he ever contact you while you were in prison?"

"No, Ma'am, he never contacted me. He's a lying S.O.B. We went to Vegas that night, but he left with most of Sarah Hudson's money and then called me from the Mexican border, or at least that's where he said he called from. He stole her Porsche and her purse and dumped me. We had swapped out the Porsche for an old Studebaker in a hick town, and he drove the Studebaker to Mexico, if that's where he went. I never heard from him again."

Brick said, "We plan to review your case. It's cold, but we'll check out your story. Can you remember anything else about what happened or what Jonathan Grayson, Dos, said?"

I thought for a few seconds before saying, "Maybe one thing, but I doubt that it is important. I remember that TwoJohnny burned his hand on the iron. He said she threw the iron at him, and he caught it with his hand and threw it back at her, and it hit her in the face. His hand looked bad. He stuck his hand in an ice bucket when we arrived at the hotel, trying to cool it down, but it had turned red and brownish, starting to blister. He said it hurt, but he whined about everything. I can't remember anything more. I've reviewed what happened hundreds of times in my head, but that's all I've got."

Maggie added, "It's okay, Charlie. We'll be in touch. If we locate or hear of Grayson, we'll let you know. Brick will take you back to the CDR so you can finish your shift. Remember, Charlie, we can help. We want you to become a regular citizen, not retain the label of ex-con. If you need something, be sure to call. Don't do anything on your own regarding Dos." She handed him a business card.

Brick dropped Charlie at the CDR followed by a return visit to the school. He wanted to see what he could learn about TwoJohnny since he now knew his name. He checked the files and was shocked at how quickly he recognized the face in TwoJohnny's old school picture. He dug further and found that Jonathan Grayson had been enrolled in Barrier High School but had not graduated. He had many discipline records, typically mischief-making activities, such as smoking on campus, teasing girls, and truancy. The offenses had been spread out with no pattern. Since he had never been caught at anything, no police records existed. Jonathan and Charlie had done mischief together. Neither of them graduated from BHS, and Jonathan had disappeared the same time Charlie had been arrested.

Both Doc and Harry were at the school when Brick arrived, so he invited them to his office to see if either could shine a light on Jonathan and his escapades. Doc McCrone knew little of Jonathan Grayson, except the court expected him to appear and testify at Charlie's trial, but he had skipped town, and no one knew his whereabouts. Doc explained, "Numerous rumors cropped up concerning Jonathan, but nothing solid. He seemed a high-strung youngster with little supervision at home and even less ambition. His mother deserted him as a teenager, and he worked for David DeClarke for a time before he disappeared. David liked him and tried to give him a foot up, but Jonathan didn't accept it."

Harry Bird gave more specific information while chuckling at his remembrances, "Yes, I can tell you about TwoJohnny. I can laugh now but didn't laugh at the time. He loved mischievous pranks and made me the brunt of his tricks. The principal couldn't pin most of them to him, but I had little doubt that he did these capers. I hired him to clean rooms after school, but he didn't last long. I wanted him to empty the waste baskets and replenish the toilet paper every night, but instead, he stole rolls of toilet paper and toilet-papered the front lawn. He filled one teacher's waste basket with water and dyed the water in the girl's toilets with red food coloring. He cut the straw off my brooms and switched out the cleaning fluids. Pink cleaners became green and green ones became blue. I thought this dangerous because mixing chemicals can get you in trouble. One time he covered the women's faculty toilet seat with Saran Wrap. He cleaned the cafeteria one afternoon after the staff had gone home and swapped out the sugar and salt and a bunch of kids became ill. All small pranks, nevertheless, their constant occurrences annoyed me. And no one could catch him. The principal viewed them as exasperating, but not harmful, and did nothing to punish him or make him stop. I constantly had to look out for his stunts."

Doc said, "Do you think he did all those? I knew of the pranks but figured Charlie Walker or one of the other kids they ran with, like Gabe Cochran or Eldon Lankford, was guilty. All of them enjoyed little tricks on the staff. I discovered TwoJohnny running a craps game at noon in the boys' bathroom with assistance from Cochran and Lankford. They pilfered items off my desk and put them in the lost and found or traded them for cigarettes. I also had to hide my school supplies, like staplers and tape, from them, otherwise they'd disappear. They would alternate who did what and when, making them difficult to catch. Cochran straightened out and ended up working as a butcher at DeClarke's until David sold it. I don't know what happened to Lankford."

"Yes, Jonathan did all kinds of things, but always came in under the radar," Harry said. "One year we planted a tree as part of the Red Ribbon Week, and somebody cut it down. I thought he did it, but the police couldn't pin it on him before he left town."

"Has anyone heard news of Jonathan?" Brick asked.

Both men shook their heads to Brick's question. Harry suggested, "You should call David DeClarke. He sold the grocery chain, but the new owners sold it to Safeway a few years ago and boarded up his old store. DeClarke liked Jonathan. He hired him for a time after Jonathan's mother abandoned him and seemed down when Jonathan left out of the blue. David dropped by the school a few times to see if he had contacted the school, which he hadn't. DeClarke changed his residence to Las Vegas after he sold his store and gave me his phone number, saying specifically, 'If you see Jonathan Grayson, tell him to call me, I'd enjoy seeing him again. I loved that boy.'"

Chapter 49

Nathan
Present Day

The drive from Barrier to Las Vegas typically lasted four hours, but Nathan, aka Nat, pulled out all the stops in the stolen Jag and arrived in a little over three hours. The previous owner had installed a radar detector, and Nat decelerated to the speed limit when it buzzed. The trip allowed him time to consider what might come next and how to divert police attention away from himself.

Nat passed through the city of Las Vegas and circled behind a casino hotel called the Vegas Villa on the southern outskirts of town. It had been a stroke of fortune that he hadn't been at the CDR when Viper arrived. He hadn't seen Viper in several years and wondered how time had treated him. Nat's head grew little hair, but he had started to grow a beard. He had gained a few pounds, and his arms, neck, and shoulders were covered with tattoos, but Viper would have recognized him for certain.

Nat didn't have much cash, as he hadn't worked an entire week, and Jay hadn't paid him, but he had a credit card with a couple hundred dollars available on it and could remain at the hotel until he figured out what to do. He needed to avoid Viper because associating with him might land him in jail or even prison.

True to his moniker, Viper, the snake would likely rat on him. They had spent time together, but it had all been in good fun, except for the time that Viper insisted on bringing the Mexican girl across the border, which they both realized had been a huge blunder. They steered her away from the ICE agents and luckily the Feds had dropped the charges when she became invisible. They justified the robbery in Henderson because, as a low-end heist, not more than a few hundred dollars, they hurt no one, and Viper needed the art supplies to do his work.

Nat parked in an obscure stall at the rear of the casino, in case someone had rescued the sheriff from the warehouse, and she was able to track the Jag's license plate. He looked in the trunk of the car, hoping to locate a screwdriver to switch the plates, but no luck. He could buy one at the stop-and-rob across the street.

He had made sure he hadn't hurt the sheriff too badly, but she would be angry, and her two deputies seemed like they could handle themselves and might come after him. He glanced down at his clothes, noting his Chicken Dinner Ranch uniform. He didn't have any other clothes, so he would have to buy new clothes, too.

He rented a room for the night and noted that the casino specials included free happy hour drinks and snacks, so he headed to the bar. Happy hour would end in a few minutes, and the snacks had dwindled to next to nothing, but he filled his plate, ordered a scotch on the rocks and had just sat down when his cell phone rang. The screen read *Restricted,* but he decided to answer it. "Yeah, who's this?" he greeted roughly.

A pause lingered before a familiar voice said, "Is this Mr. David DeClarke? Thank you for taking my call. My name is Vincent Pierson and..."

Nat interrupted, "Viper? What the hell? I'm not DeClarke. This is Nat; why are you calling me? How'd you find me?"

Viper cut him off, "Yes, thanks, Mr. DeClarke, I need help. I'm calling from the sheriff's office in Barrier, Nevada, because I'm in jail, and I'm going to need assistance. I thought you might be able to help me. I am wondering if your firm can represent me at my hearing, but first, I need bail money. Could you wire me bail money? I have not seen a judge yet, so am unsure of the amount he will set, but I can call you later, if they will let me use the phone, that is." He looked up at Cagey and raised his eyebrows as if saying, *Can you make that happen?* He hoped that Nat would read between the lines and try to get him out of jail.

Maggie appeared outside the door and motioned to Cagey to step into the hall. Cagey glanced over at Viper and squeezed around the corner, out of Viper's hearing range. Viper saw his opportunity and whispered into the phone, "Dammit, Nat, I'm in jail, and I need fucking bail money. Call DeClarke and get it. I know he sold his grocery business for a boatload of money. I met him a few years ago, and I know what he did with his money. It's in your best interest to..." Cagey reentered the room, and Viper softened his pitch, "I think it's an easy case. The sheriff says I'm wanted for a robbery in Henderson, which I didn't do, but I need help. Could you come to Barrier soon? I need a lawyer now and will need bail money after I visit with the judge."

Nat replied, "What are you talking about, Viper? Hell, no, I can't come to Barrier. I hit the Barrier sheriff over the head and tied her up, so I'm on a wanted list, too. You're the fixer, Viper, not me. I think you are fucking S.O.L." He clicked his phone off.

Viper paused for a minute, saying nothing, as if he listening to the speaker and then spoke loudly enough for Cagey to hear, "Thank you again, Mr. DeClarke, I appreciate your help. I'll see you in a few days."

Chapter 50

Nat and Mr. DeClarke
Present Day

"Now, what I am I supposed to do?" Nat mumbled to himself. "DeClarke? What the fuck is that about? Viper causes me nothing but trouble and bringing up DeClarke is just strange." After giving it more thought, he realized that Viper must know something, he must have a reason. "I don't trust the snake, but on the other hand, maybe he has an angle to keep us out of jail for the art store job. DeClarke is old, hell, I don't know if he is even alive at this point. This is so confusing because he isn't an attorney, he sold groceries for Christ's sake. Sure, he offered to help me after my mom left, but I don't know what he can do for me now. Viper said that he met him, but I haven't seen DeClarke for fifteen or twenty years. I doubt I can get ahold of him, and even if I do manage to reach him, I doubt he'd remember me."

Nat fretted over Viper's phone call, considering a myriad of problems. He needed money. He had no cash and no job prospects or other means of support. His credit card hadn't quite maxed out but was getting close, and a week at the Vegas Villa would max it. He had pilfered another credit card from a guy he bumped into at the Chicken Dinner Ranch, but the guy might have canceled it. He could find a place to rob, but without an accomplice, any business or person worth robbing needed a second person.

On the other hand, a visit with DeClarke might offer possibilities. Maybe DeClarke would remember him and want to help him. He had once before, and who knows. Maybe he could live with DeClarke for a few nights and alleviate his cash flow issues. Maybe DeClarke remembered Viper from their meeting years ago? He needed time to think and figure this all out. Surely, something would emerge.

He walked across the street to the strip mall in search of clothes and a screwdriver, so he could swap out the license plates on the Jag. Backtracking to the hotel, he stopped at the Jag and switched license plates with a California licensed Toyota on the far end of the parking lot. He strolled through the casino and sweet-talked the barmaids into free drinks, before returning to his hotel room. He had faith that a plan would spring to life when he awoke.

The next morning Nat ate the hotel's $4.00 special of ham and eggs and thumbed through his cell phone contacts to see if he had DeClarke's cell number. Somebody, maybe his old buddy Gabe, gave it to him when he stopped at the Safeway on a previous visit to Barrier.

Gabe told him that DeClarke had relocated to Las Vegas, but he didn't know where he resided or if he was dead or alive. David DeClarke had been the one person who helped him after his mother deserted him and absconded to parts unknown. The high school counselor convinced DeClarke to employ Nat to stock shelves and deliver groceries after school, and DeClarke watched over him. He even invited Nat to live with him, but Nat refused and stayed in the duplex hoping his mom would come back. He ate dinner with DeClarke occasionally, and DeClarke supplied him with groceries, like milk and cereal for his breakfast. The store baker saved stale bread and cookies every day, and Nat managed to survive, even gain weight. DeClarke made sure he went to school every day and added a few dollars extra in his weekly paychecks.

Nat knew the high school counselor lobbied to put him in foster care after his mother left, but DeClarke volunteered to employ him rather than placing him in the foster care system. Nat had been grateful that DeClarke had befriended him during those lean years, but he had never expressed gratitude and always regretted that he hadn't.

During his last year of high school, it became clear that Nat would not graduate, and Mr. DeClarke suggested summer school or correspondence courses to earn his needed credits. He went a step farther, offering to pay for his college or trade school, but Nat dismissed it, thinking he wasn't smart enough and never took advantage of this opportunity. It would have meant another year of high school or spending his summer taking classes, and he feared the other students and the teachers would consider him a failure. He wanted to get on with his life, and he couldn't see that education would make any difference.

DeClarke's offer came just before the incident with Mrs. Hudson and his escape to Mexico. He lived in Mexico for a long time, worried that he had killed Mrs. Hudson and surprised to learn that he hadn't; rather, Charlie had been blamed for everything, her assault, her eye, the car, the money, and then was sentenced to serve time in the state penitentiary. Was it skill that he avoided punishment for his crimes, or was it luck? He wasn't sure which one.

At one point, while in a drunken stupor, Nat revealed Mr. DeClarke's generous offer to Viper. Even though several years had already passed, Viper had encouraged him to take advantage of it. But Nat couldn't bring himself to ask DeClarke for help. Too much water under the bridge, he thought. On the other hand, Viper, a law school graduate gone bad, understood the value of an education and realized he had abandoned his childhood values. He had lost his family and his occupation through poor choices. And now, after all this time, Viper thought Nat should talk to DeClarke. *What else did Viper know about the situation that he hadn't shared?*

Before deciding against it, Nathan dialed the phone, hoping for inspiration to impress DeClarke. He couldn't ask him for money right away. It might take a couple visits or phone calls if DeClarke was still alive.

"Hello, Mr. DeClarke, it's Jonathan Grayson. Do you remember me? I used to work for you at your grocery store while I was in high school."

Chapter 51

Mr. DeClarke
Present Day

David DeClarke was surprised to hear from Jonathan after all these years. It had been a quarter of a century, and he was over seventy, meaning Jonathan was over forty. "What a surprise. Yes, Jonathan, I've never forgotten you. I wondered what happened as you disappeared without saying goodbye." DeClarke's rather faint voice squeaked and quivered a bit.

Nat answered, "Yes, Sir, Mr. DeClarke, I did disappear, and I'm sorry about not saying goodbye. I left in a hurry."

"Where are you, Jonathan? In Barrier? Any chance you'll be coming to Vegas anytime soon? I would enjoy seeing you. Perhaps we could meet for coffee or lunch."

"Actually, I'm in Vegas now. I drove up yesterday, and it would be wonderful to catch up," Nathan said casually, although his heart raced with anticipation.

"Well, let's do it," DeClarke said. "Can you meet this morning? We can meet at Starbucks for coffee. Let's say eleven o'clock at the coffee shop that lies to the south of Caesar's Palace on the Strip?"

Nat couldn't believe his luck. David DeClarke remembered him and wanted to see him today. "Of course, that would be wonderful," he answered.

He clicked off and viewed himself in the mirror, knowing Mr. DeClarke would remember him as a youth. He appeared quite different now. He was the same height, but other than that any similarities had disappeared. Today, he donned his new Levi's and UNLV long-sleeved shirt and plunked his new ball cap on his head. The shirt concealed the sleeve tats and minimized his middle age paunch, and the hat disguised his diminishing hairline. He trimmed strands of gray from his beard and removed the rings. It was the best he could do.

Nat arrived first and located a table at the rear of the Starbucks, where he could watch the door and observe Mr. DeClarke as he entered. DeClarke arrived right on time as Nat knew he would. He wore a short-sleeved, blue oxford shirt with a striped bow tie. The shirt appeared to be a size too big, and he seemed gaunt and bony. It had been a long time, but Nat recognized him right away and stood to wave him over. Mr. DeClarke's eyes searched the entire coffee shop before he focused on Nat signaling him.

Nat greeted him, "Mr. DeClarke, it is so good to see you. You haven't changed from when I worked for you in Barrier." He hoped flattery would help win him over, but in truth, Mr. DeClarke appeared emaciated and pale. His stooped stature resembled a walking skeleton. His sparse gray hair, sallow skin, and sunken eyes made his face look too big for his body.

The two shook hands, and Nat ordered a coffee for DeClarke and a latte and muffin for himself.

Mr. DeClarke opened the conversation with his scratchy voice saying, "Well, Jonathan, I am thrilled to see you again. I always wondered where you ended up. I can't tell you how often I thought of you and wished you had taken me up on my offer of an education, but maybe you received an education on your own. Tell me, what have you been doing all these years?"

Nat answered, "I've done many different things. I spent time in Mexico and lived in San Diego for a while." He decided to steer his conversation toward art to see if DeClarke would volunteer any info about Viper. "In the past few years, I've been helping with art projects in Los Angeles."

It didn't work. "You're an artist? What kind of art do you do?" Mr. DeClarke asked.

"No, not exactly. My friend works as an artist, and I help him with his projects, but he taught me art appreciation through the years," Nat answered. Wanting to shift the conversation from himself for the time being, he asked, "But tell me, Mr. DeClarke, what have you been doing? Are you still in the grocery business?"

"No, I sold the chain when I retired and came to Vegas because it has a large airport. I like to travel, and it's easy to catch a flight from here. Living in Barrier, I had to add a five-hour block of time to my trips. I returned from Portugal not long ago, and I've been involved with charity work in Las Vegas, the food bank for the most part," he said. "I am curious, Jonathan, after all these years, why did you phone me?"

Mr. DeClarke had always been kind to Jonathan as a teen, but he had not reciprocated and now sat in silence for a few seconds wondering how to answer. His mind zoomed through a dozen scenarios, but he remained silent. He sipped his latte and peeled off a bit of the muffin before jamming it into his mouth. He feigned a coughing spell to buy him a few more seconds, before scanning the Starbucks hoping for inspiration. He didn't know what to say, exactly. Viper had mentioned a lawyer, money, and bail and indicated he should talk to Mr. DeClarke, but Nat didn't know why, and he wasn't sure why he had called DeClarke at all. He wasn't exactly a fan of Viper's anymore so it's not like he wanted to do him any favors. And, after seeing Mr. DeClarke, Nat couldn't ask him for money, at least not today. Maybe Viper wanted a place to hide from law enforcement? Nothing seemed to make sense.

Nat decided not to share anything with DeClarke concerning Viper and his problem because it didn't seem like the correct thing to do at the moment, so he said, "I saw your number in my phone contacts and decided to take a chance. Gabe Cochran gave it to me on my last trip to Barrier. As you mentioned, I never said goodbye, and I regretted it. You were extraordinarily kind to me after my mom left. I had free time today and decided to call you. You made me a great offer when I lived in Barrier, and I have always been sorry I didn't take you up on it. I never finished high school which obviously means I didn't attend college either. Life might have been different if I had taken you up on your offer."

Mr. DeClarke said, "I regretted that you didn't take me up on it also. I liked you and wanted to help you get ahead. It wasn't right that your mother left. I watched you grow up from birth. Your mom used to bring you into the grocery, and I would carry you piggyback through the store. You probably don't remember that. And, you liked the cookies I gave you. Chocolate chips, if I remember correctly."

Nat wrinkled his forehead at this trip down memory lane and wondered if DeClarke would babble until he finished his coffee. "Sure, I remember those cookies, chocolate chips especially," Nat said, patting his abundant belly.

"Jonathan, I have something to tell you, and I'm sure it will come as a surprise."

Nat wanted to roll his eyes, but he abstained, and said, "Tell me what?"

DeClarke stared at him for a long time before inching closer and grabbing Nat's arm with his spiny fingers and whispered, "You see, Jonathan, I'm your father."

Chapter 52

Mr. DeClarke
Present Day

Nat looked at him with wide eyes and sat up straight. He leaned forward and cried, "What? My father? You're my father? That can't be true. Mom told me he died while serving in Afghanistan." His voice grew louder, and heads turned toward them. The coffee shop din lessened as ears perked up.

DeClarke tightened his grip on Nat's arm and rasped in a whisper, "Your mother wasn't the most truthful person, do you think, Jonathan? I never joined the Army, and I didn't die. I loved her, but she wanted nothing to do with me. She abandoned you at a mere sixteen years old and never returned. Have you ever heard from her? Did she ever call you?"

"No," Nat said slowly. "She never contacted me, and I don't know where she went. I hoped she would come back, but she didn't. I sneak into Barrier every year or two, hoping she has returned, but she hasn't. I wondered if maybe she was sick or had cancer and didn't want to worry me. I thought she loved me, but I don't know. I don't know how she could have abandoned me. I always thought I did something wrong. Do you know where she is now?"

David DeClarke said, "She did worse than worry you because she abandoned you, leaving you nothing, but I know she loved you. On the day that she went away, she stopped at the store and asked me for cash. I thought she needed it for food or to pay a bill, so I gave her all I had with me, a couple twenty-dollar bills and a roll of quarters that I kept in my desk. She told me she planned to leave, but I didn't realize that she meant she was leaving town for good. She asked me to keep an eye out for you and made me promise not to reveal our relationship. I don't know why. But now that I think about it...

"Anyway, when I learned that she deserted you, I couldn't believe it because I never thought she could do something like that. She said she needed money and wanted to change her life. I thought she meant she would go to school and get a degree. I've never heard from her in all these years and don't know where she went. I remained in Barrier for many years, hoping she would have a change of heart."

DeClarke's cell phone rang, and he looked at the screen. *Restricted.* Another robocall. They were becoming more and more frequent and annoying. He held off from answering and pressed the *Not Available* icon. If the caller needed to talk with him, he or she would leave a message.

Nat was stunned. His father? DeClarke was his father? How could that be? "You never told me. Why didn't you tell me before, while I was a kid in Barrier? Even when I worked for you."

DeClarke continued, "She didn't want you to know about our relationship because we never married, although I asked her many times. We had a complicated relationship. I'm sure you don't know much about me, but my parents died in an automobile accident when I was fifteen. They willed me a little money, and I received a life insurance package that I used to obtain an education. Your mother, on the other hand, grew up in a very dysfunctional household that placed little or no value on education. While my grocery business thrived, she had few marketable work skills. She had this inane idea that she wasn't accomplished enough for me because she had never finished high school. Her father drank too much and her mother, I guess you could say *played around*. Her parents never married, and they split up when she was a teenager. She never accepted that I loved her for herself and didn't care where she came from."

Nat closed his eyes for a moment and said, "She never talked to me about her parents, and I never met them. I think she had a sister, but I never met her either and know nothing of her, not even her name. I have no idea about her parents, where they were, or what they did."

"They lived in Amarillo, Texas, but after her parents split up, she didn't have anything to do with them and left home. She liked being on her own," Mr. DeClarke filled in. "She arrived in Barrier at age sixteen and needed a job. She had ridden the bus from Amarillo and planned to go to Seattle, but she ran out of money when the bus arrived in Barrier, and so she had to get off. She had a great sense of humor and could sing like an angel. I met her and fell in love with her, although she was a few years younger than I."

Nat said, "I remember that she worked at your grocery store until I was five years old, but she quit and started cleaning houses and doing odd jobs. With those jobs she barely eked out enough money for us to live on. She never revealed why she quit the grocery, but I remember her saying she didn't want dirty money. I didn't know what she meant. She earned more money working for you than doing housework. After she started cleaning houses, she was gone all the time, even nights, and I got busy getting in trouble and seldom saw her."

"She told me that, too, but I never figured out what she meant either because my success in the grocery business didn't come from dirty money, whatever that was, I guarantee you. I earned money through hard work. I offered her money or a job several times, but she refused to accept it," DeClarke continued. "She maintained that she wanted to be independent, which her house cleaning business gave her. She was able to work her own hours, set her own salary, and was able to be home with you. I thought she could do better and prodded her to go back to school, to get her GED, to do some job training, or go to college, but she didn't want to do that. She insisted she didn't accept charity."

Nat was dumbfounded at this conversation. His mother had retained this secret information all these years, as had DeClarke. is "How did you meet her?" Nat wanted to know.

"I don't think you want me to answer your question," DeClarke responded without missing a beat. "You might be upset."

Nat was still processing if any of this incredible story was true, but responded quickly, "Why wouldn't I want to know her early life. Of course, I want to know."

David DeClarke paused for several seconds, inhaled a deep breath, and exhaled it saying, "I'll tell you if you promise not to react."

Nat had been curious why his mother had abandoned him. He had done rotten things as a kid, but he thought she loved him. He thought he was the reason for her leaving, but he didn't know what he had done. Maybe DeClarke could clear it up.

Nat repeated, "Yes, I do want to know. Tell me, please."

DeClarke inhaled another deep breath and said, "I met your mother when she worked at the Chicken Dinner Ranch." He kept his eyes glued on Jonathan, trying to interpret his response. His fingers tightened the grip on Jonathan's arm.

Nat pried DeClarke's fingers from his arm and retorted, "At the CDR? There is no way my mother worked at the Ranch. No. That's impossible. She had her faults, but she wasn't a hooker."

DeClarke further explained, "It's true, she worked at the CDR when she first arrived in Barrier until I talked her into quitting. When we first met, she was sixteen years old, too young to work at the CDR. She sang in the bar at first, but when she turned eighteen, she wanted more money and went to work upstairs. I fell head-over-heels in love with her the first time I saw her and urged her to come to work for me as a checker at the store. I wanted her to think more highly of herself. Eventually I convinced her to quit the CDR, and she came to work for me. We had an affair, and she became pregnant with you. I begged her to marry me, but she wouldn't have any part of it. She wanted her independence and refused. I loved her and never loved anyone else. As you know, I never married."

Nat rejected DeClarke's comments, "Liar. She hated the Ranch. She said it brought dishonor to the town. She wasn't a hooker and would never have done that!" He rose to his feet, abruptly knocking over his chair and spilling their coffees over the table. He stretched over and shoved DeClarke's shoulder, but he was too weak to catch himself and his chair toppled, knocking him to the floor spilling coffee over his lap. "I'm leaving, *Dad*."

DeClarke clawed his spindly fingers into Jonathan's wrist as he turned to storm out and said, "You have a powerful punch but no, you aren't leaving." Nat looked down at his wrist, surprised at DeClarke's strength. "I've always wanted you to be a part of my life, and I want, rather I need, you to give me a chance. I knew you would be upset, but you wanted to know your mother. I intend to talk you through this, make you understand her, who she was, and how she thought. She was not evil, in fact, but rather a lovely person, but stubbornly independent."

Nat immediately regretted what he had done and gently pulled DeClarke to his feet. "My apologies, Mr. DeClarke, I haven't spoken of Mom in a long time, and it's hard."

The Starbucks' manager appeared at their table, righted the chairs, wiped up the spills, and inquired if everything was okay. Both men nodded that it was.

"I have another thing to tell you," Mr. DeClarke said. Nat's brain bordered on exploding, and he wondered what else could be coming. "As you know, I have no other children or family. I'm alone. A short time ago, the docs diagnosed me with brain cancer, and I have but a few weeks to live. I have written my will but want to talk to you concerning my intentions."

Chapter 53

Brick
Present Day

Maggie's head throbbed because the Tylenol wasn't doing its job. She phoned David DeClarke once, but he didn't answer. She did not leave a message as she wanted to rest and didn't want to be disturbed. She had several things on her mind and needed a clear head. Brick volunteered to watch the three prisoners during the next shift at the jail. They couldn't leave them unguarded, and Cagey had been on alert the previous night.

Before she left, Maggie suggested that Brick spend time on the phone trying to ferret out information to aid in the Walker investigation. Splendid idea given his recent discoveries. Uninterrupted time on the phone can be valuable.

Brick retrieved the Charlie Walker files from Cagey's desk and leafed through them hoping to find something to reveal what the judge had been thinking. The files held the complete transcript of the trial, along with notes from the sheriff's office. Walker's attorney filed an appeal a few days after the trial, but it had been denied. No reason given.

The Innocence Project had been organized a few years after Charlie had been sentenced, and the Rose and Reubens law firm requested that they review his case. The sketchy Innocence Project notes offered no reason why they had abandoned the investigation, giving Brick something else to request, and he made the phone call to UNLV's criminal justice department.

He punched his way through the menu, finally reaching the Innocence Project, but was placed on hold with too loud elevator music. Eventually someone came on the line and told him where to find an online form requesting information. She said they most likely abandoned Walker's case because of little or no DNA evidence. She admitted she was new to the agency and didn't have any knowledge of why a case would be abandoned except for the lack of DNA. "Thank you very much," is what Brick said, but he wanted to say, "Thanks for nothing."

Brick checked the court files to see if any DNA evidence had been taken at the time of Charlie Walker's arrest but didn't see anything. Although the crime had occurred a long time ago, it was peculiar that the investigators had not taken DNA evidence. It could not be taken now, so long after a crime.

He called Attorney Ling in Reno, but she was with a client and would call him back. Her assistant informed him she had a full schedule, so it might be the following day.

Brick dialed David DeClarke's number, but it went to voicemail, and he left a message. He next phoned Jay Guzman to ask him additional questions, and he was also hoping he would remember who sold him the graffiti paintings. The vendor, Brick hoped, might help connect the dots about the missing graffiti. Jay knew the phone number and company name and gave it to Brick, but the phone had been disconnected, and the company had gone out of business.

A friend in the LAPD, assigned to the theft division, received his next phone call. Brick thought he might have information on graffiti thefts. They chatted and laughed about old times, but on the graffiti issue, his division had not investigated any thefts in several years, so that idea fizzled out, too. On a whim he asked his friend if he remembered Nathan Griss. He did not.

It was a morning of nothings.

Chapter 54

Jonathan and Brick
Present Day

Nat stared at Mr. DeClarke. Could it be that he honestly wanted to include Nat in his will? Nat knew he had wealth, but exactly what did he intend to do? As he gaped at him, he felt heartened, even optimistic. Perhaps his luck would change soon. The sooner, the better.

When he looked at DeClarke, he now saw a different man, a wealthy man who wanted to make him wealthy, too, with no strings attached because he'd be dead. He had no concept of the extent of DeClarke's estate, but it could be enormous. DeClarke had resided in Barrier for a long time where the cost of living was low, with few places to spend money. His reputation of a miserly workaholic with no family had created local gossip as to the size of his estate and how he spent his money. He had built and managed his small chain of grocery stores, which he had sold after a successful career. Nat didn't know how many stores he owned, but he thought it close to a dozen. Nearly every small town in northern Nevada housed a David's Foods.

Nat had avoided Viper after the incident with the Mexican girl because he didn't want to go to jail, but now his mind flashed to Viper. The times they spent together were the highlights of his life, and they shared a lot of the same interests, unusual as they were. Viper had his faults, but he was also wildly entertaining and with his charisma, their linking up could be great sport. The two of them together knew how to party and he was ready for some action. In order for this to happen though, he needed money to get Viper released from jail. This windfall would be the key. They'd have to dispose of the police charges, but cops could be bought, especially in small towns like Barrier, and they would be home free and clear. Had it been a coincidence Viper suggested he see DeClarke, or did Viper know something he hadn't told Nat?

Nat forced himself to calm down because he didn't want his *father* to think he was greedy and change his mind. He had made a lot of mistakes in his life, but his *father* didn't need to know what they were; he didn't want to screw up this opportunity. DeClarke's demise could be swift. Cancer killed quickly and could be painful from what he understood, but DeClarke deserved it because he should have come forward earlier to reveal their relationship. Perfect timing. Perfect opportunity.

Nat needed to demonstrate some compassion, so he said, "That's terrible, Mr. DeClarke. Brain cancer? I'm so sorry. Isn't there anything that can be done?"

"I got back from Portugal three months ago, and I felt ill, so I went to see my doctor who performed a bunch of tests and diagnosed the cancer, which affects my sight. He said it would progress rapidly and said I had four months to live at the most, but our conversation occurred over two months ago. I have most of my affairs in order, but now that you've come back in my life, I'd like to adjust my will. That's why I'm delighted you called me," DeClarke answered. "I'll ask Dortha to meet with me tomorrow or the next day, and I'd like you to go with me. I keep in regular contact with her, she's a whiz who constructed my will solidly, but she is also a friend. You'll like her; her name is Dortha Ling. She is a wonderful woman, and we've become close. She came over with the Vietnamese boat people, but she's worked hard and made a successful life for herself."

Nat half listened, but his heart pounded like a drum. He tightened his fists and dropped them to his lap to mask his excitement. In a month, he'd be a rich man. He said, "Of course, I'll do what I can, whatever you need. I am still in shock that you are my father, and it is going to take a while to process, but I have always respected you, and I'll do whatever I can to help."

Nat wanted to keep him talking and excused himself to buy more coffee. DeClarke's phone rang again. *Restricted.* "These damn robocalls. I won't miss them when I'm six feet under," he muttered to himself.

"Hello," he answered. "What do you want?"

"David DeClarke? This is Deputy Sheriff Brick O'Brien. I am from the Barrier Sheriff's Office. I don't think we've met."

"O'Brien, from Barrier? You're the high school principal, right?" DeClarke was surprised. What could he want?

"Yes, I am, but I'm also a reserve deputy. I'm calling because Sheriff Monroe has a few questions regarding one of your former employees," Brick responded.

DeClarke chuckled, "I thought you were a spam caller. My phone said *Restricted,* so I assumed you wanted to wheedle something out of me. What can I do for you?"

"We need to locate a person and thought you might know where he is," Brick answered, "Harry Bird, the custodian at the high school, gave me your phone number. You must remember him."

"Sure, I know Harry. What an interesting character he is. I gave him my phone number before I moved to Las Vegas. I figured anyone who needed to phone me would think of Harry. We became good friends, and he's the go-to person in Barrier because he knows everybody. Who are trying to locate?" DeClarke asked.

Brick said, "We're looking for Jonathan Grayson, also known as Nathan Griss. You hired him to work in your store many years ago, as I understand it. He uses both names now but was Grayson when he lived in Barrier."

"I don't know anyone named Griss, but I hired Jonathan Grayson many years ago. You are in luck, because I am with him right now. We're enjoying coffee at a Starbucks, down the street from Caesar's Palace." DeClarke scanned the coffee counter, searching for Jonathan and saw him nearing their table, balancing two more coffees and sweet rolls. Nathan placed the load on the table and sat down. Mr. DeClarke spoke, "Jonathan, someone would like to speak with you," and handed him his cell phone.

Nat accepted the cell phone having no idea who listened on the other end of the conversation and hesitated to answer it. "Jonathan speaking," he said doubtfully.

"Jonathan, how are you? This is Deputy Sheriff Brick O'Brien from Barrier. Sheriff Monroe asked me to call. We met at the Chicken Dinner Ranch a few days ago, and we didn't quite get our business finished. It's pleasure to speak with you again. You told me your name was Nat Griss, but that's not quite right, is it?"

Chapter 55

Dortha Ling
Present Day

Dortha Ling had not answered Brick's call, so Maggie placed another call to her. She probably knew the Charlie Walker case better than anyone else, save Charlie. "Yes, she is in the office," the secretary said. "What is this in regard to?"

Maggie gave a terse two-word reply, "Charlie Walker," adding a third word, "trial."

The phone went silent and Maggie waited. Ms. Ling worked in Las Vegas and was obviously busy, but after a couple minutes, she came on the line. "Hello?" her voice was diluted, not full body, meek and soft. Maggie had to strain to hear her, but when she told Dortha who she was, Dortha's voice resonated strength, maybe power.

Maggie said, "Ms. Ling, I am the sheriff in Barrier, and our office is attempting to clarify the sentencing of Charlie Walker. I know you hold the keys to why the judge sentenced Charlie so harshly and for such a long time."

Dortha answered quickly, "Yes, I would like to speak with you but not on the phone. Would it be possible for you to come to Vegas, so we could meet one-on-one?"

"I would love to meet you one-on-one, but a trip to Vegas is impossible at this time. I have a small staff and my jail is full. Could you make the drive and come to Barrier?" Maggie asked.

"Yes, I can. I will cancel my appointments and drive over tomorrow. I haven't been to Barrier since Charlie's trial, and it's time that I faced those demons. By the way, has Charlie arrived in Barrier yet? I received notice from the warden that he would return to Barrier."

"Yes, he's here. Charlie has a steady job and so far, has stayed out of trouble. I'll see you tomorrow. If you can arrive by one o'clock, I'll buy your lunch."

"It's a deal. I hope to be there before noon," she laughed. "I can't wait to meet you."

Chapter 56

Mr. DeClarke
Present Day

Nat listened on the phone. *Oh, shit*, he thought but didn't dare say it aloud because DeClarke's eyes homed in on him. Nat said, "No, I don't know anything about that. You'll have to ask someone else," and clicked off the cell phone.

Mr. DeClarke said, "The deputy sure timed that right! What did he want? I've never met Sheriff Monroe or any of her deputies, but I've heard respectable opinions regarding her office and how she conducts business. She solved a murder case in Barrier during her first term as a sheriff, and she did it on her own from what I understand. Anyway, what did the deputy want?"

"Nothing really," Nat lied. "He asked me what I knew about art at the Chicken Dinner Ranch, but I don't know anything. I've never even been to the Chicken Dinner Ranch. I have no idea why he asked me."

"Was he referring to your artist friend's paintings? What kind of art does he do? I'm especially fond of seascapes. If he paints seascapes, I wouldn't mind buying one," DeClarke added.

"No, Mr. DeClarke, he doesn't do seascapes. He's more into modern art, action pictures, like the superheroes at the movies, or caricatures of movie stars, that type of thing."

"That's too bad. That style does not interest me. Anyway, I'm your father, Jonathan, and I'd like you to call me Dave, not Mr. DeClarke, or you can call me *Dad* if you like, which no one has ever used. It undoubtedly will be difficult as you have never called me anything except Mr. DeClarke, but I think it's time, don't you?"

Nat was thankful for the subject changing from his conversation with the sheriff's office and Viper and whatever else might lead to his missing out on a big inheritance. "Dave, it is. I'm concerned for your health, Dave. Have the doctors considered doing chemo or radiation or other treatments? Cancer treatment has improved in the past few years, and doctors and researchers come up with new ways to treat cancer and other illnesses all the time."

"No, the doctors and I have explored all possibilities. Radiation is the main treatment, and the doctors say I'm too weak to survive it. I'm seventy-five years old and have decided to let nature take its course. I've lived a long life and had lots of successes. I had many businesses and friends and have traveled the world in the past years, but I regret not having a family. Your mother rejected me, and after she left, you weren't around. The importance of family relationships can never be overstated. But now here you are," Dave said, beaming at Jonathan, once again reaching for his arm. "We need to make the most of the time I have left, which isn't long, I'm afraid."

The two men sat in silence for a few minutes, each sorting out the conversation and transpiring events. Dave focused on how fortunate he had been to have found Jonathan and finally have a family, while Nat focused on how much money he would inherit and how fast he could get it.

"Please excuse me, Jonathan, I need to use the restroom. The docs prescribed a bunch of pills that either constipate me or make me pee. Today, with all the coffee, it's the latter. I'll be back in a few minutes," Dave uttered as he left to use the bathroom.

Nat welcomed the reprieve. He didn't enjoy talking to Dave, but he wasn't going to let go now. His thoughts hovered around how he planned to talk with the attorney regarding the estate and will. In a few weeks Dave would be dead and buried, and he would be a rich man.

Twenty minutes passed, but Dave didn't appear. Where was the guy? How long did it take him to piss? He looked around at the other tables, many now empty. Maybe he had Alzheimer's and lost his way back from the bathroom. Where had he gone?

A shout from the direction of the bathroom interrupted his thoughts. "Hey, I need help! Would somebody call 911? There's a dead guy in the john."

Chapter 57

Jonathan
Present Day

Nat jumped up and sidled between the tables toward the bathrooms. It couldn't be Dave, his father. Fuck! This was not fair. He shoved people aside and entered the bathroom. Sure enough, Dave lay face down on the floor next to the urinal where drops of blood bespattered the white receptacle. Nat touched Dave's wrist, hoping to find a pulse, but Dave didn't respond and there was no pulse. Someone had called 911, and emergency vehicles arrived with flashing lights and sirens. People backstepped out of the way onto the street. Nat wanted to linger where he was, but the police and ambulance personnel hustled him outside the building with the other patrons.

The police spoke to the growing crowd that idled on the front patio of the coffee shop, asking, "Does anyone know who this man is? Who was with him?"

Nat shifted toward the policeman and uttered, "Yes, I was with him. Uh, he is my, uh, *father*."

The policeman, who had three stripes on his sleeve and a black plastic name badge reading *Loving,* faced Nat and said, "I'm sorry for your loss, Sir, he's gone. We obviously don't know for sure, but it might have been a heart attack or a stroke. Did he have heart trouble?"

"I don't know. He had cancer, but I don't know about heart trouble," Nat said. "I'm not sure of his other health issues."

"Could I have your ID, please?" Sergeant Loving asked gently. "I'll need it for my records. Also, your phone number and address. Do you live in Las Vegas?"

Nat carried two IDs in his wallet and considered which one to give to the policeman: Grayson or Griss? "No, I arrived in Las Vegas today. We hadn't seen each other for several years, and we met for coffee so we could catch up. I can't believe he's gone."

"Here's his ID, Sergeant," a young female officer interrupted, handing Loving the wallet. "His name was David DeClarke, and he resides in Vegas. He has a couple credit cards and a little over $100 in cash in his billfold."

Loving accepted it and repeated to Nat, "I need to see your ID, Sir. I'll photograph it and give it right back."

Nat inhaled deeply. *Oh, shit.* The police in Henderson wanted him under the name of Griss, but he hadn't used the Grayson ID in a while, and that driver's license had expired. Nat had introduced himself to Jay as Griss, and he felt sure the Barrier deputy had called the Vegas police by now to tell them of his location. He frowned and fished out the expired Grayson ID and handed it to the policeman. He would need to take the chance.

"Just to confirm, your dad's name was David DeClarke, and you're Jonathan Grayson and you live in Barrier?" Sergeant Loving said. "That's a long way from here, but it's a pleasant little town. It has that medieval castle B&B. Anyway, you need to get your license renewed, Sir, if you plan on driving. It's been expired several years." He photographed Nat's ID and handed it back to him.

"Yes, Sir, I don't drive much," Nat responded, "but I've been meaning to do that." His mind flashed forward to the prospect of paying a visit to Dave's house. He didn't know where he lived but thought the officer might tell him if he phrased it right. "My dad moved since I last saw him, and I don't know where he lives, that is, lived, but I'd like to drop by. Could you give me his address? He has a dog named Alpo I will need to take care of."

The officer looked at DeClarke's ID and said, "You've never been to his house? He lives in the foothills on Beechnut Way in Beechnut Heights. It's an upscale neighborhood." He wrote out the address and handed it to Nat.

Chapter 58

Jonathan
Present Day

In the few minutes since his father had died, Nat Griss renamed himself Jonathan Grayson. He needed to be called Grayson to inherit DeClarke's money. No doubt about it. He could also change his name to DeClarke, but that would take time.

He drove his "borrowed" Jag to Beechnut Heights, a gated community with a guard house, but no guard stood duty today. He didn't know the gate code, so he parked on the street a block away from the subdivision and ducked under the gate. The upscale neighborhood had large lots with well-manicured grounds and flower gardens. The streets meandered around, and he checked street names and house numbers for ten minutes before finding Beechnut Way and DeClarke's house. The cul-de-sac contained five homes, all towering high with DeClarke's house dwarfing the others. A winding drive and four car garage faced toward the side of the house. The three-story beige dwelling constructed of stucco had a red tiled roof. Jonathan crawled over the gate into a fenced back yard with a large kidney-shaped pool and jacuzzi, which both rippled pristine waters. The fresh-cut grass emitted the aroma of freshness, and flowers bloomed along the fence. Jonathan had never known anyone who lived in a mansion such as this. Another small building sat in the back of the large lot, perhaps a guest house. No mansions existed in Barrier except for the castle, and compared to DeClarke's home, it was a pile of rocks.

And now all this would be his. A security company sign perched on the front lawn, but Jonathan wondered whether DeClarke armed the system. In his experience as sometimes-thief, he discovered lazy people often ignored the systems they had paid a fortune for. Was David DeClarke, *his father*, one of those people? He knew DeClarke was meticulous, but also old and sick (and now dead). He needed a key to the house, which was most likely stashed in his dead father's trouser pocket. And the security code. His mind was racing around his impeding wealth, which lead to wondering what kind of car his father owned—that he would inherit.

Jonathan jogged out of the subdivision, not wanting to attract attention, and hightailed it back to the Starbucks, hoping they had not moved DeClarke's body in the brief time he had been gone.

When he arrived at the coffee shop, he saw a gray, plastic body bag resting in the back of the EMS services vehicle. Jonathan glanced around, searching for Sergeant Loving, but he had left. Several policemen lingered in the area, interviewing the remaining clientele, but he didn't recognize any of them. Nobody appeared to be in charge, so he selected the nearest blue shirt and asked, "Is someone in charge? That man in the ambulance is my father, and I need his keys to get into his house. He owns a dog, and I'll need to take care of him, but I don't have keys, and I don't want to break into his house."

The policeman said, "Sergeant Loving returned to the police station, and he can answer your key question. He removed all the victim's personal effects including the keys. He works out of the Denison Street Police Station, so you should check there. Do you know where it is located?"

"Yeah, I know where it is," Jonathan growled at the officer. Oh, crap. He did not want to go to the police station, but he needed to get the keys and could think of no other way. He had given Loving the Grayson ID, so maybe they had not yet tuned into his current name. He maneuvered the Jaguar out of the parking space and stepped on the gas, going south to Denison Street, silently swearing at his situation.

Chapter 59

Vegas Police
Present Day

Maggie had written Grayson's various names in her notebook and observed, "He must get a kick out of making clever plays on words. Jonathan Grayson. Gray in Spanish is Gris. Jonathan became Nathan then Nat. Walker called him TwoJohnny then Dos. All one and the same. Nat Griss, aka Jonathan Grayson, whacked me on the head and holds the key to Charlie Walker's tale of being innocent. We need to bring Jonathan Grayson to Barrier." She phoned the Las Vegas police to advise them that Jonathan Grayson, aka Nathan or Nat Griss, was drinking coffee at the local Starbucks.

Brick said, "Grayson holds the key to a bunch of things, including Viper and his misdeeds, which link to those two lovely young ladies cooling their jets in your cells. All five of these folks connect with each other, and we need to unravel their identities and connections to each other. One of us needs to go to Las Vegas to pick Grayson up. Perhaps Cagey should go and leave one of us to overlook the office and one to care for the twins. We don't want to wear your mom out."

"Mom won't mind, and since things have been hopping today with Viper and the ladies, I'd rather the three of us remain here. I'll request that Vegas transport Grayson back here. He's wanted in Henderson for robbery under the name of Griss. They're gonna want a piece of him, too," Maggie said.

"That's true, but attempted murder of a law enforcement officer, particularly when she's my favorite officer, trumps the other charges, at least in my mind," Brick reminded her.

The phone rang, and Maggie answered, "Barrier Sheriff's Office. How can I help you?"

"I'm Corporal Castillo with Las Vegas police. I'm looking for Sheriff Monroe who called us about somebody named Grayson or Griss, whatever name he's going by," the voice on the other end of the line said.

"Yes, I called you. I'm Sheriff Maggie Monroe, and we want him in conjunction with his attempt to murder a law enforcement officer: me," she said into the phone.

Castillo: "He tried to kill you, the sheriff? Unbelievable. I hope you are okay."

Sheriff: "Grayson struck me on the head hard enough to knock me out. It hurt like hell and left me with a huge lump and a powerful headache, but I'm okay now, well enough that the ER doc sent me home. Thanks for asking."

Castillo: "That's good. I'm happy that you're okay, Sheriff. We went to the Starbucks near Caesar's that you mentioned, but he wasn't there. Did you have the right Starbucks?"

Sheriff: "I think so, he met a man who was originally from Barrier, David DeClarke. Do you have more than one Starbucks near Caesar's? He didn't mention the address."

Castillo: "Yes, Sheriff, at least a dozen Starbucks lie within a mile of Caesar's. Six within a block."

Sheriff: "I had no idea. Listen, I have DeClarke's phone number, and I'll call him again. Hold on, don't hang up. I'll call him on my cell phone and get the address of their Starbucks."

Brick had already started dialing, but no one answered DeClarke's phone, so he left a message.

Sheriff: "It's a no-go. He's not answering."

Castillo: "What do you want us to do? Do you have Grayson's number?"

Sheriff: "I'm not sure. Let me see what I can find. What is your cell number? I'll call you back right away."

They signed off, and Brick and Maggie looked at each other, both wondering if Grayson had slipped away once more.

The phone chimed again.

Sheriff: "Barrier Sheriff's Office. How can I help you?"

Castillo: "Castillo, again. As I hung up, a message flashed on my computer. A man named David DeClarke died at a Starbucks a few minutes ago. It was a different store than the one we visited. Wasn't DeClarke the person who met with Grayson?"

Sheriff: "Yes, they were having coffee together. This is unbelievable. How did DeClarke die? Was he murdered?"

Castillo: "No, the officer who went to the scene thinks he died of natural causes, a heart attack or stroke maybe."

Sheriff: "Was he with anyone?"

Castillo: "You should call Sergeant Loving, the OIC. Perhaps he can help better than I."

Maggie clicked off and dialed the number Castillo had provided.

Loving: "Sergeant Loving, how can I help you?"

Maggie explained how she had acquired his number and asked about Jonathan Grayson or Nathan Griss.

Loving: "As a matter of fact, Jonathan Grayson was in the Starbucks. He introduced himself as David DeClarke's son and asked for his father's address. He said they hadn't seen each other for a while, and he wanted to take care of DeClarke's dog."

Sheriff: "DeClarke's son? As far as I know, DeClarke had no children. Does Grayson have a key to DeClarke's house?"

Loving: "I don't think so because he said he'd never seen it before and didn't know the address. DeClarke lived in an upscale subdivision inside a gated community. If Grayson went there, I doubt he could get in, unless he broke in."

Sheriff: "From what I know of Grayson, he'd definitely break in given the opportunity. We need to find him. Can you send LVPD officers to check on DeClarke's home? Hopefully Jonathan Grayson, aka Nathan or Nat Griss shows up there."

Loving: "Absolutely. I'll send patrol right away."

Sheriff: "Grayson has had multiple arrest warrants issued, so the sooner you get him under lock and key, the better. I'll fax the warrants to you."

Loving: "Yes, Sheriff. We're on it."

Chapter 60

Charlie
Present Day

I enjoyed my new job. It offered enough excitement to keep me engaged, and it fascinated me with the weird collection of people who passed through the brothel/casino. Out-of-control drunks caused me the most difficulty, but I managed them easily enough. I found I could talk them through most situations and didn't need to muscle them often. Perhaps I had learned something at Fenwick after all.

It was a Saturday afternoon, and business at the Chicken Dinner Ranch buzzed along as usual. Truck drivers came in looking tired, hungry, and dusty, and after visiting the bar, kitchen, salon, and upstairs rooms, they left refreshed, fed, and clean. The routine varied little, but today topped them all.

It was my tenth day of freedom and sixth day of employment, and today's event, one that will not be forgotten any time soon, occurred with a local guy who had resided in Barrier his entire life. He had a few years on me, but I recognized his face and name. His name was Gabe Cochran, whose mother had worked as a hairdresser and whose father had been killed in a mining accident. The Cochrans lived down the street from our family, and my mom and I knew who they were, but we were not close. Gabe and I had not been hard and fast friends, but our paths crossed occasionally and neither of us was a stranger to troublemaking.

Gabe went to work at David's Foods after high school and became a successful butcher, except for the missing three fingers on his right hand. He divorced his wife of twenty years after his kids graduated from high school and involved themselves in bigger and better things, not in Barrier. Gabe's loneliness led him to the CDR, which led him to me.

Gabe had remained at David's Foods until it sold, at which time, he changed jobs and began cutting meat at the local Safeway. Although he had been in and out of trouble with law enforcement as a teenager, he had clung to the straight and narrow as an adult. Gabe sometimes hung out with TwoJohnny when they were both employed at David's Foods. He realized TwoJohnny was capable of some heavy-handed mischief; however, they both skirted the law, and neither came under any real law enforcement scrutiny.

At one point, Gabe discovered Jonathan pilfering change from David's Foods, and in a moment of honesty, told Mr. DeClarke of it, but DeClarke dismissed it, complimenting Jonathan as a fine growing boy. A few days later, Gabe was standing behind them, and he noticed a strong resemblance, being the same height and body build. The twenty-five-year age difference distorted a strong comparison except for one facial trait: a cleft chin. Mr. DeClarke had a strongly defined cleft chin; Jonathan Grayson also had a cleft chin, but less pronounced. They both had deep set brown eyes with heavy brows and quick smiles accentuating their dimpled chins. Both had toothy smiles, revealing their front teeth and gums. When Gabe mentioned to Mr. DeClarke that he saw Jonathan shoplifting and received no response, he suspected a closer relationship than employer-employee. Honest, but miserly, Mr. DeClarke didn't *give* anything away to anybody.

Gabe had watched my trial with interest because we both had run-ins with Sarah Hudson, and no love was lost between the two of us. He felt sorry she had been injured, because nobody deserved that kind of injury, but he was not sorry she had to leave the juvenile probation business. He thought her zealousness replaced her judgment, specifically when it came to him.

As Gabe passed through the door to enter the Chicken Dinner Ranch bar, he brushed me as I watched the entry and checked occasional IDs. He did a double take and turned around to look me in the eyes. I could sense that he recognized me, but a look of confusion came over him when he looked down at the *Nathan* on my shirt.

"Aren't you Charlie Walker?" Gabe asked. "Your name tag says Nathan, but you're Charlie. I'd know you anywhere. When did you get out of prison?"

I had been fearful someone would recognize me, which is why I had not shaved off my beard and wanted to keep the false name tag on my shirt. I recognized Gabe but didn't want to draw attention to myself. I decided to try a half-lie, half-truth approach saying, "Yeah, I'm Charlie, but I don't know who you are," I lied.

"Gabe Cochran. I used to live down the street from you when we were kids. Don't you remember me?" He reached out and clasped my hand and shook it hard.

I noted the missing digits on Gabe's hand and responded, "Looks like you tried to wrestle an alligator. I'm afraid I don't remember you, Mr. Cochran."

Gabe shoved his right hand back in his jeans pocket, and he pressed me a little more, "How long have you been working here? I've been out of town for a few weeks, visiting my mom who's in a rest home in Florida, but I'm glad to be back. You've got to remember me, Charlie, I graduated from high school a couple years before you, but I saw you around. TwoJohnny and I sometimes drank beer together on weekends and you joined us once or twice. Great times, weren't they? TwoJohnny was a piece of work. He came back to Barrier once, and I met up with him for a beer. We discussed your trial, and he said he regretted that you had been blamed for a crime you didn't commit."

"Did he say that? TwoJohnny actually said that?" I asked. "Did he admit that he did it?"

"He stopped at the store to see Mr. DeClarke, but he had already left for the day. I was alone in the butcher shop, so we talked for a while. He didn't *say* that he did it, but he *did* say you didn't. You know TwoJohnny, he was as slippery as snot and never admitted to anything he ever did," Gabe responded.

I nodded in agreement, "I remember him well. He's a worthless piece of shit."

Gabe asked, "What actually happened with Mrs. Hudson? Did TwoJohnny go to her house?"

I repeated my story, "Oh, yeah, he went all right, but I wasn't there. I waited for him at home, so I could get ready for our trip to Vegas. TwoJohnny stole her car and asked her for money, but she refused to give it to him. He threw the iron at her and hurt her, but the jury blamed me for everything because they discovered my fingerprints in her house. Barrier didn't have all the proper police procedures and my damn lawyer didn't know the difference between me and my shadow. The bottom line is I didn't do it. Would you be willing to talk to the sheriff?"

Chapter 61

Jonathan
Present Day

Jonathan jumped into the Jaguar and wove his way to Denison Street, aiming for the nearby police station situated a couple miles from the coffee shop. He had nearly arrived when orange traffic cones appeared, funneling traffic into one lane. He noticed two sets of flashing red and blue lights ahead. Accidents and fender benders slowed the traffic to a crawl.

"Damn traffic," Jonathan grumbled to himself. "Why today? I need to get to the Denison Police Station to get the keys and security code before the cops send them to the evidence lockers." Between the new construction and the influx of people moving into this growing mecca, every Las Vegas street and thoroughfare was jam-packed. A potential accident loomed at every corner.

People ran red lights, hoping to gain a few seconds' edge on the competing cars. They tried alternative routes that crowded into a different traffic jam. Cars cut into lanes and created new lanes where none had previously existed. Bikes sprang out of nowhere to distract drivers, and scooters and skateboards had recently been added to the mix. Although the city council widely publicized rules for bicyclists, it had not determined guidelines for the scooters and skateboards, thus they dominated the sidewalks and now wove in and out of traffic traveling with, against, across, and through traffic. Pedestrians lived in danger if they tried to cross the streets, even at a cross walk, not from vehicles but from scooters, bicyclists, and skateboards. Driving anywhere in Vegas in recent days had become a nightmare.

Traffic accidents and incidents overwhelmed emergency services, and the wait for police or medical assistance could stretch into an hour or more. The city responded by adjusting police and emergency coverage to provide quicker access in the main traffic patterns, but in doing so they left thousands of unsuspecting residents unprotected, and the crime rate had spiked in the past year.

The homeless population had also risen and forced wary pedestrians to maneuver themselves around shopping carts, sleeping bags, and tents. The problem of human feces on sidewalks and streets grew as stores and public buildings restricted who could use their restrooms. Las Vegas had grown, but not necessarily for the better.

The news media tried to keep up with the road construction and alternative routes, intending to inform the public, but the plans and changes came too fast and were too sporadic, so no one trusted the television or radio reports on traffic congestion. Jonathan flipped through the local news stations, hoping to find out about the problem, but station after station announced nothing. He peered at the gas gauge noting that the yellow warning light glowed. He had idled in the same spot without moving for twenty minutes and impatiently awaited the opportunity to progress on his quest.

Jonathan looked around, trying to appraise his location and how long before he would arrive at the Denison Police Station. He lowered the car window and shouted at the car next to him, but that driver's radio blared, and he didn't look over. Summer heat poured into the car, and he raised the window again and turned the air conditioning to a lower setting. Stuck in the middle lane, he complained to himself, *I could walk faster than I'm driving.*

Murder Almost

A Ford F-150 directly ahead of him inched forward one car length, and Jonathan followed course creeping the same car length ahead. Other cars did the same when unexpectedly, he was hurled forward in his seat, airbag exploding sending a burst of pain in his right arm and torso. He passed out.

Chapter 62

Charlie
Present Day

Gabe squinted his eyes and said, "Talk to the police? Do you mean Sheriff Monroe? I'd be happy to talk to her and tell her what TwoJohnny said. I thought he was a slime ball, but I didn't realize his involvement with your case. I attended part of the trial, but no one mentioned him. Why didn't your attorney locate him to testify?"

"That's a first-rate question, one that my incompetent attorney might be able to answer. TwoJohnny had bolted to Mexico by then, as far as I know. Let's go to see the sheriff right now," I said. "I don't want to wait."

"Aren't you working? Maybe we should postpone our visit until you finish your shift. I haven't been in here in a couple months, and I'm ready for a little fun and games now," Gabe cocked his head and rolled his eyes toward the wide staircase leading to the bedrooms. "But first, I'm going to treat myself to some whiskey. We can see the sheriff after you finish work and I finish with my fun and games." Gabe winked at Charlie and turned toward the bar.

I sighed and gazed at the back of Gabe's retreating body. He was right; talking to the sheriff could wait. It had already been a quarter of a century, and a few more hours wouldn't hurt anything. Leaving the CDR before I completed my shift could jeopardize my job, which I didn't want to do. I called after Gabe, "Gabe, could I have your phone number, in case we miss each other? I can call you later," but he had already disappeared into the crowded bar.

As the sky began to darken, the crowd of patrons swelled, and the clamor in the bar grew from a quiet din to a level of constant commotion. It was so loud I could not determine the songs being played. Legally, the bar could hold ninety-seven patrons, but my eyeball count estimated at least 150 people crowded into the space, maybe more. The Barrier B&B had hosted their first ever chariot race with a terrific turnout, and the celebration had migrated in full swing to the CDR. Although I knew Jay would be happy with the crowd, I had never heard such a clamor. The sound thundered and reverberated throughout the room.

I wound my way through the crowd toward the bar, hoping my mere presence would diminish the noise, but it didn't. I scanned the throng and saw a trio of men and one woman, seated in a booth toward the rear of the bar, arguing. I could not hear their conversation or see their faces through the noise and the tightly packed mob, but their body language revealed a high level of anger with fist shaking and shoulder movement. Two men on one side of the table rose with fists clenched and began yelling profanities at Number Three who sat next to the woman. Number One grabbed Three's shirt, jerking him to his feet, and Number Two punched Three twice in the nose causing blood to spurt across the table. He then fell back into the booth. The woman unfolded herself from the booth and climbed over Number Three. She quickly moved her hands, then bolted toward the exit, followed by One and Two. Someone screamed, *Knife!* and I attempted to steer myself toward the table, but the density of the escaping crowd slowed my progress.

Without warning, the roar of the crowd stopped, and they began backing toward the door, some slowly, others quickly, all trying to avoid stepping into or onto others trying to exit the bar. I strained to see what had happened, standing on my tiptoes, turning and twisting to peek over the heads of people taller than me, but I could see nothing. I pressed forward and shoved several people out of the way. When I finally managed to arrive at the table, the woman and One and Two had disappeared, and Three lay on the floor, bleeding profusely, blood soaking his shirt and lower face, with a knife protruding from his neck. The black pool of blood was expanding, but he wasn't moving. I grabbed the victim's wrist to search for a pulse but felt nothing. "I think he's gone," I whispered to no one in particular. I looked down at the wrist I held and saw two digits, a thumb and one finger. Gabe. "Gabe, no," I screamed. "How can this be? No, dammit, wake up, Gabe. I need you." I dropped the limp hand and reached into my pocket for my coin.

Chapter 63

Viper
Present Day

Viper had been arraigned two days earlier, but he had not heard from Nat, and no attorney had emerged to help him. The judge set his bail at $5,000, which Viper didn't have, not even the ten percent a bail bondsman would require, so he sat in his cell, waiting for Nat. The judge had offered the public defender, but Nat refused, insisting he would hire a more competent attorney from Vegas.

After Vincent Pierson left the judicial bench, he practiced law in Reno for a time prior to the bar taking his license. As a former judge, an estate law firm hired him as a paralegal to supervise young lawyers and review the legal documents that they prepared. As a part of his duties during the few weeks he worked at the law practice, he reviewed David DeClarke's last will and testament for Attorney Dortha Ling, but it had been many years since he had seen it, and he wasn't sure whether DeClarke had rewritten it or kept it the same. It had been pure coincidence that he had run into Jonathan Grayson in Mexico a couple years later, and he quickly remembered Grayson's name mentioned in DeClarke's will. He wasn't 100 percent sure, but it had promise. The DeClarke grocery stores had been enormously successful, and the inheritance would be large. If DeClarke had not died, Nat could probably lay claim to it.

His brain was besieged with *maybes*. Maybe Las Vegas had more than one David DeClarke. Maybe his idea of having Nat contact DeClarke wasn't as effective as he thought it was. Maybe Nat had been arrested for knocking the sheriff on the head. Maybe DeClarke had died, and nobody knew where to find his money. Maybe Nat had taken the money from Mr. DeClarke and absconded with it himself. Maybe he should take up the judge's offer and use the public defender. Maybe Nat had ignored his phone call and had left for parts unknown.

On his routine cell check, Cagey offered Viper the Reno daily newspaper, and he thumbed through it half-heartedly. Reading the newspaper might divert his attention from his troubles while he waited for something, anything to help him. He quickly solved the puzzles before scanning the national and local news stories. Nothing interested him, and he skimmed over the editorial page. He read the comics, but none of them seemed comical today. Obituaries could be interesting, even amusing, at least better than the classified ads, so he began to scan them, reading the personal histories of the deceased: Baker, James; Caldwell, Edna; DeClarke, David. What the hell? David DeClarke? He focused his eyes on the rather long obituary and read each word carefully while focusing on a few: from Barrier, was living in Las Vegas, age seventy-five, former owner of David's Foods chain in northern Nevada, no family. Everything fit. Could this be Nat's benefactor? Time to call Nat again.

He called out to Cagey, "Deputy, I need to use the phone again. It's obvious my Vegas attorney is tied up, but I want to talk to him." He hoped Cagey had not read the obit in the Reno paper, but he might have. "Deputy, did you hear me?" He called out again, louder than before.

Cagey yawned and meandered back to the cell housing Viper, "Yeah, what do you want? You should have agreed to use the public defender because he's free and accessible. You might have been released by now."

"I might do that, but I want to talk to my attorney first. Let me use the phone again. Please," Viper said. "Something might have happened to him."

"It is up to the sheriff," Cagey answered and sat down at his desk.

Sheriff Monroe agreed to allow the phone call saying, "What harm can it do? Maybe a second call will light a torch under his attorney, and we can get him out of here. By the way, did you see that David DeClarke passed away? He owned David's Foods chain, but he sold it a few years ago and moved to Vegas. I liked him, and he sure did great things for this town. I remember going to the store's bakery as a little girl, and he always gave me a chocolate chip cookie. I thought I was so special."

"David's Foods had closed by the time I arrived in Barrier, so I never met him," Cagey answered. "Okay, I'll let Viper use the phone."

Cagey cuffed Viper and escorted him to the office area and sat him down in the visitor's chair. "Here's the phone, Viper. Have at it."

Viper removed the receiver from its cradle and dialed from memory, "Hello. This is Vincent Pierson calling, May I speak with David DeClarke?"

Cagey snapped his head around at the mention of DeClarke's name and stared at Viper, "What the hell?" He grabbed the phone from Viper's hand and listened.

On the other end of the phone came a weak voice, "Viper? This is Nat. I'm in the hospital in Vegas. I was in a car accident."

Chapter 64

Charlie
Present Day

Maggie, Brick, and Cagey arrived at the CDR within minutes of Jay's call. I had remained in the bar with Gabe, not really knowing what to do. Cars were crammed in the parking lot, and people gathered in small groups, creating chaos for all involved.

"Cagey, block the parking lot and don't let anyone leave. We might have already lost a few, but let's not lose any more," Maggie ordered over the radio, as they turned into the CDR. "Do the name and address thing and find out who saw what."

"On it, Boss," said Cagey as he blocked the entrance to the lot and scrambled out of his car.

Maggie and Brick proceeded into the CDR, and Jay signaled them toward the bar. A team of three EMTs followed. I stood next to the body, feeling tense and blotchy with stress. My eyes leaked tears, and blood clung to my knees and hands.

Maggie began photographing the body and the bar scene and told Brick to corral the potential witnesses and take statements from them. She examined the body and extracted the knife from his neck and placed it in a plastic bag.

After she finished her part of the processing, Maggie patted me on the back, "Is this your first dead body, Charlie? I'm sorry you had to witness this.

It's hard to see a person who has died." She motioned to the EMTs to begin their job.

I shook my head, uttering, "It's not my first, but it's disturbing." I was mildly upset because of the dead body, but extremely distraught because Gabe might have been the one person who could clear my name. I didn't want to tell the sheriff anything, at least not yet.

Maggie said, "I know this guy, Gabe Cochran, butcher at Safeway. Did you know him? Did you see who stabbed him?"

"Yes, it's Gabe. He and I went to school together, but he was a couple years older than I, and I hadn't seen him since I went to prison. He recognized me when he came in today and reintroduced himself. He wasn't a bad guy," I vouched.

Maggie continued, "Did you see this happen, Charlie? Do you know who stabbed him?"

I thought for a moment, deciding what to tell her, "I did, and I didn't. I saw a woman with bleached blonde hair fluffed all over her head, like the girls wore in the eighties, copying Farrah Fawcett. She's the one. So many people crowded into the bar that I couldn't see everyone. The noise level was unbelievable, and I wanted to quiet the crowd down, maybe shift them outside the building. I tried to squeeze through the crowd, and the next thing I know, someone shouted *knife*, and everybody scuttled toward the exit, jostling me, nearly knocking me over. When I managed to make my way to the booth, Gabe was already dead, and the woman and the other two men had left. I tried to find a pulse but couldn't get one. Jay must have called you."

"Two other men? Did you recognize them?" Maggie asked.

I said, "I didn't see their faces because they had turned away to leave the bar, but maybe another can describe them. I focused on the woman, since I saw her stab him. They must have gone out the side door, the one marked *emergency only* because they didn't go out the front exit. The woman wore a black shirt with a leopard-skin scarf around her neck, but I don't know if she wore pants or a skirt. Both men wore black pants, maybe denim, with similar colored tan polo shirts, like a uniform, but I didn't see their faces."

Cagey herded several parking lot witnesses into the bar, seated them at tables, and kept an eye on them while Brick joined Maggie, the EMTs, and me. Brick had pulled several IDs and handed them to Cagey to complete the paperwork.

Brick said, "I learned who the woman was. Gabe Cochran's ex-wife came in tonight with her two brothers who live here. Apparently, they had a messy divorce, and she had a restraining order placed on him, but she lives in Reno and hasn't returned since. She showed up this afternoon to visit her brothers, and they spent the day here, drinking. Gabe appeared and sat down at their table, and she reminded him the order remains in place. He didn't know of her being at the CDR. The witnesses agreed with Charlie, that the four of them argued, and she ended up stabbing him."

"So, her brothers live here?" Maggie asked. "Who are they?"

"According to the witnesses, the Bard brothers, Will and Luke. They own WLB, a trucking operation based in Eureka, but they live here. The sister's name is Patsy Bard, and she lives in Reno. The witnesses don't think she uses Cochran anymore, although she and Gabe had been married for a long time. The divorce was nasty."

I said, "I remember the Bard brothers. I didn't recognize them because they had their backs to me when they left the building. They came in to drink most nights since I started working. I know Patsy, too, or used to. I dated her in high school, but she moved to Salt Lake City before she graduated." He rolled up his sleeve displaying a tat on his bicep. "I inked this in prison for Patsy Bard as the first and only girl I ever dated."

Brick added, "She worked at David's Foods, that's where she met Gabe. They raised their kids here, but when DeClarke closed the store, she and Gabe divorced, and she went to Reno."

Maggie said, "We're done, so let's go talk to the Bard family. I'll tell Jay we are leaving. Three cars, no lights, no sirens."

Chapter 65

Jonathan
Present Day

Two days passed, and he ached all over. The accident was a blur, and he recalled little of what had occurred until the police visited him in the hospital and filled in a few more blanks. He didn't remember anything between the crash and the emergency room. Apparently, stalled traffic prohibited any forward movement and while he waited for traffic to thin out, the inattentive driver of the car behind him stepped on the gas full force and rammed him. The stagnant traffic delayed the EMTs from reaching him, and he was pinned in the Jaguar, unconscious, for over an hour. People in the other cars thought he had died, but he had only blacked out from the impact of the airbags.

He'd broken his right arm, now cast in plaster, and three ribs. The ER nurse had wrapped his chest, and everything throbbed, but at least he could stand and walk, albeit slowly. The impact had broken his nose, now covered with a large bandage, and he had a powerful headache. Bruised from head to toe, he could walk, which he needed to do now. As soon as he said *this is Nat* into his cell phone, Jonathan knew he had made a mistake. The screen had read *Restricted*, but his brain wasn't functioning properly. He clicked off his phone without saying another word and jerked the IV from left arm. *Damn Viper*, he thought. *I need to get out of here.*

Jonathan gingerly stepped to the floor and tested his legs and balance. He could stand, although his body ached and moaned, and his weakness made him teeter. He scanned the room for his clothes but didn't see them and had no idea where they had been taken. He wanted to find his wallet and car keys but had no idea where his car was or what condition it was in. He couldn't leave the hospital in the attractive backless gown they provided, and now there were dots of blood that had seeped through the nose bandage. He peeked out the door to find that a linen room sat across the vacant hall. He entered the room and helped himself to a set of blue scrubs, perfect for blending in with the hospital staff. He studied his reflection in the mirror to peel off the nose pack and noticed his bruised face, now dark gray and black with hints of purple. He rinsed the dried blood from his face and hoped the bleeding had stopped.

He tried his best to recall what his *father* said in their last conversation, but he couldn't extract what he said from the dark corners of his battered brain. DeClarke had mentioned his attorney's name, he knew that, but he had been half-listening, and with the airbag smacking his head, he couldn't remember. A woman, he knew that, but, hell, women probably made up half the attorney population in Vegas so that didn't help. He had to get into DeClarke's house to locate her name, so she could fix the will. Things would move quickly as soon as the attorney found out DeClarke had died.

Jonathan dressed and sneaked across the hall to his room to search for his keys and wallet but came up empty. He needed to avoid hospital staff and saw no one on the stairs and descended as quickly as possible. The four flights had nobody in the stairwell. People, mostly patients or family members, passed in and out of the building through the hectic lobby. The lady at the reception desk had the phone at her ear and didn't look up. *Easy escape*, he thought as he passed through the revolving door to the Las Vegas sunshine and the stifling heat of the afternoon sun.

The hot temperature sucked the air from his body, and he felt lightheaded, afraid he might pass out. He staggered to a bench on the other side of the walkway, nearly falling in the process. Two Las Vegas policemen noticed Jonathan struggling to stay upright, and they each grabbed an arm to steady him and prevent him from falling. Together they escorted him to the bench, and he cried out in pain when they touched his torso.

"Are you all right, Sir?" the policemen, whose badge read *Jackson,* asked. "You look like you've been hit by a Mac truck. Easy now."

Jonathan didn't look at him and mumbled with incomplete sentences, "Yeah, fine. Air too hot. No worries." His broken nose made his nasal voice sound like a squeaky toy. He squinted in the bright sunshine but did not want to gain the attention of the police. "I'm okay."

The other policeman, whose badge read *Castillo*, said, "What's your name, Sir? I'll get a wheelchair for you, and we will take you back into the air conditioning. It's a scorcher today, and you seem a little weak."

"No, not necessary. Told you I'm fine. Don't need help," Jonathan assured them as he attempted to rise. He teetered before collapsing onto the bench. His nose released a few drops of blood, and Jackson and Castillo grabbed him. The three of them headed to the hospital door.

"What's your name, Sir?" Jackson asked again.

Jonathan's brain seemed water soaked, and he didn't want to reply. The Griss name would get him in trouble but so would Grayson. Which identification would be better?

He didn't say anything for a minute. "Jonathan Grayson," he managed to reply in a half-constricted voice. If he wanted to claim his relationship as DeClarke's long lost son, he would have to stick with Grayson. His fuzzy brain scrambled his thoughts, except for his rights involving DeClarke's estate.

"You're Jonathan Grayson? We wanted to see you. Let us help you into the building," Castillo said as he neared Jonathan, pushing an empty wheelchair.

Chapter 66

The Bards
Present Day

The Bard house lay on the outskirts of Barrier, barely within the city limits. The gravel road leading to the house met a long driveway with a large mailbox at its mouth. Mesquite trees, junipers, and yucca plants crowded the narrow driveway and sway gently in the tranquil air. The temperature hovered above ninety degrees, but the slight breeze eased the heat. A few stars twinkled in the black sky, and the moon shone through a grouping of clouds, alternating dark shadows with moments of light.

The two-story World War II vintage house needed paint and a new roof. In the dark, the trio could not see the color of the house, light colored for sure, and had to pick their way through the craggy sidewalk. They could make out a combination garage and barn sitting behind the house with gas pumps near the structure.

The trio parked their vehicles behind the trees and shrubs and walked the last fifty yards to the house, crouching down close to the bushes. The inside of the Bard house sat dark with no visible vehicles outside. "It looks like a bust," Maggie whispered to the deputies. "I don't think anyone is here."

Brick whispered back, "Don't be too sure. We need to check. The car could be in the garage."

They crept noiselessly toward the house, staying hidden as best they could. Cagey headed toward the back door of the house as Maggie and Brick maneuvered through the scrappy, front shrubbery hoping the dry grass would not crackle beneath their shoes. Brick squatted below the window and Maggie positioned herself next to the door. No one said anything. They both removed their Glocks from their holsters and readied them to fire if the need arose. Maggie reached over to test the knob when two shots rang out, and the door burst open. The sheriff and her team saw nothing, except for the flash of the bullet leaving its chamber. Three more shots echoed through the open door, and Maggie instinctively pitched herself to the wall, while Brick rose and crept closer to the door and the gun fire. Brick sneaked a quick look into the dark cottage but backed off when he sensed a bullet whizz by his head.

Cagey, at the rear of the house, tested the door and slowly twisted the knob open. He unholstered his Glock 22 and eased into the dark room but could see little. He squinted to distinguish the scene more clearly because of the dim, indistinct shapes, but he thought the furniture had been shoved to the center of the room. He could see slight motions of three people kneeling behind the obstacles, but they faced toward the front door and did not notice him. Cagey scratched at the wall to find a light switch, flipped it on, and shouted, "Drop your guns." Simultaneously, Luke Bard turned and fired at Cagey, but the unexpected flash of overhead lights confused his eyes, and he missed.

All three now faced Cagey and the back of the house. Maggie stepped two long paces through the front door and repeated Cagey's demand, "Drop your weapons." Three guns clattered to the floor. Clearly, they had not planned to see three officers; they had hoped for none but expected only one.

"Patsy Bard, I'm placing you under arrest for the murder of Gabe Cochran and for resisting arrest," Cagey said while handcuffing her. He patted her down and discovered a knife with a seven-inch blade in her cargo pants, a like companion to the one Maggie had extracted from Gabe Cochran's neck.

Patsy snarled, "He fucking deserved it. I have a restraining order against him, but he fucking ignored it. He came into the CDR bar like he owned the fucking place and sat down at our table like an old friend. He didn't even ask. I told the fucker to leave, we all told him, but he refused. He said I couldn't boss him around anymore because he had divorced me. He called me some fucking names and said a bunch of other fucking stuff a lady can't repeat."

One of her brothers said, "Patsy, shut up. Don't say anything else. Just shut the hell up."

Cagey raised his eyebrows and said, "I'm gonna escort this lady out of here and take her to jail where she'll be safe. I'll Mirandize her in the car, and meet you at the office," Cagey said as they went through the front door, Patsy in tow.

Maggie said, "Luke Bard and Will Bard, we are placing you both under arrest for the attempted murder of three police officers and discharging a weapon within the city limits." Brick read them their Miranda rights.

"We didn't try to kill anybody; we wanted to protect our little sister. Gabe was an asshole and shouldn't have come into the bar. Patsy had warned him many times she would kill him if he came near her. He roughed her up a few times, broke her jaw once. That's why the judge issued a restraining order. He could be a real jerk. And dangerous," Will said.

"Will is telling the truth," Luke offered. "He broke her jaw and a couple other e broker bones, but she never complained. This all came out at the divorce proceedings. He constantly hit or belittled her. Mental, physical, and psychological abuse."

Brick said, "That's enough. You can tell your lawyer, the prosecutor, the judge, and anybody else who will pay attention. They'll love listening to all your excuses. In the meantime, you can cool your jets in our jail."

Chapter 67

Charlie
Present Day

Jay bought me a beer, and we sat at the bar and talked for a while, discussing the day, an exciting, yet discouraging day, and an exhausting experience for both. Jay was talkative, as usual, but not me, I felt frustrated and hopeless. My coin lay between my thumb and middle finger, and I rubbed it so hard that it felt hot. I needed time to consider what had happened and what came next. *Dammit all*, I thought, *being out of prison is harder than being in prison.* The beer had stimulated me, and Jay offered me a second, which I accepted but consumed less than half. I needed to keep a clear head.

My one chance at clearing my name had died, and nobody else knew of TwoJohnny's near admission of guilt. I needed to find TwoJohnny, even though he would probably lie. Maybe I would beat the hell out of him after all. He deserved it. I decided to walk back to Gene's as I needed fresh air and time to think, to consider what steps I could take next. The day had swung high and low, and I wasn't ready to make any quick decisions, so I deposited the coin back in my pocket, thanked Jay for the beers, bade him a pleasant evening, and started walking and thinking.

Tonight was a fine night for both. The temperature had subsided in late hours, under eighty degrees, and a gentle breeze chased the stifling heat out of town. I smelled the mesquite trees and heard a lone coyote baying at something or nothing. A collarless yellow lab followed me through the empty streets.

As I proceeded through the town, I considered a myriad of things. Gabe. Gabe covered with blood. The knife. Gabe's wife and my ex-girlfriend, Patsy Bard. I didn't know what had transpired between Gabe and his wife, if anything. Family dynamics puzzled me. We can treat the people we should love the best, the worst. Case in point: my mother, testifying against me. Family emotions could sway from a boiling pot to an ice bucket and back again in the beat of a heart, I thought, remembering my own upbringing.

I had a few more blocks to walk when the beer hit me. *Oh damn, I have to pee. The beer went right through me. I've already passed the Panorama, and everything else is shut down for the night.* I ran my eyes down the coming block and saw the sheriff's office with lights ablaze. Refusing to break any laws, peeing outside was not an option. *Well, I guess I'll be stopping at the sheriff's office to see if I can use their facilities.*

I opened the door tenuously and saw Brick, cup of coffee in hand, leaning up against the file cabinets. I poked my head in, and asked, "Excuse me, Brick, are you open for business?"

Brick cocked his head and said, "Yes, what kind of business?"

I felt my face getting warm and said, "I had a beer with Jay, and it passed right through me. I need to use the can. I can't hold my beer like I could as a kid. I'm walking home, and it's still quite a distance to Gene's house."

Brick smiled, "I get it. Of course, you may use it. The head's through the gray door, next to the interview room, help yourself."

I used the facilities, and as I stepped back into the hall from the bathroom, the door to the interview room opened, and I bumped into Cagey, with Patsy Bard in hand. Clad in orange jail garb and handcuffed, she did a double take and said, "Hey, I know you. You're Charlie Walker. We went to school together and even dated a few times. You went to prison for a long time. Gabe talked about you all the time. He said you received a bum rap, and he knew the guy who did it."

Cagey interrupted her, "Enough chatter, Ms. Bard, back to your cell," as he nudged her past me.

Chapter 68

Jonathan
Present Day

Jackson and Castillo escorted Jonathan Grayson to the hospital reception area. Castillo read him his rights and attached him to the wheelchair, while Jackson walked to the reception desk. He flashed his badge and cut to the front of the line.

"May I help you, Officer?" the receptionist asked as she cast her eyes toward Jackson and Grayson on the other side of the waiting area.

"Yes, can you tell me if the gentleman in the wheelchair by the other policeman has been released from the hospital? We found him wandering outside, and he seems disoriented. His wrist tag reads Jonathan Grayson." He gestured toward Grayson.

She flipped through several computer screens and said, "No, he has not been released; he is a patient here. I can't imagine why he went outside. He's supposed to be in room 465 on the fourth floor."

"Thank you, we'll take him back to his room," Jackson said motioning to Castillo to bring him to the elevator.

"Do you want any assistance?" the receptionist asked. "I can find a volunteer to assist you."

"No, Ma'am, I think we can handle it," Jackson responded with a smile.

Castillo had searched Grayson and found nothing on him. They wheeled him to the bank of elevators and waited until an empty car appeared. Grayson fought the handcuffs for a few seconds, but it aggravated his broken ribs, so he gave up.

The elevator door opened to the nursing station, and a tall, full-bodied woman greeted them, "We wondered where you went, Mr. Grayson, the doctor wants to check your mobility before he dismisses you. You had a powerful blow to your head from the airbag, and you could be a little disoriented or at least lightheaded for a day or two. We have your personal...uh, Mr. Grayson, what's going on here?" Her eyes scrolled over the policemen and the handcuffed patient. "I had no idea you had left. If you needed assistance, Mr. Grayson, you should have pressed the call button by your bedside."

"I'm Corporal Castillo with the LVPD, and this is Corporal Jackson. We found Mr. Grayson wandering around outside. He seemed disoriented, and since he is wearing a hospital ID bracelet, we decided to bring him back inside. But, he is wanted in connection with some crimes that were committed, and we handcuffed him to keep him from disappearing."

Grayson's face reddened. Viper betrayed him, and now he had been placed back in the clutches of the police. "I don't know what you are talking about. I didn't do anything, and I need to get out of here," Grayson answered. Not realizing that two days had passed, Nat continued, "My dad died this afternoon, and I have business to attend to. I have a lot of things on my mind, like my father's dog, his lawyer, his funeral, and his accountant. I hadn't seen him in a long time, and I don't know where they took him, and I don't have time to be in the hospital. I'm okay; I can manage."

"Yes, you do have a lot on your plate right now, but you forgot to mention the Barrier sheriff and what you did to her. No wonder you have so much stress," Castillo said.

Chapter 69

Patsy Bard
Present Day

I watched the pair as Cagey led Patsy down the hall to her cell. She shifted and turned her body to look at me but failed to gain control of the deputy, and profanity once again spewed from her mouth. The deputy didn't leave her any wiggle room, and they disappeared in a few seconds.

I returned to the main office and asked Brick, "How did you locate Patsy so fast?"

Brick smiled and said, "Sheriff Maggie specializes in finding crooks. Ms. Bard and her brothers weren't hard to find because they went back to their own house. They stashed the car in the garage and switched off the lights in the house, trying to make it appear empty. They even took a few shots at us, but the sheriff was on top of things."

I asked, "Is Sheriff Maggie around? I'd like to talk to her."

"She isn't here. She went home for a while. Someone hit her on the head and knocked her out a few days ago, and she's been dealing with a headache ever since. Can I do something for you? We have a small force, and the three of us work together, so I will relay any message if I can't solve it." Brick smiled at me again, "Is it relating to your prison sentence? Why don't you sit down, so we can talk?"

Brick seemed like an okay guy, so I sat down and began to explain, "Maybe, I hope so, but I'm not sure. It's Gabe, not his death, rather what he told me when he came into the CDR tonight. We talked for a few minutes, and he said that he and TwoJohnny, I mean Jonathan Grayson, spoke sometime after my trial, I'm not sure when, but TwoJohnny told him that I wasn't the one who injured Mrs. Hudson. He didn't come right out and say that he hit her with the iron, but Gabe said that he hinted that he had done it. And, now, that is, a few minutes ago, when I bumped into Patsy, she said Gabe told her I received a *bum rap*. She used those words. *Bum rap*. But she killed Gabe, and now she's in jail, and I sure as hell don't know where TwoJohnny is. All of this is so complicated. Is there any chance I can talk to Patsy, Brick?"

"That would be up to the sheriff, but I might know where Grayson is," Brick said. "In fact, I'm pretty sure I know. TwoJohnny, as you call him, uses a bunch of different identities. He switched to Nathan or Nat Griss, and he worked right here in Barrier at the same job you have now. He worked as the last bouncer at the CDR and called himself Nathan Griss. The ID tag on your shirt says Nathan, that's him," Brick said as he pointed at the name tag on my shirt. "We believe he's the one who hit Maggie on the head and departed for parts unknown, but he turned up in Vegas, and we hope the LVPD has arrested him by now."

"Is he coming back to Barrier? Because if he is, I'm gonna kill the son of a bitch," I exclaimed, tugging off my shirt. "After I get him to confess, that is."

Chapter 70

Jonathan
Present Day

Two days later, the officer who had been guarding Jonathan phoned Castillo and informed him that the doctor wanted to release Grayson to their custody. He had arrest warrants in two jurisdictions, Henderson and Barrier, but the chief decided that they should send him to Barrier because of the more serious charge of attacking a law enforcement officer. Henderson could wait.

Corporals Castillo and Jackson showed up at the hospital to accompany Jonathan to the police station. "Where are we going?" Jonathan asked. "This is bullshit. My father died, and I need to tend to his business and take care of his dog. The dog's been in the house for four days without food and water. He's going to die."

"Don't worry, Mr. Grayson, we sent an animal control officer yesterday to check for pets, but he had none. None. The neighbors said that your father didn't own a pet because he often traveled and didn't want to leave a dog in a kennel, so he never owned one. Did your father tell you that he had a pet?"

Jonathan remained silent for a full minute and muttered, "He has always had a pet. He had a dog named Alpo for a long time. I just thought..." His voice trailed off, and he didn't finish his sentence.

Castillo and Jackson looked at each other and smiled. They could easily identify a scam artist, and Jonathan Grayson fit the image. "To answer your question, we are taking you to Barrier, so sit back and relax because it's a five-hour ride," Jackson said.

Jonathan tilted back his head onto the head rest and considered his plight. How could he have come so close to a real fortune, perhaps millions of dollars, and now he was headed to jail in Barrier, the last place on Earth he wanted to go? As he looked out the police vehicle's windows, he saw a lone jack rabbit hopping through the forlorn desert and compared it to his predicament. He felt as desolate as the jack rabbits ravaging for food among the mesquite trees and sagebrush, although they might have had easier lives. Five more hours and he'd be back in fucking Barrier while his fortune waited at some lawyer's office.

Jonathan sat up and leaned forward toward the front seat and said, "You don't understand, we need to go back to Vegas because I have urgent business to attend to. I need to visit my father's house. He had appointments, and I need to cancel them. He had cancer. And, oh, yeah, his attorney. He made an appointment with his attorney this week to discuss his will. I don't know his lawyer's name, but I need to see him. That is, her. I think he's a her." Jonathan rambled on, grasping at anything that came to mind, but he didn't care. He didn't know the contents of the will, but he might be able to convince the attorney that he should receive an inheritance. Perhaps not as much as he would have been awarded with DeClarke's signature, but perhaps something.

"It ain't happening," Jackson said. "Shut up and enjoy the jackrabbits and sagebrush."

Chapter 71

Nat
Present Day

The judge had fined Viper's two concubines, Rhoda and Anne, $200 each and had given them 100 hours of community service, which he suspended, and released them without further penalty, stipulating that they go back to L.A., which they agreed to do. If they showed up in Barrier again, the fine and community service would be reinstated. Their tirade at the CDR had been their first offense, and the judge felt satisfied that he had scared them into compliance.

Viper remained in jail for a week with no hope of release. The judge wanted him transferred to Henderson where the art theft had occurred but moving him to Henderson proved problematic because of Barrier's small departmental staff. Maggie spoke with the judge and suggested sending Viper back with the deputies from Vegas. She cited cost effectiveness as her reason, and the judge agreed.

When Maggie informed Viper of her plan to return him to Henderson, he began to complain. "I told you I didn't do it. I didn't steal anything. I don't know where Henderson is, I've never been to Henderson, and I don't wanna go. You're trying to railroad me," he screamed at Maggie.

Around mid-afternoon, the Las Vegas cruiser parked in front of the sheriff's office. Two deputies and Nat crawled out of the car. His face remained swollen with cuts and bruises from the accident, and he wore a cast on his arm. Jackson and Castillo, one on each side, escorted him into the sheriff's office, where he met the sheriff and both of her deputies.

"Hello, Nat," Maggie inched closer, getting in his face and said, "I'm glad to have you back in town. By the way, I didn't appreciate the lump on the head. You accosted me, and we're charging you with injuring a law enforcement officer: me. That's a felony by the way."

Brick stepped toward Nat and said, "You could have killed her, you son of a bitch. What the hell's wrong with you?" He clenched both fists and drew back his right arm, ready to punch Nat.

Cagey grabbed at Brick's elbow to restrain him from the threat, but he spun away, "You're not worth it, you useless piece of shit," he fumed.

Brick was taller and more muscular than Nat, but Nat was heavier and would have been a formidable opponent, if not for his broken arm and ribs. Corporal Jackson twisted Nat away and said, "Can we lock him in a cell while we complete this paperwork? We'll eat and then grab Pierson before we retrace our steps back to Vegas this afternoon. We can either house Pierson in the Las Vegas jail or transport him to Henderson. They will probably be glad to have him."

Maggie said, "Good idea. Cagey, would you settle Nat into a cell?"

Cagey raised his eyebrows and twisted his mouth, "So, Boss, exactly which cell do you want him in? We're maxed out right now because three of them contain the Bards, and Viper sits in the fourth."

"What about Pierson? Where's he? Isn't he locked up?" Castillo asked.

"Pierson and Viper are one and the same. Pierson's whole name is Vincent Ivan Pierson, but he goes by Viper. He claims to be a graffiti artist in L.A. He landed in Barrier because he also claims somebody stole his graffiti, which now hangs in the local brothel, and he wants it back," Maggie explained. "He likes to be called Viper, so we call him that, too. The name fits, you'll see."

She considered what Cagey said for a moment, thinking of how this could work and came up with a plan, "Okay, Cagey, I don't want the Bard's in the same cell, so handcuff both Viper and Grayson and put them in Viper's cell. Leave the cuffs on so they'll be able to talk but not hurt each other. This will work until the officers finish eating. It's not ideal, and one of us will have to stay outside the cell to keep an eye on them. They are slippery S.O.B.s." Maggie couldn't help but think that maybe they'd say something useful. Brick just thought she had lost her mind.

"Okay, Boss," Cagey replied and picked up the keys and disappeared through the door to the jail. "Let's go, Nat-buddy, you can join your friend," he said, smiling.

Chapter 72

Viper
Present Day

As soon as Nat entered the cell, Viper started yelling and swearing. Cagey locked them up and stood outside the cell. Maggie and Brick and the other officers were there in an instant.

Maggie put her finger to her lips to remind the others to remain quiet and then listened to the whispered conversation of Viper and Nat.

Viper: "Nat, did you get the money? Do you have a plan to get us out of here? How did DeClarke die? Did you have to kill him?" Viper voiced one question after another, not pausing for Nat to answer.

Nat: "Hell no, I didn't kill him;" he croaked. "But, listen to me, I'm his son, his only heir, and he willed all his money to me. I need to see his fuckin' lawyer, whoever that is."

Viper: "DeClarke came to Las Vegas when I practiced law, and I met him. He left his massive fortune, which I'm sure has grown, to his son, if he ever appeared, but he didn't mention his whole name, just *Jonathan*. After we left Mexico, it occurred to me that you were *Jonathan* from Barrier, you were the right age, and you didn't know who your dad was."

Nat: "He told me I was his son, that's what he said. He wanted to take me to see his lawyer the next day, but he died while taking a shit. He told me I would inherit his entire estate, but he needed to confirm our relationship with his lawyer. Do you hear me? All his money is coming to me, but I need to find the fuckin' lawyer."

Viper: "Did DeClarke tell anyone else about your relationship, or did he tell only you? If no one else knows, you're shit out of luck, you dumbass. If you don't have written proof of his acknowledgment, including a witnessed signature, you won't get any money."

Nat: "I thought of that, but listen, if we can get into his house, we can find his signature and copy it. It wouldn't be that hard. You're a lawyer, and you can be the witness."

The officers looked at each other with disbelief. Nat was planning to forge DeClarke's signature and falsify his will. He was oblivious to the five law enforcement officers outside of his cell, listening. Maggie's ploy had worked.

Viper moved to the cell door to view the hall and moaned, "You're a dumbass, that's for sure. Number one, it wouldn't work. And number two, five deputies are standing in the hall, and you have just announced your crazy plan to them. Dumbass."

Nat wasn't listening and jumped in, "Number three, they won't tell anybody if I pay them enough. And DeClarke had a whole shitload of money. Now who's the dumbass?" He moved to the door and looked into the hall where Cagey and Maggie and Brick stood, and for the first time, it registered that the officers had heard the entire conversation. "Well, fuck," he exclaimed.

Only a short time later, Viper was removed from the cell and sent on his way with the officers from the Las Vegas Police Department. The police in Henderson had built a strong case against him and charges linking him to several other crimes were mounting, including the additional charges he accrued in Barrier. It would be a long time before Viper saw the light of day as a free man.

Chapter 73

Dortha Ling
Present Day

Dortha Ling had not been in Barrier since Charlie Walker's trial ended. She had vowed never to see it or Charlie again. She had written him once while he was in prison, telling him that she no longer worked for Rose and Reubens, and if he wanted to file an appeal, he should contact Josh Gaines. She never heard back from either of them and didn't know if Josh had filed an appeal or not.

She had really liked Charlie and believed him, although he had a penchant for lying. She thought he had a spark for life, and she saw a streak of goodness under the brash and insolent facade. She felt guilty because she could not defend him well enough to receive a lighter sentence and had wanted to do more for him yet hadn't known what or how. Josh, the paralegal, had not helped a bit, damn him. Perhaps with more experience or more guidance, she could have done a better job. She had failed Charlie, hadn't aided him at all.

She went to bed early, and thought about her own youth, the poverty, the abuse, the real probability of her demise after the Vietnam War. She thought how many people had helped her when, at age sixteen, she had scurried out of Vietnam by boarding a leaky boat to come to America. When she hid in the barrel with rats to avoid the pirates. When she went to college and then law school. Now, just before her fiftieth birthday, she had a legacy of success, and Charlie was an ex-con, forty-three years old and starting over. Could she do anything to remedy his situation? She wondered.

With an early rising and a lead foot, she arrived in Barrier before lunch. She thought about Charlie Walker and regretted how she had handled his case. While she built her law practice, he sat in prison. Now she was a successful lawyer, and he had nothing. For an unknown reason, Dortha sought to tell her story to the Barrier sheriff. Perhaps she could assist Charlie now, pay it forward, they called it.

Dortha Ling entered the sheriff's office, looking around. Nothing much had changed from when she had interviewed Charlie a lifetime ago. New computers, perhaps. Pictures of the past sheriffs lined the wall, six more than when she last visited and one female, Maggie Monroe.

Maggie exited her office to greet Dortha. "You must be Ms. Ling; I'm pleased to meet you." Dortha was dressed in black slacks and a pale pink silk blouse, tiny pearl earrings, and a single pearl drop necklace. A tiny woman, under five feet tall and barely 100 pounds, she had the smoothest skin Maggie had ever seen. She looked professional, and Maggie was certain that her clothes had not been purchased in Johnstone's. Maggie, carrying a near six-foot frame, towered over her.

"Yes, I'm Dortha Ling, please call me Dortha. It's been a long time since I've been in this office, and I'm glad to see a woman at the helm," she responded smiling and extending her diminutive hand to Maggie.

Maggie offered her coffee or tea but Dortha accepted neither. "I left Vegas at dawn and didn't have breakfast, so could we go to lunch? I'm famished. I enjoyed eating at the Panorama the last time I was in town. Are they still in business?"

"Yes, and I'm hungry, too. I'll tell my deputy that I'm going to lunch, and we can walk to the Panorama if you're game. It's a quick two blocks," Maggie said.

"If I remember correctly, they had the most interesting menu, in fact, they created different menus every day, like out of a European bistro. It was so delicious," Dortha said.

Once seated at a table in the restaurant, they both ordered the daily special, which happened to be a Thai dish. As soon as they ordered, Dortha started talking, and Maggie started listening. Maggie had read the transcript of the trial, so much of her story sounded familiar, but she listened closely, hoping to learn a new fact that might be pertinent to Charlie's claim of innocence.

The details of Dortha's story and the transcript dealt with TwoJohnny and the lack of interest by both the prosecution and the judge in locating him to have him testify. TwoJohnny had not appeared at the trial, but the local grocery owner, David DeClarke had, indicating that he had pertinent information regarding Jonathan Grayson and requested that he be allowed to testify. Judge Little denied DeClarke's testimony, but they talked behind closed doors. The prosecutor attended the meeting inside the judge's chambers, but the judge excluded Ms. Ling. Dortha admitted that due to her inexperience, she did not know how to confront the judge. She had this on her mind when she asked for a mistrial, but she didn't know the right words when the judge denied it. She meekly accepted anything the judge said.

Maggie quietly pondered what might happen if she introduced TwoJohnny, aka Jonathan Grayson, to Dortha. He was, after all, sitting in her jail.

Chapter 74

Charlie and Dortha
Present Day

The Panorama served as a gathering place for residents of Barrier who did not enjoy pepperoni pizza, and today it buzzed with a dozen conversations, gossip, news, all important stuff. The restaurant was a holdover from the 1950s with a cosmopolitan, though limited, menu, and still, after all these years, *no coffee*. The owner, Jay Guzman, stubbornly continued the *no coffee* tradition when he first purchased it. He justified his decision that patrons wanted whatever he didn't have and decided a good variety of tea made for an easier menu. He stubbornly stuck to his choice, which puzzled visitors and new residents to Barrier, but they soon accepted it and enjoyed the other benefits of its international menu and ambiance, not to mention an array of international teas. In most patrons' eyes, the excellent cuisine compensated for the lack of coffee.

The front door to the Panorama banged open, and two men entered, one in his mid-forties and the other in his eighties. They glanced around looking for a table and found one near the window. The younger one had a nicely trimmed black beard, with strands of gray peeking out. Both wore the usual Barrier uniform: plaid flannel shirt and blue jeans with ball caps on their heads.

Maggie reached for Dortha's hand and whispered, "That's Charlie Walker, right there." She tilted her head toward the two men. "He lives with his stepfather, Gene Jacobs. Do you remember them?"

Dortha turned to look at the two men, "That's really Charlie and his stepdad? Wow. I never would have guessed. He has grown into a very handsome man. He was just a kid when he went to prison, scrawny and pimply with red eyes most of the time from crying. He's seems different now, confident and secure. He's no longer a skinny kid but has grown into a muscle-bound, attractive man, that's for sure." She seemed to be in a daze as she rambled on, "His beard gives him a scholarly, distinguished look, and his tan gives him a glow. Don't you think he's handsome?"

Not quite believing what she was hearing from Dortha, Maggie stared at her before she turned her head again to look at Charlie. Dortha continued to gaze at him. Maggie was surprised at her somewhat inappropriate comments. Dortha looked like a schoolgirl with a crush and appeared giddy. Trying to remain professional, Maggie turned back to Dortha, "I've spoken with him several times, but our conversations were strictly business. I like him, though, he seems bright and well read."

Snapping out of her reverie, Dortha asked, "Gene served as a Marine, didn't he? He looks the same, older, but still robust and grizzled. He stood up for Charlie during the trial. He was my best witness, even better than his mother. I didn't see him after the trial, but I wanted to thank him, even though his testimony did not help Charlie." After a minute, she continued, "I'm not sure if I'm ready to talk with them."

***

I turned my head and stared at the two women eating with chopsticks and tipped my cap to the sheriff. I looked at the other woman wondering... The server asked what we wanted and brought water and tea, while Gene and I continued our conversation. We both kept an eye on the sheriff and her companion, when suddenly Gene said, "Come on, Charlie, let's get out of here. That's Ms. Ling, and it's probably a bad idea to talk to her. Let's go across the street to eat."

He grabbed my wrist and tried to yank me up as he stepped toward the door. I shook him off and didn't follow but stood and walked toward their table. I said, "You're Ms. Ling, aren't you? I'm Charlie Walker."

Chapter 75

Charlie and Dortha
Present Day

"Would you like to join us, Mr. Walker?" Dortha said to Charlie, while shoving the chair that sat next to her from the table with her foot. "The sheriff and I have nearly finished, but I wouldn't mind having dessert and coffee."

"Tea," Maggie said automatically, "No coffee, just tea."

I glanced toward Gene who stood in the doorway with his vein pulsing purple. Some things never change. Maggie's eyes grew big, and she made mouth moves indicating that she had not planned, nor even considered the possibility of seeing Gene and me at the Panorama during their lunch.

"That would be nice," I said and scooted the chair into position beside Dortha. Sheriff Monroe watched us like an eagle looking for prey. From her eye movements, I deciphered that either she didn't like me, or she didn't trust me to be kind to Dortha. I knew she was thinking that this was trouble but was also curious as to why I sat down, and I honestly wondered the same thing.

The sheriff's phone chimed, and Maggie excused herself to answer it. She reappeared quickly saying, "Something's happening at my office, and I need to leave." She tossed two tens on the table and stepped quickly toward the door. "Dortha, could you come by the office when you two finish talking. I'd like to finish our conversation." She took another look at me and pursed her lips before heading out the door. Gene shook his head in defeat and held the door open for the sheriff as she left, and then he filed out behind her.

Dortha and I began our conversation with the niceties, what a coincidence, that type of thing before moving to the trial and her leaving abruptly to live and work in Las Vegas. She seemed nice and spoke to me like a human being, not like a maybe-guilty client or an ex-con. I immediately liked her, more than I had when she represented me. She was easy to talk to, obviously smart, and funny. And pretty. We talked of the twists and turns our lives had taken. They sort of paralleled. She had twice removed herself from her life as she knew it, first from Vietnam and later Reno, severing ties with all the people she knew. I had been removed twice also, in a different way, and now I wanted to piece together my life, and of course, find Dos.

She explained how she was forced into taking the case, even though she was far from experienced. She went into detail about how Josh, her former co-worker, coerced her throughout the trial. We talked about the specifics of the trial, and all the things she would do differently. We talked about Dos. She admitted her disinterest in him at my trial and said she didn't know how to locate him and knew nothing about how to conduct an investigation or about the tools that she had available. I had been correct; even though she believed I was innocent, Josh advised her that her job was to alleviate my sentence, not prove my innocence. She told me that she had thought of me every day of the last twenty-five years but had made no attempt to remedy my sentence. I had difficulty hearing this, but it gave me a better understanding of how she had run my case.

I felt so comfortable with her that I was easily able to share my experiences in prison, how I chose the better part of the coin. I told her about how I had spent the weeks that I had been out of prison and how thankful I was for my relationship with Gene. There was not a subject that I didn't want to talk about. With Dortha, I surprisingly was an open book.

And, the more Dortha and I talked, the more intriguing she became. We chatted for the better part of three hours before I looked at my watch and realized that my shift started in half an hour. "I am so sorry, Ms. Ling, but I have to work in thirty minutes. As much as I'd like to continue this conversation, I can't jeopardize my new job."

"Please, call me Dortha," she said. "What time does your shift end? Maybe we can have a drink when you get off?"

My head just about spun off its axis because even though I had been thinking the same thing, I was hesitant to ask given our history. "A drink? Sure. This bar stays open until late, so I'll come by here when I get off around ten p.m. I guarantee that you would not want to come to the Chicken Dinner Ranch for a drink. It is no place for a beautiful lady like you."

Chapter 76

Charlie and Dortha
Present Day

I managed to take off from work a little early and raced home to change my clothes. Working in a brothel can make you feel grimy, even if you aren't.

Gene met me at the door. "Did you get fired?" Gene asked, clearly pissed. "Jay fired you, didn't he?"

"On the contrary, Jay suggested I leave early and talked about giving me a raise. He sees me as a real asset.

I'm going out again as soon as I shower and change clothes. I have a date," I said, smiling.

"A date? You're kidding me. Who with?" Gene's forehead vein surfaced and grew brighter.

"Dortha Ling. We're going to have a drink at the Panorama. Maybe dinner, I'm not sure. I didn't ask her; she asked me, which completely shocked me. I like her, but I don't know if I would have been gutsy enough to invite her on a date. I mean, I don't even have any decent clothes, just the ones I bought at Johnstone's, but they're just going to have to do."

Gene puckered his lips, and the vein in his forehead pulsed hard and bright, "You're going out with Ms. Ling? What's up with that? Isn't she married?"

"No, she's not married. She's been engaged twice but broke them off. She couldn't find anyone to suit her. She's a fascinating woman, her background, her education, her work. She's done a lot of things in her life, and now she asked me to go have a drink with her. She apologized to me several times for her inexperience with the trial, and I can tell that she still feels guilty. The court gave me a raw deal, and she knows it. Maybe she's trying to make up for her involvement and the outcome of the trial, but whatever her reason, I'm going to meet her. I like her, and I'm excited to have some female company. Better than you, you old fart."

***

Dortha had already been seated with a glass of wine in front of her. She had selected a seat in a booth away from the noise of the bar. She wore blue jeans, a red t-shirt with a UNLV monogram, and cowboy boots similar to what she had on when we first met. She stood and gave me a peck on the cheek. It was nothing to write home about, I thought, but still a kiss, something I had not enjoyed for a long time. She signaled the barmaid who asked me, "Beer, wine, or something that lasts longer?"

"Coors," I said to the barmaid. When she walked away, I told Dortha, "I'm in a rut with my beers. Gene gave me a lot of information about the new beer companies, but I'm a traditionalist. A frosty Coors is perfect."

The conversation covered a myriad of things, and it zigzagged from vague to personal and back again. There was never in lull and no subject was too uncomfortable. I felt like I could talk to her for days on end. We had a lot in common in how we approached life, which surprised me, and she responded to me thoughtfully and pleasantly. I showed her the coin I had received from Ms. Moneyjoy and explained its meaning to me. We both opened up and shared things that were important to us, and we both knew that our innermost thoughts would not be met with judgment. The connection between us was indescribable. I couldn't help but wonder if it was there from the beginning when we met twenty-five years ago, but didn't recognize it due to the circumstances, or if this was something we could only experience with time and maturity? As our conversation continued and I had just finished up a funny story about my stepdad, she leaned across the table and kissed me again, this time right on my lips. I had no idea what was happening. It seemed too good to be true.

Time seemed to fly by, and before we knew it, it was already approaching midnight. She reached over, grabbed my hand, and asked, "Do you want to hang out tomorrow? I have to drive home to Vegas tomorrow evening, but we could spend some time together before I have to leave. I am really enjoying my time with you, and I am not ready for it to end."

Thankful that I wasn't scheduled to work tomorrow, and knowing that I didn't want my time with her to end either, I would agree to anything, but instead asked, "What do you have in mind? This is a small town, and there isn't much in the way of entertainment. How would you like to go on a hike or rock climbing, something outdoors?"

"Yes, something outdoors sounds great. We could go to the shooting range," she said. "You know, target practice."

"You like to shoot? I haven't shot a gun in a long time."

"Then it's time you did. I'll pick you up at Gene's after breakfast, and we can hit the rifle range. There is one out by the hot springs. What do you think?"

There was no way that I could say *no* to this woman. The feelings I was having toward Dortha didn't make sense, but they were unlike anything I had ever felt before. I couldn't explain them. I looked over at her, and with certainty said, "Count me in!" knowing full well that I meant more than just going to the shooting range.

Chapter 77

Maggie and Brick
Present Day

Maggie handcuffed Nat and led him to the interview room. It absorbed all her energy to keep from slapping him silly. If Brick or Cagey had retrieved him, another murder might have taken place, or at least assault and battery. He did not ingratiate himself with either of the law enforcement staff watching from the other side of the glass window.

Maggie began the interrogation with, "How do you know Viper?"

Nat shook his head, "Viper? I don't know him well at all. We've only met a few times. He told me he had practiced law, but I didn't believe him. Where did you take him, by the way?"

"What do you care where he went, especially if you don't know him? It doesn't seem like you are being honest about your connection with him. I'm curious though, why did you leave Barrier the minute you heard his name? A departure that included thwacking me on the head, knocking me out, and tying me up before stranding me in Jay's warehouse. No one found me for quite a while," Maggie said.

Nat shrugged his shoulders and answered, "I don't know. It seemed like the best thing for me to do, leaving Barrier, that is, not the thwacking you on the head thing. I didn't realize you had come into the warehouse because I thought you would wait outside. Anyway, I didn't like my job at the Chicken Dinner Ranch because I didn't like working in a whorehouse. I have much higher values, and it might destroy my reputation. Also, I wanted to get away and visit my father, and now he's dead and you plan to detain me in my grief."

Maggie looked at him curiously, "You saw nothing wrong with thwacking me on the head and locking me up?"

He didn't answer but said, "I want to tend to my father's burial and other legal affairs. He doesn't have anyone else. I have important business concerning my father's affairs. I am his one and only heir, uh, I mean, that is, I am his only family."

"In your cell, you and Viper talked about inheriting David DeClarke's money. Is that what this is about? Money?"

"No, of course, it's not about money, not at all. It's about family," Nat protested.

Maggie rolled her eyes and said sarcastically, "Oh, brother. Yeah right, family. Tell me about Mr. DeClarke, whom you claim to be your father. I've lived in Barrier nearly all my life, and I know that David DeClarke never married. He worked hard, and you could have profited from learning from him."

Nat considered his predicament for a few seconds, but finally said, "So, okay, I'll tell you the truth: I didn't know until a week ago that he was my father. I needed money and thought he might give me some, so met him for coffee at a Starbucks. I thought about hitting him up for bail money for Viper when he admitted that he was my father. The next thing I knew he told me he had brain cancer with two months to live and that I would inherit the whole pot, all his fucking money. Everything. And now he's dead. He and I planned to see the attorney the next day to add my name to his will, but he died in the Starbucks shitter."

Maggie snapped back, "So, you never saw the attorney add your name to the will. And you think you can have Viper forge his will and everything will be good? What a piece of work. You've earned everything you are about to get, TwoJohnny."

"Stop calling me TwoJohnny. I'm not a kid anymore. My name is Jonathan Grayson, and I plan to change my last name to DeClarke. So, I will be Jonathan Grayson DeClarke. I'll see an attorney for a name change as soon as I get out of this fucking jail and am back in Las Vegas."

Brick came into the interview room. "That's a pretty interesting story, Mr. Grayson. You have more names than the Octomom's kids. It's hard to believe that anything you've said is true."

Chapter 78

Charlie and Dortha
Present Day

Gene watched through the window as Dortha arrived, and I entered her car. Dortha's interest bewildered me. I was entranced by her and thought she was one of the most beautiful women I'd ever seen, but I hesitated after that. Obviously, she was completely out of my league. While I had spent the last twenty-five years in prison; she built a successful career talking to rich people about their money. Years ago, given the circumstances, I had not considered her as a person to date, but rather a person to guide me through my legal problems. As soon as my sentence was issued, I dumped her from my memory. I had a new reality to navigate, and I needed to focus on surviving the next twenty-five years. Now, oddly enough, our paths have crossed once again, and she apparently had become interested in me. Was she feeling what I was feeling? Were her feelings romantic? Were they sexual? I thought that was too much to ask and wondered if she had another plan up her sleeve. It was a jigsaw puzzle with several pieces missing.

Today, dressed in camo jeans, and a t-shirt, Dortha looked stunning because everything molded exactly to the curves of her tiny body. She passed through town, aiming at Highway 95, where we would take the turn toward the hot springs, but when we reached that point, she didn't make the turn. I asked our destination, obviously different than I thought, but she didn't answer, just smiled. I asked her a couple more times, but instead, she reached over, rested her hand on my thigh, and gave me a wicked little grin. I was puzzled, but it appeared she would remain silent. She drove a few more miles until reaching the town of Altoona. She passed a restaurant, a gas station, and a couple bars before arriving at a small, but curious looking hotel constructed in the shape of a bighorn sheep. A large sign read *Bighorn B&B,* and a small one read *No Vacancy.*

She pulled into the parking lot and turned off the ignition. She turned to Charlie and said, "Charlie, I don't understand what is going on with me, but I am fascinated with you, and really don't want to go to the shooting range at all. I have a pistol and two rifles, but I left them in Vegas. They are not in my car, and to be totally truthful, I am a horrible shooter and am not really fond of guns. I'm going to be absolutely honest with you: I have never done or said anything like this before, but there is just something about you, Charlie Walker. I am drawn to you like I've never felt with anyone else, and the reason we are sitting in the parking lot of the Bighorn B&B is because I would like to get close to you, as close as two people can be, and I am hoping you want that, too. I made a reservation here, but if you don't want to, we'll go back to Barrier, and I won't bother you again. I wouldn't blame you for saying no. My incompetence and inexperience had a huge impact on your life, and it is because of me that you had to spend so many years behind bars. I've told you I'm sorry before, and I'll say it again. I am so sorry. I will always be sorry for that, but now I want to spend more time with you because I like you. I really like you, Charlie."

I was shocked. Yes, I liked her and felt a pull toward her that made absolutely no sense. And, to top it off, I was as horny as a hoot owl, but was this a trick? I had heard of women who duped men by telling them one thing and then turning the tables and denying they ever said it. I knew at least six inmates who had told me similar stories. But, on the other hand, inmates lie, and maybe they lied about that, too. I looked into her eyes and said, "Dortha, of course, I want to sleep with you, who in their right mind wouldn't? I'm finding myself drawn to you in so many unexpected ways, but I have to ask, is this a trick, to dupe me into sleeping with you, only to claim that I coerced you?"

"No! Oh, no! Is that what you think? Do you think I would do that? I like you and promise that I am not setting you up," she said vehemently. "I don't know how to make you understand."

"The thing is, you are a successful attorney, and I am someone who spent most of my life in a prison cell. This isn't adding up, and I don't want to go back to prison with a rape charge, that's all. I haven't made love to anyone since before I went to prison, and I'm out of shape in the romance department. Are you sure you want to do this?"

She stretched over the car's console and kissed me long and hard, "Yes, I do. I'm out of shape in the love-making department, too. Let's go make up for lost time."

Chapter 79

Charlie and Dortha
Present Day

We went fast and slow, hard and soft, the most fun either of us had in years. We examined each other's body slowly, touching, sensing, and tasting, enjoying the anticipation and fulfillment of each sensation. The first time created the need for a next, followed by another next, and then we both slept deeply in each other's embrace, free from inhibitions and care. Our love making building an irrational, yet undeniable connection that we both fully embraced. When we awoke, we felt good, alive, and invigorated. One more time, for the road, she said, or maybe two, and we did.

"The Bighorn B&B will never be the same," I said as I reluctantly reached for my clothes to get dressed. "Hell, I may never be the same." Unable to contain what I was feeling inside, I wrapped my arms around Dortha and said, "I don't know how this happened so fast, and I don't know if this is love, Dortha, but if it's not, then I don't know what love is." He held her tight as he pressed a gentle kiss on her forehead, not wanting the moment to end.

"Well, I believe in love at first sight, Charlie, and I am pretty sure that I fell in love with you the first time I saw you in that interrogation room chained to the table. You were so young and naïve and vulnerable, a mess, trying to keep yourself out of jail, trying to cover up for TwoJohnny, and also trying to appease your mom. I was there to do a job, and obviously didn't do it well, but even then, I felt drawn to you. You stirred emotions in me that I hadn't felt before and didn't understand. Over time, I realized what it was. It was love, but I never let my true feelings out and have hidden them for all these years.

"When I saw you yesterday, my feelings for you flooded back, but I didn't think there was any way possible that you could feel the same way, given our history. But after yesterday and this morning, maybe there is a chance? I'm crazy about you, and I don't want to miss out on any more time with you."

I sat quietly processing everything that she was saying. Was it really possible that she was feeling the same way that I was? This truly was a whirlwind romance, and I was not only blindsided but excited about where it could lead. Could it be that our love story was one that actually started twenty-five years ago?

"Charlie, I do love you and have for all this time but was never able to admit it to anyone, not myself and especially not you. In the past, I tried building relationships with other men, but something was always missing. I know what that is now, it's you. I want to be with you and spend my life with you."

The pure joy that welled up inside me at her declaration was impossible to contain. I pulled her into my lap and held her tightly, never wanting this moment to end. She nuzzled into my neck and softly said, "Carl Sandburg, who authored your coin's statement, also said, *Only you can determine how your time will be spent.* I hope you want to spend your coin with me."

This had materialized too fast, I thought. But everything about it felt right. Why not take a chance and jump right in when I had twenty-five years to make up for? I clawed the coin out of my pocket and held it in my hand rubbing the remaining letters: T C L. *Time is the Coin of Life.* What would Ms. Moneyjoy say? Time with Dortha would be time well spent, and I couldn't wait to get started.

"Yes," I answered as I handed her my coin, "Yes, I do want to spend my coin, my time with you, and let's not waste any more of it. Let's jump in with both feet and see where this goes, shall we, Dortha? I don't have money to buy you a ring, but my coin is my most valuable position, and I'm giving it to you. Until I can put a ring on your finger, this will serve as my commitment to you.

Chapter 80

Nat
Present Day

"Let's talk about Charlie Walker," Brick said to Nat. "What do you know about him?"

"He's in prison at Fenwick for beating up an old lady, Sarah Hudson. He's a dumbass. She was his probation officer, and he gouged out her eye. That's all I know," Nat said. "His sentence was for twenty-five years, as I understand it. I didn't attend his trial."

"Did you know Sarah Hudson?" Brick asked expecting him to fabricate the answer. So far in today's interrogation, TwoJohnny had skipped the truth on everything. It would be interesting to see what he said about Sarah.

"No, I didn't know her. I knew that Charlie didn't like her, but I didn't figure he would try to kill her."

"Is that what he did, tried to kill her?" Maggie queried.

"That's what I heard, but of course, I wasn't there, so I don't know for sure."

"You were Charlie's friend, so why didn't you attend the trial," Brick asked.

"I wasn't around. I had business in Mexico and drove down for a few days. I wanted to learn Spanish and living in Mexico made it easy. Language immersion they call it."

Brick reached toward the metal bar and grabbed TwoJohnny's hand, splaying his fingers. "How did you get the scar, TwoJohnny."

Nat licked his lips, and his eyes bulged before he answered. "Oh, that. It's nothing. It's from the Boy Scouts when we went camping. I picked up a pot of hot coffee without a potholder and burned the hell out of it. I burned it thirty years ago, and it's faded. I forgot I even had it."

"I see. It has definitely diminished, but I think an iron made that scar," Brick said, as he traced the shape of the burn with his fingers. He looked TwoJohnny directly in the eyes and said, "You are a liar, you son of a bitch."

"Listen, Sheriff, you have this all wrong, and I can't stay in Barrier. I need to go back to Las Vegas. I'm worried about my dad."

"Well, he's dead," Maggie answered curtly, "and you've got a lot of explaining to do. You're not going to Vegas or anywhere any time soon, and you should probably start considering who you want for a lawyer."

Chapter 81

Charlie, Dortha, and TwoJohnny
Present Day

This was all happening so quickly, and Dortha and I had a lot of things to think about. I suggested we go to the sheriff's office to confide in Brick and Maggie. They both seemed levelheaded and had proven to be great sounding boards in my previous conversations with them. Perhaps they could help us sort out the tangles that we would face as we pursued our relationship. Dortha's issues dealt with her work and life in Vegas, and my issues, well, my only issue, dealt with locating TwoJohnny and trying to clear my name. I wanted to have a clear name if Dortha and I were to marry someday.

Cagey sat at his desk surrounded by a mountain of paper when we arrived.

"We're looking for Maggie and Brick. Are they here?" I asked Cagey. "We need advice."

Cagey locked his eyes on our clasped hands and asked, "What kind of advice do you need? They're in the interview room with Nat Griss. He arrived yesterday, and this is the first time they've had a chance to talk with him."

I dropped Dortha's hand and exclaimed, "Nat Griss? That's TwoJohnny! I can't believe he's here. I want to talk to him," and I headed toward the jail door.

Cagey leapt to his feet, and Dortha grabbed my arm and said. "No, not now, Charlie. Let's talk to Maggie. You need to do this right. If you do it wrong, you'll end up back in prison."

Cagey said, "Dortha's right, Charlie. Sit down, and you can wait for Maggie."

I frowned and said, "I want to talk to TwoJohnny face-to-face. I'm not gonna kill him or anything, I want to look him in the eyes and call him what he is: a piece of shit, rat-faced liar who blamed me for what he did, and I paid for it. I want to know why he left me in the lurch and has lied all these years."

"Talking to him won't get you anywhere. Like you said, he's a liar and manipulator," Cagey reminded me. "You can talk to Maggie when she comes out of the interview room."

By habit, I reached in my pocket for my coin but came up empty because I had given it to Dortha. "If you won't let me talk with TwoJohnny, could I talk to Patsy Bard? Gabe Cochran told me that TwoJohnny admitted that I had not hurt Mrs. Hudson, and Patsy, Gabe's ex-wife, said the same thing. She also said that I got a *bum rap*. She's in your jail, can I ask her if she is willing to tell Maggie or the judge what TwoJohnny told Gabe? If I can get another person to confirm what I've said, perhaps people will believe me, and my name can be cleared. Dortha and I have decided to take our relationship to the next level, maybe even get married someday, and I want a clear name to do it," I said, eyeing Dortha. "TwoJohnny's the one who deserves time in prison."

I wasn't able to talk to Patsy without Maggie's approval, so we sat down and waited. After a time, Maggie came out, and I repeated my wishes to her. I had waited a long time for this and wasn't going to walk away without confronting him. Maggie opened the door to her office and closed the door, not saying anything, not a word, and the three of us waited for her, sitting silent for another twenty minutes. I watched her through the glass and could see her mind working, but she didn't come back into the main room to reveal anything. Dortha looked back and forth as if she wanted to ask a question but didn't say anything either.

Finally, Maggie walked through her door and said, "Charlie, I'm going to deputize you. Don't ask why because this might not work, but it's the best thing I can think of. And you, Dortha, I'll also deputize you, and then we will speak to TwoJohnny."

Dortha and I had no idea what might happen, but Maggie deputized us, gave us badges, and ordered us to attach them to our shirts. We followed Maggie into the interview room where five chairs sat empty around the table. Cagey went to retrieve Nat and escort him back into the interview room while Maggie warned us to be cautious. The door opened and suddenly we stood face-to-face with TwoJohnny. He and I recognized each other in an instant, and it couldn't have been better. He wore handcuffs, and Dortha and I stood between Maggie and Brick with deputy sheriff badges pinned to our shirts. Sweet. TwoJohnny started cussing, and every other word started with an "F."

TwoJohnny bristled and tried to throw a punch. I wasn't sure who he had aimed at because, even though he wasn't cuffed behind his back, the cuffs restricted movement, but a moment later TwoJohnny was on the receiving end of a punch that landed squarely in his eye. Brick had not yet handcuffed TwoJohnny to the bar on the table and took his revenge for what TwoJohnny did to Maggie. TwoJohnny collapsed into one of the chairs with a few drops of blood leaking out of his nose, and he began yowling.

As soon as TwoJohnny started settling down, Dortha said to Maggie, "I need to tell you all something that's important to TwoJohnny and by extension, to Charlie. May I have the floor, Maggie?"

Maggie didn't know what Dortha had on her mind, but she agreed, and Dortha began her story.

"Charlie doesn't know any of this, but I want him to know. He and I have a future, I hope, and he has the right to know who I am and what I have done. As most of you know, I am an attorney and practice estate law in Las Vegas. One of my clients, David DeClarke, whom I think you all know, came to me several years ago and asked me to draw up his will, power of attorney, and medical power of attorney. He didn't know any other lawyers but remembered my name from when I tried Charlie's case in Barrier, and he requested my assistance."

TwoJohnny nearly jumped out of his skin when he heard that. She was the answer to his problems. This woman was the fucking lawyer who could help him get his money back. "Fuckin' A," he said loudly with a smile that closely resembled a sneer.

Ms. Ling looked at him blankly and continued, "When I wrote David's will, he told me that he had no known relatives except for a son named *Jonathan* who disappeared years ago. He hoped his son would come back but didn't know where he had gone or how to get in touch with him, so he wrote his will accordingly. I don't have his original will in my hands today, but I can tell you how he approached it."

"That's me," TwoJohnny shouted, "This is getting better and better because I'm his fucking son who disappeared. When do I get my money?"

Ms. Ling resumed her explanation, "The substance of the *original* will is: If DeClarke's son, Jonathan, appears before DeClarke dies, the son, Jonathan, would inherit everything, money, houses, cars, debts, the whole banana. DeClarke feared fraud by people who knew the size of his estate and stipulated in the original will that, if his son returned, then he would re-sign the will. If Jonathan didn't appear before he died, showed no interest, or he had not re-signed the will, the estate, in toto, would be left to another person whom he would name at a future time, and David left that blank. I held the power of attorney authority and didn't know how an open-ended beneficiary would work but checked with my supervisor, a former judge named Vincent Pierson. He didn't work for our firm long, but he researched it and advised me that the clause would work."

"Viper? This is excellent," TwoJohnny crowed, nodding his head, and looking from person to person. "Excellent. God bless Viper."

"Last year David became uneasy with the will because his son, Jonathan, had never appeared. He thought his current will too loose, too easy to be manipulated. He had accumulated a sizable amount of money, upward from $8 million."

"Eight million! Yes!" TwoJohnny screamed.

"Through the years, David and I became close friends, and he liked and trusted me. We went to ball games and dinner and did things that friends do. He often called me his daughter, the one he never had. "Of course, his thoughts shocked me, but on the other hand, he was right. I had been more of a daughter to him than anybody, including his own son." She glared at TwoJohnny as she said this.

"I helped David with many things through the years, such as buying a house and hiring household workers. I accompanied him to his medical appointments and checked on his house when he was out of town. I drove him to the doctor and was with him the day his doctor diagnosed his brain cancer.

"Early in our friendship I told him of my trip to the United States after the Vietnam War, and it became a cause with him, kind person that he was. He resented that Jonathan had never returned to see him. He hoped he would come back, but finally gave up. A few months ago, before he traveled to Lisbon, David came to my office and made an odd request. He asked if he could adopt me as his child, even though I was forty-eight years old. My real parents had died in Vietnam, so I had no reason to say no. So, last January, he and I went through the formal adoption process, and if you check the courts records, my name is now Dortha DeClarke. He said he admired and respected me and wanted to leave his estate to me, and legal adoption would clarify any issues that might arise, particularly if Jonathan appeared and somehow found out he was David's son. He placed me in total control of the estate and asked me to consider Jonathan as an heir, should he appear, but it would be my choice."

"Are you fucking kidding me? I don't believe you. This is so unfair," TwoJohnny screamed. "Un-fucking-fair. You probably just screwed him to get his fortune. It's mine, I tell you, mine."

"I thought you might say that," Dortha said, "but David traveled extensively throughout Europe, South America, and even Vietnam where he visited last year. He sent me post cards from nearly every port, and I have them all, a stack of 100 or more. When you read them, you will recognize our relationship as friends, not lovers, not sexually involved in any way. He addressed the most recent cards, those from Lisbon, to Ms. Dortha DeClarke."

Dortha leaned on the table, smirking as she stared directly into TwoJohnny's eyes, and issued the final blow.

"Now, because it is my choice to make, and because of all that you put Charlie through, you will not inherit one thin dime."

Maggie, Brick, Dortha, and Charlie waited until TwoJohnny's rant about unfairness subsided. Then, Charlie stuck his hand in his pocket, extracted a nickel, and balanced it on its side in front of TwoJohnny.

He said, "This is the lesson I learned in prison, TwoJohnny, and I hope you can stop being a dumbass long enough to figure out what I am saying. This nickel represents you, on your first day in prison. You can stand tall or you can fall flat and, believe me, prisons offer many ways to fall. Carl Sandburg called this nickel *The Coin of Your Life*."

"Who the fuck is Carl Sandburg?" TwoJohnny said.

Read on for a sneak peek at the next book in the
Maggie Monroe series: **Murder in the Brothel**

Chapter 1

Brandi, Candice, and Ginger
Five Years Ago

Candice Dumont's house lay smack in the center of a tight-knit, Reno subdivision where everybody knew everybody. Her small, aging two-story colonial, while nothing special, boasted a well-kept yard, updated paint, and even a potted daisy or two that always made her neighbors feel welcome. Candice's community prided itself on being a team that watched out for one other, often checking in each afternoon to see that all was well. Candice never worried about locking up before her daily catnaps or as part of her nightly routine because her neighborhood had proven itself safe year after year. That night, she had drifted off into a deep slumber, so deep that she heard nothing, not even footsteps on her creaking hardwood. All fell silent to her dead-to-the-world ears. Her panicked eyes flashed open only as the first bullet ripped into her chest, but she never knew of the other three bullets or the number of blows that had been inflicted on her torso—the cool serene morning destroyed by the person hell-bent on butchering her body.

Candice's older daughter, Brandi, lived in an apartment nearby, having moved from her mother's home a few weeks before. Throughout her years at university, she had bunked with her mom, but now, halfway through her second year-long teaching contract, she had earned enough money to rent a small place of her own. It wasn't that she hadn't loved being in her mom's home, after all she and her mom were more than mother and daughter. They had grown to become friends with similar interests, who not only enjoyed their time together but shared clothes and hairdressers, always laughing when someone remarked on their physical similarities. They were both tall and slender, with similar hair color, and they both wore it pulled back into a ponytail. Brandi's hair was brunette, and Candice's was the same color, except that hers had recently become woven with gray. Brandi's nearby move was merely a next logical step in her well-planned life.

After the move, Brandi was sure to see her mom whenever she could, but always stopped by on Friday mornings for an early morning cup of coffee and toast before heading to school to teach her fifth graders. That morning, the door was unlocked and ajar, which was not unusual, but on this morning, Candice did not respond when Brandi called her name. She popped an English muffin in the toaster, poured her coffee, and called out, "Mom, where are you? Do you want an English muffin, too?" She was met by silence and shouted louder this time, before heading up the stairs to her mother's bedroom, coffee sloshing from the cup as she ascended the stairs. "Mom, are you okay?" Seconds later, Brandi dropped the coffee cup when she discovered her mother's battered and shredded body motionless in her bed.

The violent murder shocked the Reno citizens so fiercely that even the casino trade slowed down for a time, as the town came to grips with the murder. During the first days, the news media carried daily stories of law enforcement's progress on the case, which was nothing. The police roped off Candice's house with lime green tape and recommended that Brandi take extra safety precautions, explaining that perhaps the perpetrator meant to kill her instead of her mother. After all, they resembled each other so closely. Brandi, filled with trepidation, in shock over finding her mother's body, listened to their advice, and holed up, never returning to her classroom. Except for the police, she talked to no one, and had no interaction with her friends, colleagues, or her sister, Ginger.

About the Author

Born and bred a small-town Idaho girl in the beautiful mountain west, my life has been a myriad of adventures. I am a Marine Corps officer, a former high school principal and superintendent who loves to write. My readers may recognize that I write my blogs, my *Wrinkly Bit* series and newspaper columns as Gail Cushman, my birth name. I love writing these humorous stories and enjoy receiving the fond feedback. My heart is full when I read your comments. Thank you!

Before I penned my *Wrinkly Bits* series, I had written a serious mystery and crime series revolving around a female sheriff named Maggie Monroe in rural Nevada. Now I find that I need to switch hats, from the silly, flowery bonnet of Gail Cushman to a new hat, a detective's fedora, for my nom de plume or pen name, Helene Mitchell. One cannot wear two hats at the same time, so when I put on the humorous hat of Gail, I write funny nonsensical stories that occur in everyday life, and when I put on my detective Helene hat I write about murder and mayhem. Every day, I choose which hat I will wear as I say good morning to my computer.

I hope you enjoy this second book in my Maggie Monroe series. And watch out, I have several more in the pipeline. Enjoy life, my friends, as Scarlet O'Hara said, "After all, tomorrow is another day!"

Gail Cushman's other books

- *Loving Again: A Guide to Online Dating for Widows and Widowers*
- *Murder in the Parsonage*

Wrinkly Bits Series, a senior hijinks:
- *Cruise Time*
- *Out of Time*
- *Wasting Time*
- *Flash of Time*
- *Bits of Time*

Loving Again

A Guide to Online Dating for Widows and Widowers
You Don't Have to be Alone

Gail Decker Cushman and Robert L. Mitchell

The authors, both widowed after long and loving lives with their spouses, decided to pursue adventures in their new widowhood situations. They met on the internet and now have written a book about the life-changing rewards of discovering a new love and romance. What better subject matter expert than two people who have the real-life experience of dealing with death, deciding to move on, meeting someone online, and falling in love in their seventies!

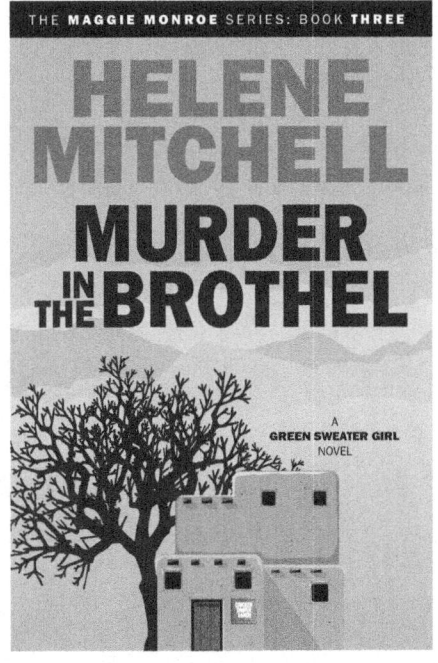

THE MAGGIE MONROE SERIES: BOOK ONE

HELENE MITCHELL
MURDER IN THE PARSONAGE
A GREEN SWEATER GIRL NOVEL

THE MAGGIE MONROE SERIES: BOOK THREE

HELENE MITCHELL
MURDER IN THE BROTHEL
A GREEN SWEATER GIRL NOVEL